BREAKOUT

ROAD TO THE BREAKING
BOOK 4

CHRIS BENNETT

Breakout is a work of historical fiction. Apart from well-documented actual people, events, and places that figure in the narrative, all names, characters, places, and incidents are the products of the author's imagination, or are used fictitiously. Any resemblance to current events, places, or living persons, is entirely coincidental.

Publisher's Cataloging-In-Publication Data
(Prepared by The Donohue Group, Inc.)

Names: Bennett, Chris (Chris Arthur), 1959- author.
Title: Breakout / Chris Bennett.
Description: [North Bend, Washington] : [CPB Publishing, LLC], [2021] | Series: Road to the breaking ; book 4
Identifiers: ISBN 9781733107990 (trade paperback) | ISBN 9781955100007 (ebook)
Subjects: LCSH: United States. Army--Officers--History--19th century--Fiction. | United States--History--Civil War, 1861-1865--Fiction. | Militia--Virginia--History--19th century--Fiction. | Underground Railroad--History--19th century--Fiction. | Dwellings--History--19th century--Fiction. | LCGFT: Historical fiction.
Classification: LCC PS3602.E66446 B74 2021 (print) | LCC PS3602.E66446 (ebook) | DDC 813/.6--dc23

To sign up for a
no-spam newsletter
about
ROAD TO THE BREAKING
and
exclusive free bonus material
see details at the end of this book.

Breakout [breyk-out] noun:
1. a military attack to break from encirclement. 2. a forcible escape, especially from a prison. 3. a violent or forceful break from a restraining condition or situation.

CONTENTS

"I see ... and pray tell, gentlemen—what business brings you here to Greenbrier County, and more particularly, to my home, may I ask?"

"Well, sir ... to be perfectly blunt, we have come here to escort you back to Richmond."

"Oh ... I see. I have just recently come from that city at great pains and have no desire to return in the foreseeable future. So I'm afraid your long journey here has been for naught."

"I don't think you understand, sir. We have a warrant. We are duty bound to place you under arrest and bring you back in our custody to Richmond, sir."

This made Tom sit up in his seat and look over at Nathan, but he said nothing, letting Nathan do the talking.

"I see ... and what are the charges, if you don't mind my asking?"

"Not at all, sir. The charges include three counts of murder and one of assault. It seems three gentlemen, by the names of Stevens, Miller, and Baker were last seen alive in a ... *confrontation* with you, sir, on the streets of Richmond on the afternoon of Sunday, April 21st, 1861. We found these gentlemen later that day, deceased. All three had been shot by pistol at close range. A fourth man was reportedly run down in the street by a horse ridden by *you*, sir. The man was grievously injured but is presently recovering in hospital."

"Hmm ... and ... tell me this, gentlemen—since it appears you had witnesses to this ... 'confrontation'—in what state did said witnesses say I was when last seen in the company of these three *fine* gentlemen?"

The two visitors exchanged a look before Benning answered, "You were said to have been apparently unconscious, having been struck on the head by a pistol during the fight, sir. The gentlemen were seen to be carrying you."

"Ah. So let me see if I have this story straight. You are saying I was carried away unconscious by three armed men ... sorry, you *did* mention at least one of them had a pistol, did you not? Ah, yes ... as I was saying, I was last seen being carried away unconscious by three armed men. And yet, by some miracle, I

2

managed to regain consciousness, overpower these three *armed* men, and murder them? And then, apparently, having excess energy about me, I decided to mercilessly ride down another gentleman who innocently walked in front of my horse on the street? Is this *truly* the story you intend to present to a judge and jury, gentlemen?"

Tom was quietly chuckling and shaking his head. Nathan was clearly turning the tables on the visitors. It reminded Tom of the train robbery incident when Nathan virtually disarmed the robber with nothing more than the force of his personality.

Benning had turned red in the face. "Look, Mr. Chambers, it ain't our job to decide the truth of it—who's guilty or not. That's a matter for a court of law to decide. Our job is to bring you in to *face* the law."

"*Law*, gentlemen? Are you referring to the *law* of a government that has just recently broken the most sacred law of our land, the Constitution of the United States of America? I wonder which *laws* this government expects its *citizens* to follow after such a monumental show of flagrant disregard for the highest law of the land?"

"It ain't our place to debate such matters with you, Mr. Chambers. Such things are for others higher up than us to decide. Right now, we mean to bring you back to Richmond, sir."

"Well, gentlemen, then it seems we are at an impasse, for I no longer recognize the legitimacy of the government in Richmond. Therefore, you have no right to come here and arrest me, as you are no longer legitimate law officers … in my humble opinion."

Cumberland reached into his inner jacket pocket and pulled out an envelope.

"We were warned you might say something of the sort, Mr. Chambers. So we were instructed to place this letter into your hands. Please read it, if you would, sir."

He handed the letter across to Nathan. He opened the envelope and unfolded a single page, reading silently before handing the paper over to Tom.

"Mr. Clark, kindly read the message aloud, so we are all under the same understanding of its contents, if you please."

"Certainly, sir."

Headquarters, Army of Virginia

Richmond, May 6, 1861

My Dear Nathaniel,

Despite our recent unhappy exchange of words in Richmond, I continue to hold you in the highest esteem. I pray we may mend our differences and return to our previous happy state of affection and comradeship.

I am also led to understand you presently find yourself in certain legal difficulties in Richmond, due to unfortunate circumstances occurring on the night of April 21 last. I am entirely confident of your complete innocence in such matters, and have spoken with his honor, Governor Letcher, on your behalf. He is also convinced of the falsehood of these charges, and of the unimpeachability of your personal character.

As such, he has authorized me to offer you a commission in the Army of Virginia, soon to be merged into the armies of the Confederate States of America, at the rank of Major General. I beg you to consider this proposal in the spirit of friendship, and loyalty to our home of Virginia, in which it is offered.

I pray you will kindly accept this offer and accompany the men presenting this letter to Richmond. Upon your arrival all other matters will, of course, be immediately resolved in your favor.

I am, very respectfully, your loyal friend and fellow Virginian,

R. E. Lee

Major General, Commanding, Armed Forces of Virginia

Tom turned toward Nathan, a questioning look on his face. Nathan sighed a heavy sigh, staring at his feet for several moments. Then he looked up.

"Gentlemen, you may tell *General* Lee, and *his honor* Mr. Letcher I do *not* break my sworn oaths. And further … I no longer consider myself a *Virginian*, rather only a citizen of the United States of America, in which state I intend to live until such time as I am dead.

"Therefore, I reject his offer, though I agree with him on one point: my innocence of these ridiculous charges! I was assaulted in Richmond by these men you name, that much is true. But I have little memory of events thereafter, having been pistol whipped in the back of the head in a most cowardly manner by one of the three. I can assure you, after that I could not even stand unaided for several days, and in fact nearly expired from my injuries. I was certainly not capable of murdering those men, nor any others, much as I may have wished to … and much as they may have deserved it."

"As we said before, Mr. Chambers, it matters not if we believe you or don't. And, from what you have said, it may be a judge and jury will agree with your innocence, sir. On the other hand, it could also be your men committed these murders on your behalf, which is much the same thing in the eyes of the law. For instance, it is known Mr. Clark here was also in Richmond at that time, and we have witnesses who saw him fleeing town in your company, sir. Have no fear, however, Mr. Clark … we have no instructions to arrest you, at this time …"

Tom gave him an ironic smile, and said, "Oh, well, I am *greatly* relieved to hear *that*, sir!" in a tone that could not be mistaken for anything but heavy sarcasm.

"Gentlemen … I'm afraid I am still weak and ailing from my recent injuries and ordeal. So if we have nothing further to discuss, I must respectfully ask you to depart. Please return to Richmond with the answers I have given you for Mr. Letcher, and Mr. Lee."

The two men stood, but instead of heading for the door, they both unholstered their pistols, pointing them at Nathan and Tom.

"We were afraid that would be your answer, sir. So now we must be more insistent. It is our duty to bring you to justice … preferably alive, but … if necessary, dead. Please do come along with us without resistance, sir, and no one need be injured or killed in this matter."

Nathan looked up at them, mouth agape. He had *not* been expecting this. He glanced at Tom and saw he was not shocked and seemed calm about the whole thing. Nathan thought about that a moment and smiled.

"Very well, gentlemen. I shall not resist. In fact, I have a strict rule against any gunplay in my home. I am also too tired and weak to make any further attempts at dissuading you."

He slowly and stiffly raised himself up out of his chair, Tom quickly rising and stepping over to assist him.

"Thank you, Tom. I'll be fine, just give me a moment for my head to clear."

Nathan rubbed his temples as his head throbbed. But after a few moments the pain eased, and he could walk. Tom took his arm and helped him from the room. They made their way out the library doors, the two lawmen following behind, glancing down the hall, and up the stairs nervously, guns still drawn.

Tom and Nathan went out the main doors and stepped onto the veranda. But instead of moving straight ahead toward the stairs leading down to the driveway, Tom pulled Nathan to the left, out of sight of the lawmen behind.

The two lawmen immediately stepped out the front door, looking to see what Mr. Clark and Chambers were up to, when they suffered a sudden, terrible shock.

To the left of the doorway stood a stocky man with dark red hair and matching beard. This man pointed two colt revolvers at them. Tom and Nathan had neatly ducked behind him and now stood looking over his shoulders. As the lawmen gazed about, they could see seven more men, at ground level, arms leaning up onto the edge of the veranda. At the end of each man's arm was another revolver.

And back on the opposite side of the doorway was another man; this individual was enormous. He was holding a very large, wicked looking pistol, and sporting an equally wicked looking grin.

For a moment nobody moved or spoke.

The red-haired man to the left said, "Gentlemen, unless you's fixin' to die right here and now spoiling the Captain's lovely veranda spewin' copious amounts o' blood, I'd suggest you hand me them sidearms. Nice'n easy like."

The man grinned broadly, an unlit cigar clenched between his teeth.

Cumberland and Benning raised their hands in the air. Jim holstered his two pistols and stepped forward to snatch the men's weapons from their hands.

He grabbed the one closest to him, Cumberland, and shoved his face hard up against the wall of the house. He'd not finished this move before Stan arrived from the other side of the door, grabbing Benning, and shoving him hard up beside his partner.

"What you want us to do with these fellas, Captain?" Jim asked. "I ain't opposed to putting a bullet in their heads and burying 'em out in the woods. Billy knows tricks on how to hide the graves so's no man on Earth'll ever find 'em."

Cumberland tried to squirm, but Jim slammed his face hard into the side of the wall, which had the desired effect of settling him back down.

"No. Thank you ... but *no*, Mr. Wiggins. In the end, these men were only trying to do their duty ... such as that is. No, please escort them back to the edge of my property, then return their firearms to them ... unloaded. I'll not be accused of thievery on top of everything else ... then send them on their way back to Richmond."

"Yes, sir."

Then Benning, hearing he'd just received an apparent reprieve, worked up the nerve to say, "This will do you no good, Mr. Chambers. Richmond will just send soldiers next time. You'll not escape justice, sir."

"Well, as you can clearly see, Mr. Benning, I *too* have soldiers.

"Mr. Wiggins, I will leave this matter in your capable hands. Tom, will you be so kind as to escort me back inside? I find I am quite fatigued by all this activity."

"Certainly, sir. Come ..."

After Tom and Nathan had returned inside, Jim released Cumberland, and signaled Stan to do the same to Benning.

Jim called out, "Cobb! Are you there, my good man?"

The groom came out from around the side of the house where he'd been hiding during the potential gunplay.

"I's here, Sergeant Jim."

"Oh ... good. Cobb, would you kindly bring them horses 'round now, like we discussed earlier?"

"Yes, sir. They's all saddled and ready to go, just as you asked, sir. I'll go'n fetch 'em now. Won't be a minute, sir."

"Thank ye kindly, Cobb. You're a good hand!"

Jim turned his attention to his prisoners. He looked toward their feet. Both wore shiny black, new-looking riding boots.

"Say ... them're nice looking boots, gents ... they as comfortable as they looks?"

Benning looked at Jim with a puzzled expression. It was such an incongruous question he didn't know how to respond. So he shrugged and said, "Yea ... sure ... I suppose so. Why d'you ask?"

"Oh, good! Glad to hear it because ... well, you see, the Captain he says to escort you to the edge of the property. Well, now, that's a whole ... oh, I don't know ... maybe three, four miles ... give or take. And, well, to be honest, gentlemen, I'm a bit of a nervous Nel when it comes to escorting prisoners. I have this fear o' them running off or straying afore I can get 'em to where I been ordered to get 'em to. So ... I'm thinking it's a nice, fine day for ... *a good long walk.*"

The lawmen stared at him wide-eyed, to which he smiled broadly, finally striking a match and lighting the cigar he'd held in his teeth.

ৡৠঌৣৠৡৠঌৣৠৡৠঌৣ

Evelyn held the letter up to her heart and breathed a great sigh of relief. Her face was lit by a smile she could not wipe away, despite the tears streaming down her face. If she'd ever before felt such joy and relief, she couldn't remember when it was.

She sat back in her chair and read the letter again:

Mountain Meadows Farm
Lewisburg, Virginia

May 4, 1861

My Dearest Evelyn,

I cannot thank you enough for your kind words and timely message of April 24 last. I am very happy to report all is well with us, and all our loved ones have now safely returned from their recent travels.

I have passed along your affectionate regards to Megs and Mr. Chambers, and they ask I return the same to you. He is feeling a little weak from his recent illness but is recovering nicely and we expect his return to complete health very swiftly.

Please give my love and best regards to Miss Harriet, and any of my friends and acquaintances back in Richmond you may happen to meet.

And, I would especially ask you to give my heartfelt thanks to those who have been helpful and kindly toward my beloved son during his recent travels.

And lastly, I heartily agree with your wish we may one day be reunited in happier times.

With love and sincerity,
Abigail Chambers

She jumped up, grabbed her hat, and walked out the door headed for the Hughes' house to share the good news. The letter had not come as a complete surprise, of course, but it was finally confirmation of what they had already suspected; Nathan and his men had beaten the odds and made it safely home.

The first positive news had come more than a week ago, when she'd been called to a meeting at the Hughes' house. There they introduced her to their man called Joseph, who'd escorted Nathan and company safely to Lynchburg. He told his long tale in great detail, after which he patiently answered her questions. And he humbly endured her rebuke for abandoning them in their hour of need, until Jonathan sternly reminded her the man had likely saved their lives multiple times. She immediately apologized sheepishly then profusely thanked him for everything he'd done.

Then a few days later, rumors began to circulate about the gang of men who'd been sent to apprehend Nathan. They'd apparently returned to Richmond empty handed. Although the rumors were wild and mostly unsubstantiated, they sounded generally positive from *her* point of view.

It seemed Nathan and at least some of his men had gotten away. And one and likely several of the pursuers had been killed in the process—but possibly some of Nathan's men as well. This latter rumor had filled her with great anxiety, knowing all Nathan's men personally.

There was also a wild rumor a *bear* had attacked several men in the woods, or possibly wolves had done it. Or even Indians!

One rumor seemed most credible and extremely encouraging: that a rescue party from Mountain Meadows had arrived in the very nick of time and fought a gun battle with the slavers. But of course, there was no way to know for sure if any of it was true.

But now there were smiles and congratulations all around after Evelyn shared Miss Abbey's letter with Jonathan and Angeline in their library. She asked that Jonathan especially thank the man called Joseph both from Miss Abbey, and from herself, which he promised to do straight away.

But then Jonathan said, "Unfortunately, not all the news today is positive. I am very sorry to tell you, Dr. Johnson has been arrested."

"What?! Oh *no!* What happened?"

"It seems your friend, the watchman Jubal Collins, began to become suspicious. He showed up one evening just as a 'conductor' was escorting a group of slaves away from the house.

Police officers arrived shortly after and carried Dr. Johnson away in chains."

"Oh, dear … oh, dear. What will they do to him, do you suppose?"

"Well, the good news is he was arrested by legitimate police officers, so he will likely be put on trial and be sent to prison. If others in the employ of the Slave Power had caught him, they'd have taken him to the nearest tree and hanged him."

Evelyn shook her head, "What terrible times we live in, when we feel happy our friends are only being thrown in prison and not murdered outright!"

"Yes … and likewise we feel joyful Mr. Chambers escaped Richmond with his life, when such an ordeal should *never* have happened to him in the first place! He is a proper gentleman, and an elected official of the Commonwealth, for God's sake! These are dark times, indeed, Evelyn."

"So what now?"

Angeline answered this time, "Well, first, we will do what we can for our dear friend. We will secretly hire the best possible attorney, though it will likely bear little fruit. But never fear, my dear. Once all the noise has died down, and he is 'safely' off to prison, it may be possible to … make certain *arrangements,* to get him out and smuggle him off to the North."

"You can arrange a prison escape? Oh, my! You are more resourceful than I'd realized."

"You have no idea, my dear … no idea at all," Angeline said with a smile.

"Speaking of," Jonathan said, "we now must talk about how to fill Dr. Johnson's shoes. His capture has left a gaping hole in our organization."

"Yes, I should imagine so."

"And … it's timely you're here today, my dear. Jonathan and I had just been talking about you, before you arrived …"

ᏚᎢᎷᎧᏒᎧᎷᏚᎢᎷᎧᏒᎧᎷᏚᎢᎷᎧᏒᎧᎷ

"You didn't really make them walk all the way to the main road, Jim?" Tom asked, smiling and shaking his head in amusement.

But Jim, for once, had a serious look, "Tom ... them fellas pointed loaded guns at our Captain! At *our Captain!* Them bastards is damned lucky I didn't disobey Captain's orders and go ahead and put that bullet in their fuckin' heads, as they so richly deserved! Damn it, Tom! What if them guns'd gone off on accident and hit him? *Damn* ... makes me sick to even think on it! I won't tolerate nobody pointing guns at the Captain, *no sir!*"

But then he grinned, and added, "Besides ... don't you know ... it's become a Mountain Meadows *tradition*—making uninvited, unwelcome guests walk their way back to the road!"

"True ... I recall you started that *fine tradition* the first time Walters attacked, during the big wedding. Oh, I sure wish I'd have been there to see his face when you made him wade the creek in his shiny new boots!"

Jim chuckled, "Yep, it was a glorious sight. Then don't forget when the Captain was so furious with them slave traders on account o' that sweet little slave girl. He forced them two to walk back down the hill and had one o' our boys, Cobb as I recall, drive the wagon, and another ride the horse! Our two slave men got to ride while them slavers had to walk! I reckon they was fit to be tied!"

They shared a laugh.

"By the by ... and speaking of such ... I don't think I ever told you before, Tom, what a fine job you done back in Richmond, killing them damned bastards what was fixin' to murder our Captain. Shot 'em down like the rabid dogs they was ... that was good work, Tom, and I salute you for it!"

"Thank you for saying so. Those men were planning to murder him slowly and in the cruelest possible manner with sharp knives as he was tied helpless. Of all the killings I've ever done, those seem the most righteous to me, and have caused me the least pause."

"Amen to that, brother! Amen to that. *Damn* ... makes me wish they could come back to life just so's I could kill them too! May their flea-bitten hides burn in hell!"

Just then the back door opened, and Nathan stepped out, moving very deliberately. Tom and Jim jumped up and hurried over to help him.

"You sure you're feeling up to this, sir?" Tom asked, as they guided him over to a seat at the table.

"Yes, thank you Tom ... Jim. I am feeling a bit better this evening. I came out here to thank you for earlier today. That was neatly done."

"Oh, don't think nothing of it, sir. There weren't no way on God's green Earth them fellas was gonna take you away from this house, sir!" Jim answered with a grin.

"Yes ... I know that, Jim. You're good men, all of you. The best and most loyal I've ever known, and I thank you for it."

"No thanks necessary, sir," Tom answered.

Jim poured whiskey into his empty glass and slid it over to the Captain.

"Thanks, Jim."

Nathan lifted it up in salute to his two men, then took a sip.

"Mmm ... that tastes mighty good. William hasn't let me drink any since I've been home. Says it's not good for my head."

"Well, we won't be for telling him, will we Tom?"

"Oh no; we most certainly will *not!*"

"Thanks, gentlemen. But I'll not overindulge. I'm sure William knows what he's saying, and I'll be well-served to follow his advice."

They were quiet for a moment.

Then Tom said, "Sir, I am very sorry about Colonel Lee ... *General* Lee, I suppose now ... I know you were close and now it feels ..."

"Yes, thank you, Tom. Since I never got along with my Daddy, Colonel Lee was like a father to me in many ways while we were in Mexico, and later in Texas. He was someone I admired greatly and felt true affection for. His ... *treason* ... is one of the most painful elements of this whole ugly episode. That and ..."

He trailed off without finishing his sentence as if lost in thought.

"*And* ... sir?"

He turned to Tom and said, "Tom ... when I reached her house, she wasn't home, so I never got it to see *her*, never got to ask her about *the note* ... what it meant. I arranged with her momma to meet her later, but those men attacked me on the way home and ... well, you know the rest."

"Oh! Oh *no!* ... I ... I didn't realize *that*, sir. I ... well I guess I just assumed they'd attacked you *after* you spoke with her. I figured once you were feeling better, you might be inclined to confide in me what she'd said."

"She?" Jim asked, not catching on to what they were talking about, since he hadn't been with them in Richmond.

"Miss Evelyn, Jim. I never could work up the courage to just go talk with her, face to face. But then we met, seemingly by chance, at a social event. She was there with ... with another *gentleman* ... one of my political opponents, in fact, and a former Army officer. I was ... not very pleased about it, as you might imagine. And, to top it off, she spoke to me with some coldness, which I hadn't expected.

"You'll not be surprised to hear I left there in a fiery ill humor. If it hadn't been for Tom's kindly intervention, I might have committed murder that very night. Then these gentlemen today would've had a *real* case against me!"

"Oh ... sorry to hear that sir. My ... condolences on it, knowing how you was feeling about her, and all."

"Thanks, Jim ... but that wasn't the end of the story. We were walking back to our rooms, about halfway there. I was fuming and fussing, doing my best to kill a perfectly good bottle of whiskey when I reached into my pocket for a cigar, and what did I find? A strange cryptic note, written in her hand, and signed 'E'. It seemed to hint she still had feelings for me but didn't exactly say so.

"So the afternoon before we left for home, I became determined to meet her and ask her straight out what she'd meant by it ..."

"But you never got the chance to talk to her … *now* I see. *Damn!* One more reason to bring them fellas back so's we can shoot them again!"

"What?"

Tom shook his head, "Never mind *him*, sir … just something we were discussing before you arrived."

"Oh, I see. Anyway, now Miss Abbey tells me this fellow, 'The Employer,' sent me a mysterious message: that I shouldn't write anything 'personal' in a letter to Evelyn lest it put her in danger! I don't understand why, though. What's she got herself into, anyway?"

"I think I know the answer, sir. Joseph told us he's been working for the Underground Railroad for years now, and clearly she's now keeping the same company …"

"Oh! Ah … yes, now I see. I guess I've had a stronger influence on her than I'd known. When she first came to Mountain Meadows, she was spouting the usual slaver nonsense, but now …"

"Yes, that's how it looks, sir."

"Well … I applaud her for it, of course. But it puts me in fear for her safety, and it confounds my ability to ask her what I want to ask her."

He was quiet and thoughtful again for several minutes. Then he looked over at Tom, as if a new thought had struck him, "And what about you, Tom? I've never asked you about your correspondence with Adilida."

Tom's expression became more serious at the question, and Nathan suspected he'd *not* received good news.

"Well, sir, as you know, in my last letter I told her not to come to Richmond, but rather to Baltimore, so as to avoid any trouble with the secession. I also told her to send her return letter to Mountain Meadows, as we were likely to return here shortly."

"Yes, I recall discussing something of the kind."

"Well, when we arrived back here, there was already a letter waiting. It was sent by way of the telegraph. It says Mr. Lincoln has declared a blockade of all Southern ports, including New

Orleans. No passenger ships dare leave port for fear of Northern war ships. Sir, Adilida can't come."

Nathan nodded but didn't immediately respond, looking thoughtful. Then he said, "I'm very sorry, Tom. But perhaps things will change, and she'll find a way out of New Orleans. Or perhaps you can go there, if you wish."

"Oh, no, sir! That I will *never* do. For one, I'll not travel to a state that's in open revolt against the United States, unless I'm wearing a blue uniform and marching with a rifle slung over my shoulder, if you get my drift! And for another, I will never leave *you*, sir. Not with all the present troubles.

"No, Adilida will just have to wait, I'm afraid. We'll just have to postpone our reunion for the time being."

"Well, I thank you again for your loyalty, Tom, and I understand your feelings."

He reached over and refilled Tom's glass, then raised his own, "Here's to Adilida ... may she stay safe, and may you be swiftly reunited."

They clinked glasses and took a swallow. "Thank you, sir."

Nathan handed the glass, still half full, back to Jim, who raised it to Tom, "To Adilida." He finished it in one swallow.

They were quiet and thoughtful for several minutes until Nathan sighed, and said, "Well ... after today's events, we've *crossed the Rubicon* now."

"Crossed the *what?*" Jim asked.

"The Rubicon ... it was a river, back in ancient Rome," Tom explained. "It's a metaphor, meaning we have now crossed beyond the point of no return."

"Well, that I'll agree with."

Then Nathan explained, "Sorry Jim, it's from the days of ancient Rome. There was a time when Julius Caesar had been off in Gaul—what is now France—fighting Rome's foreign wars for years. But one day his political enemies back in Rome gained power, and tried to strip him of his commands, titles, authority, and influence.

"But Caesar was not a man lightly gainsaid. He brought his very best fighting men, the Thirteenth Roman Legion, back to

Italy from Gaul and marched on Rome. In those days the Rubicon River was the boundary of the Roman Republic proper. The law said no Roman general, with troops under his command, could cross the Rubicon or he'd be in defiance of the Roman Senate, which was treason.

"So when the great Caesar crossed the Rubicon, he knew he was passing the point of no return—that it was now either victory, or death. It is written he spoke the Latin words, *'Alea iacta est,'* which means, 'The die is cast.'"

"Ah ... now I see what you mean, sir. Yes ... I'd agree; it seems we have passed the point of no return, and, as Caesar says, now the die *is* cast. But now I'm curious ... how'd it turn out for old Caesar, anyway?"

"Well, the Roman Senate had him badly outnumbered with nine full legions at its disposal and Pompey the Great to lead them, against Caesar's one legion." Nathan chuckled, "So of course his enemies fled Rome in fear! And after a brief, decisive civil war, Julius Caesar became Dictator of Rome."

"Well, that didn't turn out so badly for him then! Maybe we'll fare just as well!"

"True, Jim. But unfortunately, we don't have the Thirteenth Roman Legion with us!"

"Yes, sir, and more's the pity. I heard-tell them Roman boys of Caesar's was some mighty stout fighting men."

"Yes ... but we have some *'mighty stout'* fighting men, too!" Tom offered.

"Truer words were never spoken, Tom," Nathan agreed, "truer words were never spoken!"

ഈഅഓഅഈഅഓഅഈഅഓഅ

Adilida stirred awake at the sound of the front door opening. Uncle had returned from town. She hadn't planned on napping, but she always felt so tired lately, and any chance to rest was welcome.

Edouard came in removing his hat, "How are you feeling, my dear?"

"I'm well, Uncle, though a bit tired."

"Well, that is normal and understandable," he said with a smile.

"What news from town, Uncle?"

"Nothing much good, I'm afraid. It has been confirmed the Union warships patrol the coasts. There are some ship captains who will risk it, but only for transporting highly valuable cargo, *not* passengers. And I've heard they've blocked the Mississippi as well, north of Memphis, so there's no going that way either. Lastly, the trains have all been commandeered for essential military purposes only. I'm afraid our journey east must wait."

"Wait for *what*, Uncle … and for how long?"

"For things to change … and for as long as it takes, I'm afraid. Nobody knows what will happen, but it seems very likely there will be a war. Some hotheads brag about the South 'whipping' the North in short order, but I believe they are fools. If the North is determined to fight it will go very hard on the South, I am sure of it.

"The only good news I heard is the postal service is still sending mail between the North and South, as if nothing were amiss; though there is now talk of a Confederate postal service starting up soon. So you may continue to exchange letters with Thomas, at least for now."

"Oh, Uncle … what am I to do?"

He knew what she meant by the question.

"Yes … I think we must discuss it. I was reluctant of your earlier plan, as you know. I agreed to it only because it was such a relatively short time before you would be reunited with Thomas. But now …"

"Yes, I know … it can't wait for months, or maybe even years."

They were quiet a moment. But as Edouard opened his mouth to speak, he was interrupted by a loud noise from down the hall.

He smiled, and Adilida got up from her chair, "Duty calls."

They walked down the hall and turned into a bedroom. Adilida walked over to a brightly painted crib in the corner of the room, reached in, and lifted out a two-month-old baby.

"You are awake, my handsome one!" she cooed, holding him close, as she moved over and sat on the bed. The child snuggled in and stopped crying.

"Speaking of ... have you decided how you will tell Thomas?"

"No ... I'm still insistent on telling him in person, but now ... Oh, Uncle, a man shouldn't learn he has a son in a *letter!* Especially a son he cannot see, no matter how much he might wish to, with this blockade, and a terrible war looming! It would be *most* cruel.

"No! No, I *won't* subject my Thomas to such suffering; he is too good a man and does not deserve such."

"Well, whether I agree or not, it is *your* decision on *that* matter. But I must insist you wait no longer to give the child a name. That has always been the part of your plan I have found most disagreeable. I know you have felt strongly about letting the father help decide the name, but now ... a child *must* have a name, Adilida! To delay it longer is ... unconscionable!"

"Yes ... I know Uncle, I know. You need not chastise me further; I freely admit you are right. Come, please sit. Since Thomas cannot help me decide, then you and I must give my son a name ..."

༄༅ᴥᴥᴥ༄༅ᴥᴥ༄༅ᴥᴥᴥ

Nathan called a meeting of his men, who now gathered on the veranda. They stood in a group while Nathan sat in a chair next to a table, still not trusting himself to stand for any extended period. Miss Abbey and Megs were there also, sitting in chairs behind him at the same table.

"Men, as you know, the country's now divided between the Southern slave states and the Northern pro-Union states. I've made no secret my loyalties lie with the Union, but unfortunately, we're living in a state that's gone the other direction. It's not clear what will happen here on the western side. There's some talk of a split with Richmond, but that's not yet been decided. And even if it does happen, we're in a very vulnerable spot here, being so close to the mountains and the eastern side.

"Anyway, I've clearly made some bad enemies over the whole matter. And it's very likely they'll come here with force of arms to make me mend my wicked ways.

"So firstly, I want to say y'all are good men—the best I've known. You're hard working and loyal, and I appreciate everything you've done for me up 'til now.

"I also realize, however, my point of view isn't the only one there is in the world, and some of you may be seeing things differently.

"So I called you together here to say if you choose to fight for the Southern side in the coming conflict, I'll not hold it against you. You may collect your personal belongings and any wages owed, and I will send you on your way with no hard feelings.

"Likewise, y'all didn't sign on here at Mountain Meadows to end up in a shooting war. So if you'd rather not be a part of *that*, I'll certainly understand. And again, there'll be no hard feelings."

There was a silence.

"What about you, Jim? You're a Texan, born and bred. And Texas has now declared for the South."

Jim looked him in the eye, and there was a scowl on his face, "Sir ... I don't give a good Goddamn what them other Texans do. If'n they was to jump off a cliff am I supposed to join 'em just 'cause I'm from there? No, thank you. I've worn the blue uniform since I was old enough to *pretend* to be a man. Now I believe if you were to cut me open, I'd likely bleed blue blood! No, sir, I'm a Union soldier, through and through. And even if I wasn't, I'd follow *you* anywhere, sir, as I have said many times before."

"Thank you, Jim. What about you, Billy? You're also from Texas. I expect the Tonkawas will side with the soldiers in Texas, who'll be fighting for the South."

But Billy stared at him, as if he didn't understand the question, so Nathan tried to word it a different way.

"Billy ... will you stay, and fight with me on the Northern side, even if the rest of your people fight for the *other* side?"

"You are my Captain. I will fight whoever you tell me to fight. The rest of my people are free to decide for themselves who *they* will fight."

Nathan shook his head and smiled. He wished more people had Billy's simple philosophy about life. The world would likely be a much better place.

Then he turned to the three original farmhands, Zeke, Benny, and Joe. "What about you men? You're all Virginians. I can't ask you to stay and fight against your fellow Virginians, if you're unwilling."

The two others looked at Zeke, and he stepped forward. "Sir, me and the boys've already discussed it, and we want to stay. We don't feel good about fighting Virginians, of course, but I reckon we've already been doing some of that against old Walters.

"We like the things you've been saying—'bout how you're gonna make the farm work without slaves and whatnot. And we're fired up mad about what them fellows over to Richmond tried to do to you when you was there. We don't have much problem fighting against fellas like *them*.

"And also ... we're keen on the idea you mentioned about the West splitting off from the East of Virginia. That makes us not feel so much like outcasts in our own state, but maybe like we'll have our *own* state after all."

Nathan was pleased, but not especially surprised. "All right, then, I guess it's unanimous. I thank y'all kindly, from the bottom of my heart, and I am most obliged to you. Now we must plan our defense of this property and prepare for the storm that is surely coming."

Chapter 2. The Siege of Mountain Meadows

"They're on our left,
they're on our right,
they're in front of us,
they're behind us...
they can't get away this time!"
– Lt. General Lewis B. 'Chesty' Puller, USMC

Saturday May 11, 1861 – Greenbrier County, Virginia:

Tony sat in a chair next to a table on the veranda. Across from him sat the Captain, calmly smoking on a cigar, looking at Tony, but not yet saying anything. Tony had heard he'd been injured and was moving about only slowly. But just now, sitting still as he was, he looked the same as always.

"Sergeant Jim has told me everything that happened on the day Walters attacked the farm while I was away. It made for an interesting tale, especially *your* part in it."

Tony felt shameful for what he'd done that day, but he knew it hadn't been *all* bad, and he'd at least tried to make amends. But he didn't know what the Captain thought about it, nor what he would say, so he feared the worst. And it didn't help that the Captain's huge, frightful dog lay close by over in the house's shade. The dog looked at Tony, tilting his head in curiosity, his large mouth open and panting, exposing a long row of sharp teeth. Still, Tony was determined to look the Captain in the eye, and not bow his head as he would've done in the old days.

"I ain't too proud o' that, sir."

"Yes, well I understand Sergeant Jim felt conflicted about it, and I can see why. On the one hand, you stole a rifle and abandoned your post which nearly led to disaster. In the Army that would carry a death sentence ..."

Tony's eyes widened at this, and his heart beat faster, but he said nothing.

"On the *other* hand, for some reason you apparently thought better of it, and came back to fight. As I understand it, you killed our old friend Sickles with that same gun you stole. That frightened off Walters, preventing him from taking Miss Abbey hostage and likely killing everyone else in the Big House."

He continued to look at Tony, a mild expression on his face as he took several more puffs on his cigar.

"But so far I've only heard the tale from *other* people ... I'd like to hear the story from you now, Tony, if you please."

"Ain't much of nothing more to tell, sir. It was ... pretty well just as Sergeant Jim says, I reckon."

"Well, yes ... but Sergeant Jim couldn't tell me the *why* of it, which is the part I am most interested in. Especially *why* you decided to come back."

Tony was surprised by this statement. He'd expected the Captain to quiz him on why he stole the gun and left, after all the good things that had been happening lately on the farm.

"Well ... I never thought nothing bad would come of us leaving ... we'd been watching that road for weeks and nothing ever happened. No sign o' that wicked Walters or his folk. So, I reckoned we'd not be missed. But then ... we was going along and heard the gunfire back this-a-way, and I knew ... well, I knew we was needed back here."

"So ... even though you'd decided to leave this place, you returned to fight for it? Why?"

"Well ... on account o' ... I reckon ... I still gots *feelings* for folks that lives here, and couldn't stomach the thought of causing them harm ..."

"I see ..." the Captain took a few more puffs on the cigar.

Tony still felt anxious over where this was headed, but the Captain didn't appear especially angry — just ... *curious*, maybe?

"Then I guess that leads us to the other '*why*' ... *why* you decided to leave in the first place. But this time let me guess it ..."

He took another long puff, then looked Tony hard in the eyes.

"You liked the things you heard me say about setting you free, but you had a hard time trusting it; perhaps I was only saying things to get the people to work harder, be more cooperative, and

23

whatnot. But you were willing to wait and see what would happen. Except then … *something* changed. A … certain young lady whom you … *admired* … did not return the feelings as you'd wished, and in fact, seemed … hmm … more interested in the new, young master? And the young master seemed only too happy to oblige the young lady's wishes, even taking her into his house so she'd be closer. This hurt you, stinging worse than any whipping ever could. So you made up your mind to leave, and never come back.

"How am I doing so far?"

Tony's eyes were wide with shock, "How …?"

"And then there's the gun. You'd been watching us at target practice … at first out of curiosity. But you kept coming back because you'd decided you needed to know how to load and shoot a gun. You figured if you observed carefully, and asked a few pointed questions, you'd figure it out.

"So when you were ready to leave, you snuck into the house at night and took the rifle and ammunition. I guess you were concerned … *hmm* … someone might follow after you to bring you back? But since we don't have hunting dogs anymore, that doesn't seem likely. Maybe slavers might try to capture you out on the road?

"No … *wait!* We *do* still have *one* dog … Harry! You were worried Harry might come after you! Ha! Then I don't blame you for wanting a gun. I'd not want to be unarmed with Harry chasing me through the woods!"

He grimaced at the thought of it, recalling the bloody scene after Harry attacked the slavers in the woods outside Paint Bank.

Tony continued to stare at the Captain open-mouthed. "But … but … how you knows all that, Captain? Did Johnny tell you them things?"

"No … I haven't yet spoken with Johnny, or Ned … though I will later. No, Tony … I know these things because … I am *not* blind, and I am *not* a complete fool."

He let that notion sit for a moment while he took another pull on the cigar and let it out leisurely.

"Tony ... I have stood before y'all every Sunday for months to give my sermons ... do you think I couldn't see everything everyone was doing right in front of me? Where they were sitting, and who they were ... *staring at*, for instance?

"And then, after Rosa's near-beating incident with Sickles, I saw a change. No longer sitting near her, even trying to look a different direction, but still not able to resist a quick glance from time to time.

"As I said, I am *not* a fool, Tony ... I am only sorry she didn't return the feelings. Truly sorry."

But now that they were discussing Rosa and dredging up those feelings, Tony felt the old heat rising again. It emboldened him to ask the question bubbling up inside him, "Then *why*, Captain ... why did you take her into the Big House?"

Nathan paused ... he wasn't ready to tell Tony his suspicions about her being his sister, but fortunately that wasn't necessary. The simple, *known* truth was sufficient.

"She *asked* to come work in the house. And I didn't see any harm in it. She said she'd been suffering night terrors since the incident and thought she'd feel safer in the Big House. So I acceded to her wishes. There was no ill intent on my part, nor on hers ... as far as I know."

Nathan knew there was no point in mentioning his growing concern she might be starting to have *other* feelings for him. He wasn't sure it was true, and if it was, he'd not yet figured out a graceful way to discourage it without further hurting her. Maybe if she and Tony could become closer that would solve the problem for him.

Tony gazed at his feet and said nothing, a scowl twisting his features. Nathan assumed this meant he wasn't yet convinced, so he'd have to take a different tack.

"Tony, look me in the eye if you would, so you will see the truth in what I am about to say."

Tony looked up at the Captain whose expression was now stern and intense. And when the Captain spoke, his words carried that same strong conviction, "After what happened between Rosa and Sickles, I made my severe displeasure known to all the white

25

men on this farm. I made certain they understood there was to be no relations between them and any black woman on this farm under any circumstances—under penalty of severe punishment and immediate forfeiture of employment. And I made it plain that that rule includes me! Tony, I have *never* bedded Rosa, nor any other slave woman, and I *never* will! Do you hear me?"

Tony not only heard what the Captain was saying, he heard the *truth* in it. He felt the anger drain out of him in a rush.

"I ... I understand, sir. But if that's so, then ... why does she turn away from me as she does ... I just can't ... understand it. What is she thinking, anyways?" He shook his head slowly and again gazed down at his feet, this time with a puzzled, troubled expression.

Nathan took another pull on the cigar and slowly let it out again before answering. "Tony, there was a time when I might have offered you advice on how to deal with a woman, or about what she had on her mind. But ... I no longer feel qualified to give such advice. What a woman has on her mind ... has become a mystery to me as well ..."

The Captain's earlier stern voice had suddenly turned quiet and soft as he spoke, and he trailed off with a thoughtful and faraway look in his eyes.

Tony remembered the rumors he'd heard of Miss Evelyn's sudden, inexplicable departure, and the devastating effect it'd had on the Captain. He suddenly felt sheepish and ashamed of himself for how he'd been dealing with Rosa. And for blaming it on a man who clearly wasn't at fault.

"I ... I's sorry, sir. This ain't none o' your concern. I's just got to deal with it as best as I can. Like a man should do.

"And ... thank you for telling me, you know, about not *bein'* with Rosa. I ... never knew how much it mattered. But now that you've said it, I ... well ... anyway, just ... thank you, sir.

"And ... about me takin' the gun and runnin' off and whatnot ... whatever punishment you think I deserves I won't argue it, nor hold it against you, sir. Not that it matters none, as you can do as you wants with the likes of me."

"It *does* matter, Tony. And I have sworn not to mete out the kind of punishment you're speaking of. So … my most severe option is to exile you from the farm, which ironically is exactly what you were trying to accomplish by running away. So if you still wish to go, you may do so."

"I can just … walk away, and you won't try to stop me, nor send your hound after me?"

"Yes. That's right. But I must warn you … if you do walk away now you won't be a freeman … you'll be a runaway slave in the eyes of the law. With no manumission papers, you'll be subject to capture and enslavement by the first slaver who comes along. And even if you make it to the North, there are still laws in place, at least for now, that say they must send you back. So even there you'd have to live in hiding lest someone arrest you and put you in chains. I wouldn't recommend it, but, as I said, it's up to you."

Tony considered it a moment. With all that had happened with Walters' raid, and knowing there might still be a chance with Rosa, the desire to run had entirely left him.

"I reckon … I'd rather stay, sir, and not be punished in *that* way, if it's all right with you."

Nathan smiled, "I was hoping you'd say that. Well … that being the case, I have made my decision. But before I pronounce your sentence let me say, if you don't like it, you can still choose to leave; I will not try to stop you. Is that fair?"

"Yes, sir. More than fair, I'd say."

"Very well, then. Your punishment shall be … you will attend target practice every Sunday until such time as I dismiss you from that duty. And this time you will *practice* firing the rifles, and pistols for that matter, so you become proficient at shooting. And then, if and when this farm is attacked again, you will fight as ordered by your superior officers. And will do any other such things as you are asked to do in the defense of this farm.

"Do you accept this punishment, or do you choose to leave Mountain Meadows forever?"

Tony's eyes widened again. And then a bright smile spread across his face. "Oh! Yes! Yes, sir! I'll gladly accept *that* punishment! Though … it don't rightly seem like any *punishment* at all!"

"Hmm … well, you may feel that way *now* … but wait until bullets are zipping past your head and then tell me if you still feel the same!"

"Oh, I reckon I'll not change my mind about it, even then, sir."

Nathan looked him in the eyes for another moment, then smiled, nodded and said, "I believe you're right about that Tony. Yes … I believe you're right. Good man."

ᔓᔓᔓᑫᑫᔓᔓᑫᑫᔓᔓᑫᑫᔓᔓᑫᑫ

Jim strode across the field toward where the regular target practice took place. He hadn't expected there to be any *this* Sunday; the Captain was still too weak for it, Georgie was still on the mend, and the others were resting up from their adventures rescuing the Captain. Even the Captain's usual sermon had been very abbreviated earlier in the morning, and he'd sat in a chair to deliver it.

Nobody had even gone to church this morning—the Captain's health being the excuse. But he suspected even Miss Abbey didn't feel comfortable leaving the farm just now, not knowing for sure what was happening out in the wider world.

But he'd heard gunfire, so came to investigate out of curiosity. As he walked, he recalled the Captain's "punishment" of Tony—that he had to practice shooting guns every Sunday until the Captain told him to stop. So he assumed Tony had asked one of the men to work with him on it, Stan being the most likely.

Then he heard multiple rifle shots, too close together to allow time for reloading. He paused to listen and count the shots, *one, two, three … four, five, six, seven … eight, nine, ten … what the hell? We ain't even got that many men!*

He wasn't surprised to find Stan and Tony there when he arrived, but he *was* surprised to see a whole row of black faces turn and look up at him, several with wide grins. He recognized them as some of the same men who'd manned the Mountain Meadows Watch since they'd instigated it right after New Year's.

"Stan … what're you doing?"

28

"Oh, hello, Sergeant Jim. Is silly question. You can see with your eyes what I am doing."

"Well, yes, I can see you have all these ... *gentlemen* ... with rifles and are teaching them to shoot. But ... son ... don't you know it's against the law to teach slaves to shoot a gun? Tony, here ... well, that's one thing, since he done already figured it out on his own, but these others ...?"

"Oh, against *law* you say?" he smiled broadly, but not humorously. "You mean *law* where Captain is criminal for killing men who attack him on street, bash his head, tie him up, and try murder him slowly with knives? Or you mean *law* where governor can ignore president's orders and bomb his forts? Or *law* where Army officer ignores sacred oath sworn to God and joins other side? *This* is *law* you worry about breaking?"

Jim paused and scratched his chin, looking up at a cloud drifting by above in an otherwise blue sky. "Well, now you put it that way ... you *do* have a point there. Oh, what the hell! In Richmond we're already outlaws and traitors, so why not?! It'll give us more firepower, that's certain."

"Yes ... and will be *big* surprise for enemies. Will not expect so many trained shooters on farm."

"True ... very true. But, Stan, where'd you get all them guns?"

"Oh ... you can be thanking our good neighbor Walters for these. Each time he comes visit ... he kindly leave behind rifles! And pistols, knives, shotguns, whips, and other odd useful things ..."

"Oh, *yeah!* I clean forgot about that ..."

"Yes, Sergeant. And if only he would come ... hmm ... two, maybe three more times, we will be having enough rifles for all men on farm!"

Stan grinned, and this time he *did* appear amused.

☯☯☯☯☯☯☯☯☯☯☯☯

An hour later Nathan was sitting under the old oak tree at the now-famous "whip-cutting" table talking to Toby, with Harry the Dog curled up underneath. They'd walked about the cotton field next to it until Nathan had to sit.

He felt sheepish asking the much-older man to allow him a rest. But such was the current state of things, and there was nothing he could do about it, despite the frustration it caused him.

"Yes, sir, Captain … the crops is coming along beautifully this year so far. I think maybe the cotton'll be even better'n last year, if you can believe it."

"I'm so happy to hear it, Toby. But what about the people … how are *they* doing now that … well, that things have changed?"

"You mean, how is it now we's no longer following The Way? Look for yourself, Captain. Folks is happier, smiling, and being proud of a field with fine looking cotton plants, and nary a weed to be found! I never would've believed it before, but you and Megs was right … it was maybe hurting our own folks as much as it was hurting the white masters."

Nathan smiled, "That's very gratifying, Toby. I'm looking forward to another bountiful harvest, and another great step toward putting this farm on a footing to survive without free labor… toward being able to free y'all."

"Amen to that, Captain, sir."

"Now, we must pray the wider world leaves us alone long enough to enjoy the fruits of our labors."

"What do you mean, sir? The secession talk, and whatnot?"

"Yes, but I'm afraid it has gone far beyond that now. Now there's a war brewing, and my fear is this farm may end up right in the middle of the fighting."

"Oh … I see. Well, let's hope it passes us by, like them plagues and whatnot passed by the Israelites back in them olden days in the Bible."

"Yes, the 'Passover' they called it. And I agree. Let's pray it does, so we can complete our plans in peace."

"I say amen again to that, Captain. Amen to that."

ဢဠၢၣၣဢဢၢၣၣဢဢၢၣၣ

The next day, Nathan called together Tom, Jim, Miss Abbey, Megs, and Toby for a meeting. These were the people he'd begun to think of as the "Mountain Meadows Commanding Officers."

And for reasons the others couldn't quite fathom, he'd invited Billy to join them.

They gathered around a table out on the veranda after breakfast. Though the table was in the sun, it was still cool and pleasant; the day had not yet heated up. Once again Harry lay close by the Captain, this time right next to his chair under his right hand. Nathan idly scratched the dog's head between the ears as he spoke.

"As y'all know, I've refused to return to Richmond with those law officers, or to accept Colonel Lee's invitation to join the new Southern Army—what they're now calling 'Confederate.'

"By doing so I've declared my defiance of the government in Richmond. They can't just ignore a thing like that and allow it to go unanswered. I believe it's not a question of *if,* but rather *when.*

"The good news is … they likely have bigger fish to fry at the moment, and little time to waste worrying overmuch about one recalcitrant farmer in western Virginia. I'd imagine they're more than busy preparing for Mr. Lincoln's invasion from the North and figuring out how to counter his blockade of the seas.

"So I don't expect the regular Army to come marching up our drive anytime soon. On the other hand, as we've seen elsewhere, the Slave Power likes to use local militias to conduct its dirty business—like-minded volunteers who are ready and willing to do their bidding.

"And now the official government in Richmond has joined in the madness, it's certain their numbers will swell. This is our biggest threat for the time being: not professional soldiers or officers, but rather a local militia of volunteers. Farmers, townsmen, and whatnot."

Jim laughed, "Let 'em come! Ask Walters how that's worked out. Bunch of amateurs! Our boys'll chew 'em up and spit 'em out without breaking a sweat!"

"Yes, likely so … but even Walters can be dangerous, and he'll likely be leading the band. Anyway, we needn't panic, but we need to prepare, and quickly, before our enemies have time to react."

"Nathan, dear ... how many of these militia men do you expect to attack us? Surely only Walters, and a handful of others would stoop so low?"

"I'm sorry to disagree with you, and there was a time when I would have agreed with you, Momma. But after what we saw in Richmond, and what we experienced trying to get home ... I no longer have faith in the common sense of our fellow Virginians. I hate to say it, but ... it's likely some of the same people who've smiled at us in church will soon be pointing rifles at us."

"Oh surely, not!"

"He's right, Miss Abbey," Tom said, "the secession has caused a mass hysteria in Virginia. When we arrived in Richmond, everyone treated us with deference, like important, honored citizens. But in the end, we had to flee the city, in fear for our very lives."

"Let us leave that aside for the moment," Nathan continued. "We can all agree it's best to err on the side of caution and prepare for a confrontation. That's why I've asked Billy to join us. Billy, you've explored every hill and dale for miles around this farm since you've arrived. From which directions are we most vulnerable to attack?"

Billy was quiet for a moment, and closed his eyes, as if recalling the things he'd seen in his explorations.

"East the mountains loom, ridge and ridge for endless miles. An army might come marching up the main road from the east, going into the mountains somewhere close to here ... hmm ... maybe White Sulphur Springs. But it would be difficult and dangerous. They could not bring wagons, nor cannons—ridges too steep, and no roads, nor even elk trails. Horses might be led but not ridden. It would be very hard. A handful of rifles on the ridgetops might stand off an army to the end of days.

"The north is not high, but still rough, and great forests of monster trees. In places a horse cannot squeeze between. Trees for mile after endless mile. No roads, not even wide paths. Only winding animal tracks. I do not know what is on the other side, I have never reached it. One time I walked for a week or more and found no end.

"West of Mountain Meadows is also thick woods and drops off steeply to the edge of a great river. 'Greenbrier' the white men call this river. It is wide and too deep to ford. So men coming from there must first cross the river, by swimming horses, or on boats. Back on land they'd climb a steep slope through thick trees, with no road, and no wide trails. Here too, a small group of men might stop an army for many days. Likely forever if they keep them from crossing the river.

"South runs the road from the farm. Though winding and narrow, still the slope is not so steep, and wagons or cannons may be brought up. In two places it passes narrow gaps in high rocks. Good men could hold these points against many, for a long time.

"There is also the Elk Trail up the back side of the Captain's grandfather's hill. Horses can climb up but not wagons. For attackers, if they gain the hilltop, they can fire down on the farm to good effect."

"Thank you, Billy. And what if … what if someone wished to keep us in, rather than attack us? What would that look like?"

He considered this a moment before answering. "Same problems in reverse. No way for us to bring wagons and no way to get out, except on foot or horseback, other than by the main road. And the road may be easily blocked and held by an enemy, same as by us."

There was a stony silence as they absorbed the implications of this.

"And what if … what if we were to build a *new* road … to the north, say? You said it was not so mountainous, only heavily wooded. But trees can be cut, and a road made through them."

Billy shrugged, "In West Texas all is open, with little need for cutting trees to make a way."

"I think I can answer that one, Captain," Tom offered. "When I was going through Jacob's paperwork, I came across an interesting report. It was written by a surveyor he had apparently hired to look into that very possibility: cutting a road through to the north. Of course, he wasn't concerned about a siege; rather, he was looking for a more efficient way to get his goods to the more profitable Northern markets."

"Oh? That's interesting. And what does it say?"

"I'm afraid it's *not* good news, sir. The surveyor concluded it was *possible* to do, but he estimated it would take several years, and cost more than all the profits from a dozen harvests, even if they sold the timber harvested while building the road to support the project. So naturally, Jacob abandoned the idea as economically unfeasible."

"*Damn* ... too bad. We could sure use that northern route just now."

"Yes, sir. That would be most convenient, and it might also allow us to bring in potential allies from that direction."

"Well, it's of no benefit to wish for things to be different than they are. I suppose we should be grateful there's little chance of the enemy attacking from that direction. Jim, you've kept up a scaled-back version of the Watch since Walters' last failed attack; it may be time to ramp it back up again."

"Yes, sir. That we will do, straight away."

"And ... you and Billy get together and decide if there's any benefit to watching the other routes. I like Billy's idea about a few men with rifles stopping an army in those directions. But that doesn't do us much good if those 'few men' aren't there to pull the trigger!"

"We'll get on it, sir."

"And once you've got the Watch in place, let's figure out our battle plans. We must never again allow our enemies to set foot on our soil. No more tricks or traps ... we must stop them cold before they ever get started. Do I make myself clear?"

He locked eyes with Jim, and the latter understood. Though the Captain had never spoken a critical word concerning it, Jim was keenly aware of his previous plan's failure. Though not entirely his fault, it *had* put Miss Abbey and the household at great risk and had nearly ended in disaster. That must *not* be allowed to happen again.

"Understood, sir. No tricks this time. We shall meet the enemy at the gates and drive him back with all the force we can muster."

"Good. See that it's so, mister.

"Gentlemen … and ladies … our safest course of action is to assume our enemies may soon attack us and to plan accordingly. Tom, I'd like you to get together with Miss Abbey, Megs, and Toby to draw up a plan for how this farm can become self-sufficient, with no supplies from outside. Draw up a list of any goods we need to purchase while we still can."

"Certainly, sir. Self-sufficient for how long?"

"Months at the least … indefinitely, if possible."

Tom's eyes went wide. "I … I'm not sure that's possible without a lot more planning than we'll have time for, sir. If we'd planted all *food* crops, there'd be little problem. But it's hard to eat tobacco and cotton, though we'll likely never run out of cigars or shirts!"

"We do grow subsistence crops, do we not? And raise our own livestock?"

"Yes, sir. But those crops are intended to supplement the necessary food, not supply *all*. They're not sufficient to make it through all the winter months and early spring. The farm has always purchased and brought in at least some portion of the required foodstuffs during those months."

"Well, it's only May, so we may not need to worry overmuch about the winter months."

"Well … you did say *indefinitely*, sir."

"Yes … I guess I did, Tom."

"All right, let's think about this, sir … assuming there *is* a war, how long do you figure before it's over?"

Nathan didn't immediately answer but gazed up to the sky for several seconds. Then he looked back at Tom. "Guess we'd better figure out what to do about those winter months after all, Tom."

"Yes, sir. *Indefinitely* it is."

"Miss Abbey, I'm afraid we must assume it is no longer safe to leave our own property, even to attend church. I'm sorry."

"That's all right, Nathan, dear. I am perfectly content to spend all my time here, now that you're home. Everyone I truly care about is right here. I have no need to go elsewhere. And, as they say, 'this too, shall pass.'"

But Nathan had a sudden vision of Evelyn, and he suppressed a sigh. He burned to see her again ... to talk to her. And ... to hold her close and kiss her sweet lips. A lengthy siege would be a sore test. He felt the heat of his anger rising; his enemies would pay the price for this injustice! Putting his enemies to the sword wouldn't bring her any closer, but it might make enduring the separation easier!

"Oh ... and Tom ... when you go into town to buy supplies, take a well-armed escort. I'd not want anyone waylaying you on the road.

"And ... go ahead and take Jim and Stan with you this time. You may have need of them in case someone decides he doesn't want to sell goods to us 'traitors.'"

Tom smiled, "Yes, sir. Thank you. It will be a great comfort having them along, and ... we may need their *particular* skills at persuasion, as you say."

He looked over at Jim who shrugged his shoulders and grinned.

ℰℐℐℭℰℐℐℭℰℐℐℭℰℐℐℭ

"Thank you ever so kindly for the hospitality, Mr. Walters."

"Never mention it. My butler tells me you're a Colonel in the new Southern Army, Mr. Burns?"

"Yes, sir, that's correct. Our esteemed former Governor Henry Wise sent me to ... *recruit* for the militia on *this* side of the mountains even before the secession. But now ... I have been granted an *official* rank in the new Army to compliment my most vital mission. The commission has just come through and I've not yet had time to acquire the proper ... attire," he glanced down and gestured at his suit. It was the fine suit of a gentleman, but not a soldier's uniform.

"Ah, I see. And what can I do for you, Colonel Burns ... or for Mr. Wise, as the case may be?"

"Well, yes ... as you have implied, Mr. Wise is my ... *advocate*, I suppose you might say. He's the one responsible for my commission, though I expect a promotion to general officer once hostilities break out in earnest."

"Oh, well, congratulations in advance on that, I'm sure."

"Thank you, sir, though I expect anyone with previous war experience is likely to attain a high rank in the coming conflict."

"Oh, so you fought in the late Mexican war?"

Walters recalled Chambers describing the desperate, hand-to-hand fighting through the streets in the Mexican capital city and raising the American flag over the capitol building. Despite his hatred for Chambers, remembering the man's narrative of that action still gave him chills.

"Yes, that's right. I was a sergeant … in the Voltigeurs Regiment under Joe Johnston. We fought our way through the castle fortress at Chapultepec. It was … most *memorable.*"

"I would imagine so."

"Anyway … you have asked why I'm here. I shall be brief, sir. In my official capacity as Colonel I have been tasked with recruiting young men in Greenbrier County for the new Southern Army—the *Confederate States* Army I should say. This work is already well underway … we have nearly a hundred recruits already, and more coming in every hour."

"Ah … excellent. I'm pleased to hear it."

"Yes, it has been most gratifying. Once I have recruited and equipped a battalion or so, I'm to march north and link up with Colonel Porterfield. He's performing my same function in the area between Grafton and Philippi. There we'll be well positioned to prevent any incursion into Virginia by Northern aggressors."

"Seems a sound plan."

"Thank you for saying so. But even before I complete my recruitment and move north, Mr. Wise has asked me to undertake a *specific* task for him once I have sufficient men for the mission."

"Oh?"

"It seems Mr. Wise has developed a *particular* enmity toward your neighbor, Mr. Nathaniel Chambers, him being, apparently, a traitor to our most-noble cause and also a former military officer. In fact, it would be safe to say he *loathes* the man and wants to see him hang."

"Well, that makes two of us!"

"Oh? Well, I'm gratified to hear it. I've come here to ask if you might provide any useful information toward arranging his immediate capture ... or *demise* if capture proves too inconvenient."

"*Demise* seems a good outcome to me; I would like nothing better. Yes, I have a good deal of *information* ... as well as ideas and plans already in the works."

"Excellent! Then I can count on your full cooperation? Of course, Mr. Wise will be most grateful for any and all assistance you're inclined to provide."

"I've considered little else these past few months. I'm sure if you and I put our heads together ... and our men ... we can come up with a workable plan. One that will finally put an end to his traitorous mischief, to the satisfaction of Mr. Wise. And myself, of course."

"Very good, Mr. Walters! Tell me what you have in mind, if you please ..."

𝆠𝆠𝆠𝆠𝆠𝆠𝆠𝆠𝆠𝆠

In the end it took the better part of the week to plan out the resupply mission: coming up with a list of necessary goods the farm was unable to supply for itself 'indefinitely' proved a greater challenge than Tom had at first assumed. Everyone had a different opinion on the matter, and no one was especially precise in their calculations of the quantities of whatever it was they needed. "A goodly supply," "a pile," "a lot," etc. were the typical responses. No one had ever had to plan that far ahead before. They typically took a wagon to town every few weeks to stock up on whatever necessities were running short. But nobody had ever back-calculated how long it had been since the last time they'd had to buy each particular item. And because it was considered normal operating expenses of the farm, it was the one thing Jacob had never kept specific records on.

The good news, from Tom's perspective, was by the time they were ready to leave, Nathan was feeling considerably better; so much so that he came along too. Tom suspected he was getting a bit of cabin fever and needed to get out and do something. At any rate it did Tom's heart good to see Nathan walking steadily without leaning on a cane. And he'd regained the old fire in his eyes.

Tom figured the Lewisburg Mercantile had likely never been visited by such a caravan—four wagons, each driven by a groom, and six armed men on horseback. Besides himself and the Captain, their armed escort included Jim, Stan, Jamie, and Georgie. Those four pulled up with rifles in hand, and pistols holstered at their hips. He and the Captain also wore pistol holsters, in keeping with Nathan's long-standing belief in a strong show of force to confront a potentially dangerous situation.

But despite the Captain's earlier concerns, the proprietor was agreeable to selling them whatever they wanted. Tom noticed he wasn't as friendly and chatty as he'd been on prior occasions, but the man soon recognized he was about to make one of the biggest sales in the history of his store. His eyes widened when Tom presented the list of supplies he wanted to purchase. In the end, they'd nearly bought out the store, and the Mountain Meadows wagons were full to bursting. Tom purchased every gun—pistol and rifle—every bullet, and all the gunpowder they had in stock. The Captain was taking no chances!

Stan seemed disappointed. He'd been looking forward to exercising his skills at persuasion, such as he hadn't done since the church pew incident. But Jim was more philosophical about it, "Cheer up, Stanny-boy, there's still a chance we may yet run into some of Walters' yahoos out on the road on our ride home. Then we'll have a little fun."

"Ah … you are always saying *nicest* things, Sergeant Jim," Stan said with a grin.

Nathan soon realized there was nothing productive for him to do in the store. Tom had the whole operation well in hand, and nobody would allow him to lift or carry anything. Even Cobb scolded him when he started to help with a heavy load, "Oh, no, Captain, sir! Both Megs and Miss Abbey told me not to allows you to do any heavy work." He grinned, "And to tell the truth … I's more a-scared of them two ladies than I am o' *you*, sir!"

Nathan laughed, "You're a wise man, Cobb."

So he stepped outside and went for a stroll down the street. He had a mind to get a pulse on the general demeanor of the town after all that'd happened. He still hoped the folks west of the mountains had retained their common sense—that they'd at least have a healthy skepticism of the whole secession business, if not outright opposition.

But he quickly realized there had been a sea change since he'd been here last. He was no longer greeted with friendly nods and smiles. People seemed to go out of their way to avoid him, or to avoid making eye contact; and nobody said hello or stopped to speak with him, even people he recognized, who he was sure recognized him.

It started to remind him of when he'd first arrived at Mountain Meadows and none of the slaves met his eye. Only this time he saw sour, even angry looks rather than the downcast, apathetic expressions he'd seen on the slaves. Had things really changed that much in a few short months? He felt a wave of hopelessness and despair threaten to overwhelm him. He realized he was in danger of drifting down into the doldrums. But the fighting side of him said, *No! Don't take this lying down! Are you not a man?*

He was walking past the courthouse at that moment, the very spot where he'd stood back in February to speak to the town and tell them his pro-Union feelings in hopes they'd agree, which they had in spades at the time. It made him wonder if he'd been wrong to not campaign against the secession for the referendum. Could the people still be swayed? Was all hope for Virginia truly lost?

He suddenly felt determined to at least try, to make one last attempt to convince these particular Virginians—his own neighbors—that secession was madness. Or maybe they'd be open to the idea of a new, separate pro-Union state in western Virginia.

He jumped up the steps of the courthouse and turned toward the town square in front. Harry trotted up after him.

"Fellow Virginians, and fellow Americans! I would speak with you, if you would listen!" he shouted out. Though some people continued to walk past as if they hadn't heard, several people paused, and turned to look up at him.

"I am Nathaniel Chambers, who stood in this very spot months ago, asking for your vote so I could represent you in Richmond. On that occasion I said exactly how I felt about the secession, that I would rather die than break up our great Union, a Union for which I'd fought a bloody war. Well, here I stand, and *I* have *not* changed … I still believe the secession is a mistake—a disaster that will destroy our beloved home and our beloved country. The country of *true* Virginians, George Washington and Thomas Jefferson, not of *false* Virginians like Henry Wise and his band of lawless slavers. Who is with me?"

But this time he was met with stony silence, and mostly angry, sullen looks. He saw a few sympathetic looks as well, a few nods and smiles, but nobody spoke in his favor. A sudden shout, "Traitor!" broke the silence.

It was shocking. Nathan didn't know how to respond. Another shout rang out, "Yankee!" then "Northern traitor!"

His opponents seemed emboldened by his lack of support from the crowd. Soon a surly-looking knot of young men had gathered at the bottom of the stairs.

He considered a heated retort. Then he recalled Proverbs chapter twenty-seven, verse twenty-two:

> *Though thou shouldest bray a fool in a mortar among wheat with a pestle, yet will not his foolishness depart from him.*

He shook his head and smiled a rueful smile then strode purposely down the steps straight toward the group gathered below.

When he stepped up to them, a hard look on his face, no one seemed inclined to stand in his way. They parted to let him through, the dog hard on his heels. But just as he'd passed into their midst someone gave him a shove from the side, and he nearly lost his balance. He spun around to confront whoever it was, and received another shove, this time in his back from the other side. He wheeled and threw a punch at the person standing there, connecting just below the man's eye with a *thud*, staggering him backward.

But now he was in the middle of an angry group of young men and realized they had him badly outnumbered, and things were about to turn ugly. He stepped back and turned to face five adversaries. All had determined looks and balled-up fists.

Harry slunk forward and crouched protectively in front of his master, a deep growl rumbling in his throat. The men hesitated in response to the new threat, until one man drew a large hunting knife from behind his back and stepped closer. Nathan unbuttoned the safety strap on his pistol holster. He gripped the handle, preparing to unholster the weapon …

His adversaries suddenly vanished in a blur too swift for eyes to follow.

He turned to see what had happened: Stan! The big man had launched himself on the men in a rush, knocking them to the ground in a heap. He now stood over them, fists on hips, scowling. They lay scattered across the hard cobblestones, moaning and rubbing sore heads and ribs. The hunting knife one man had been holding now lay harmlessly out of reach, knocked several yards away by the force of Stan's momentum.

The remaining crowd in the square scattered.

"Is not so funny now, eh? What is matter? Little sissy boys have no balls? Come, stand up! You dare threaten *my Captain?!* Fight Stan instead. I will crush you like bugs!" he waggled a huge right fist at them.

He was fired up—fighting mad. His face had a dark, deadly look, like a thunderhead about to burst forth in storm. Nathan feared if anyone took him up on his offer, they'd need to arrange a burial detail. But seeing the angry giant looming above, none were eager to accept the challenge.

Nathan stepped up and put his hand on Stan's shoulder, "Come, Mr. Volkov … these little boys no longer want to play."

Stan looked at him, a fire still blazing in his eyes. But the uncharacteristic humor from the Captain registered and the tension drained from him. He smiled … then laughed, "Seems so, Captain … seems so.

"Wagons are ready, sir ... I come to fetch you. Would have come sooner if I knew *this* was place with all the fun!" he reached down and patted Harry on the head, then laughed.

ಬಿನಿಂದ್ರಿಜಿಬಿನಿಂದ್ರಿಜಿಬಿನಿಂದ್ರಿ

"*They're here*, Captain!"

Nathan looked up at Jamie standing in the library doorway, nearly out of breath. Nathan had been sitting reading a newspaper Tom had acquired in town during their resupply mission. It was a Richmond paper, and over two weeks old. But he'd been absorbed in it before the interruption, and for a second he didn't understand what Jamie had just said.

"What? *They?* Oh ... oh, yes, thank you, Mr. O'Brien," he rose from the chair, tossing the paper aside.

"Your horse is saddled and outside, and I've brought your pistols from the hook in the hallway closet, sir. Your men are already confronting the enemy. I'm here after riding back at the gallop to fetch ye and Sergeant Clark, sir."

They heard hurried footsteps coming down the stairway into the foyer.

"Jamie ... I saw you from out the upstairs window with the grooms, bringing our horses ... what has happened?" Tom asked, poking his head into the library, breathing heavily.

"The story is, the enemy has come marching up the road, and they are many, aye! The lads have engaged them, and there is bein' one devil of a gunfight. Come ye sirs ... they are needing us!" Jamie turned and ran for the door, Nathan and Tom hard on his heels.

When they arrived at the scene, gun smoke drifted in the air and the sound of steady rifle fire echoed all around them. But they could see nothing of the actual battle for the thick trees and the curve of the road. Jamie led them off the roadway into a small meadow where they tied their horses to tree branches and bushes. There were several other mounts they recognized tied there.

"C'mere, sirs. Sergeant Jim is *this* way ... or at least he was," Jamie dashed off through the woods, drawn pistol in hand.

Nathan and Tom drew their pistols and followed, along with Harry the Dog who refused to stay behind no matter the danger. Jamie led them on a twisting path through the trees, heading steadily downhill. They were on the very southern edge of the Mountain Meadows property where it sloped steeply down to the main road. When they came to a small clearing, Jamie raised his hand to signal a stop as he cautiously poked his head out to reconnoiter. He turned back and said, "He's here. Move quickly to him … and kindly be for keeping your heads down, sirs!"

The continuous rifle fire, now much louder, confirmed the wisdom of his instructions. They moved forward into the clearing at a crouch, and immediately saw Jim and Billy, rifles in hand, squatting behind a large fallen log. Jim was looking their way, and gave them a grin, motioning them to come to him. Billy was looking the other direction, down the hill. He quickly leaned up over the top, took aim, and fired, a cloud of smoke swirling in the air as he ducked back down.

Nathan and Tom slid in beside Jim with Harry flopping down next to Nathan. His tongue hung out and he panted heavily from his exertions, but seemed entirely unbothered by the steady gunfire reverberating all around him.

Jamie moved in next to Billy and immediately holstered his pistol. Billy handed him his rifle. He looked down and saw that it'd been reloaded in his absence. He smiled at Billy, "Thanks, laddie! That was most kindly of you."

Billy returned the smile and nodded, without missing a beat in his own reloading. Jamie leaned up over the log, aimed at a point down the hill where a puff of smoke rose, and pulled the trigger. The rifle spoke sharply, flame leapt out the barrel, and smoke curled up around Jamie. He quickly ducked back down. A few seconds later a bullet impacted off the top of the log near where he'd been when he fired. Billy popped up, his own rifle answering the enemy in kind.

"Situation, Sergeant?" Nathan had to shout to be heard over the noise of continuous gunfire.

"Earlier this morning Billy spotted a large group of men, fifty or more with two wagons. They was coming along the main road from the west, moving in the direction of Richmond—which as you know would lead them right past the turnoff to this farm, sir. Four horsemen led them. He couldn't tell if their intentions were hostile, nor if they were armed—they carried no visible weapons. He sent a Watch man back to inform me. At the time I was stationed near the top of the rise up to the farm.

"I brought the other men up and moved them into position just in case. But until we knew their intentions, I didn't wish to bother you with it, sir, which I now regret, of course. Billy and the Watch men continued to observe the group as they moved along the road. Then just as they neared the turnoff, the walkers moved up around the wagons and appeared to be offloading something. Even with Billy's sharp eyes it took him a moment to realize they was rifles! They was handing them out as they walked. As soon as he saw this, Billy sent the other Watch man back here at the run!

"When they got to the turnoff, the riders turned and led the men afoot at a trot up our road, with the wagons following along behind. When they got close enough Billy recognized one of the horsemen: Walters! He didn't know the other riders—none of Walters' men that he'd seen before. That's when Billy beat it out o' there and came up the hill to join us.

"I'd positioned us initially at the first pinch point, closer to the bottom of the hill as you know, about a couple hundred yards further down from here. We were there waiting for them as they rounded the corner. When they was about sixty yards in front of us we opened fire. One horseman went down—an 'officer' I'll call him, but not Walters, more's the pity! Several foot-soldiers in the front went down as well, but the rest got off the road and took cover. Though there's a good, defensible pinch point there, the road ain't very steep nor narrow just before it. That allowed them to disperse to the sides for decent cover. They began returning fire to good effect, forcing our heads down.

"Apparently, whoever's in charge down there knows his business, so I'm guessing it's not Walters. They seemed to have come prepared for trouble and didn't panic as we'd expected when we opened up on 'em. I'm thinking several among them have done this before, sir."

"Damn ... at least a few *real* soldiers, then ... that's *not* good news. Then what happened?"

"Well, they have a lot more guns than us, sir, so we was having a hard time returning fire without great risk of getting our heads blowed clean off. So I ordered a withdrawal to this spot, our second designated pinch point. Once we was established in our new position, I sent Jamie back to fetch you two sirs.

"There's much steeper terrain below this spot, and the roadway's narrower, dropping off sharply on our left side, and climbing steadily on the right through thick woods. So they can't get all their guns on us at the same time. But they've been able to creep up close enough to keep us fairly occupied. We don't dare ease up on them for fear they'll get close enough to overrun us.

"So we've pretty well battled to a standstill at this point sir. They can't lay down enough lead to push us off this hill, but we don't have enough guns to drive them back down it. Too bad we didn't 'requisition' a cannon or two when we left the Army— would've come in most handy today!"

"Yes ... well, I'm just grateful that fellow down there doesn't have any. Casualties?"

"None to speak of, sir. Stanny-boy took some rock splinters in his upper arm from a close call with a rifle bullet. But I understand it hasn't slowed him down none, though he's bled a bit.

"William said he had a look at it. Stan asked if it was gonna kill him, and when William answered 'no,' Stan told him to go away and get back to shooting his rifle."

"Hmm ... that's Stan, all right. Speaking of ... where've you got our men positioned?"

Jamie and Billy continued to poke their heads up at differing points along the log, firing off shots as quickly as they could reload their rifles.

"Joe and Benny are just beyond yonder tree." He pointed off to the right of their position to where the trunk of a huge old oak tree stood, "Behind those rocks.

"Stan, William, Georgie, and Zeke are over to the other side of the road, up on top of that sharp ridge that looks back down toward the first pinch point. Oh, and *Tony*, too! He's been doing his bit. We've also got the Watch men running back for more ammo and powder, and Stan has a few of them helping load guns—the fellows I told you he was training, as you recall, sir."

"Oh! He does, does he? Hmm … how can I get there from here without getting shot?"

"Go back up the trail you came down on, about twenty yards until you'll notice a shallow dip in the trail—a gulley of sorts. If you follow that gully back over to the road, you'll find the roadway also dips at that point. There you can cross at a crouch without your head bein' visible from below."

"All right, thank you. I see you have a few spare rifles. Tom, go ahead and grab a rifle. You can help hold down this side, while I go over to check on the others. I have an idea for driving the enemy back, but I wish to speak with Stan first. I'll return shortly."

"Sir!" both sergeants answered, snapping him a salute. Nathan smiled at them and shook his head, *old habits*, he thought.

He holstered his pistol and headed back toward the trail they'd come in on, continuing to duck his head, his four-legged shadow close behind. Tom reached for a spare rifle and started loading it.

Nathan had no trouble locating the gully Jim had described, and was soon settling in next to Stan up on the ridgeline, behind a rock outcropping. Stan greeted him with a broad grin, while the other men continued firing and reloading, acknowledging the Captain's presence only with a quick nod.

As Jim had described, the three "old" soldiers were there, along with Zeke and Tony. And the sleeve on Stan's right arm was stained a dark red from just below the point of his shoulder to well below his elbow.

"Some fun, eh, Captain! Is even better'n tossing bullies from church!" he laughed as he took a loaded rifle from one of the black men. He pulled back the hammer and examined the percussion cap, pushing it down firmly with his thumb. He turned toward the man who'd handed it to him. Nathan recognized Johnny, one of Tony's friends.

"Hey, Johnny … be sure'n push cap down harder. If not down snug, rifle is misfiring. Is not good, yes?" He smiled and turned to fire without waiting for a response. If his injured arm bothered him at all he showed no sign of it and appeared to move with as much ease as ever.

"Yes, Mr. Stan! I'll be sure to push 'er down harder next time," Johnny said, picking up an empty rifle sitting next to him and starting to reload it.

Two other black men were doing the same. Ned was one, and the groom Phinney, the other. They were moving about handing loaded rifles to the shooters, while picking up the empty ones for reloading. It was an efficient method, allowing the riflemen to fire much more rapidly than they otherwise could, but it required plenty of spare rifles and lots of ammo.

When Stan ducked back down after firing, Nathan said, "Mr. Volkov, I would have a word with you."

Stan exchanged rifles with Johnny, looking down and checking the percussion cap again. Apparently satisfied this time, he said, "Yes, Captain?"

"Firstly, I'd like a report on your condition, if you please. I'd heard you'd been wounded, and I can see it's true. How're you holding up?"

Stan laughed, "Is not worth the wasting of breath speaking on. Have had worse in bar fight, and never have I died, yet!"

Nathan shook his head, "No pain then?"

"Pain? Oh, da … but *man* ignores pain in fight. Why spoil fun?"

Nathan chuckled, "Yes … why, indeed? So Sergeant Jim tells me you've been training some of the other men, aside from Tony, to load and shoot rifles."

"Yes, Captain … and *yes*, I know *is* against law, but—"

"Never mind that … as you can clearly see, *the law* stands for very little just now. What I wanted to ask you is … how are they *doing*?"

"*Doing*, Captain?"

"Yes … how are they coming along? Can they load and shoot without immediate supervision?"

"Oh! Hmm ... yes ... *could be*. Have had only two lessons, and are ... *'coming along,'* as you say. Why? You want bring them into battle?"

"Yes ... that's *exactly* what I'm thinking."

"Oh, well ... they can *load* guns pretty good ... and know how to pull trigger, of course. But ... not so good at *hitting* anything yet. Hmm ... except Tony."

"That's what I was hoping to hear. And ... it won't matter if they hit anything or not, as long as they can load and fire the guns in a reasonably efficient manner. Let's get all your trainees up here on the double, along with all the spare rifles and enough ammo for all. Place half here and send the other half over to Sergeant Jim's location."

"Yes, sir! It will be so. But ... then what? Not enough room up here for so many to shoot all at same time. Not allowing room to move about so enemy don't know where to aim, anyway."

"Yes, I can see that. But I've been thinking on a plan. Listen while I lay it out for you, then you can tell the others on this side. Here's what we'll do ..."

ᔰᘔᐧᗚᘓᔰᘔᐧᗚᘓᔰᘔᐧᗚᘓ

Two hours later, the battle had devolved into an acknowledged stalemate. Each side now offered only sporadic gunfire to keep the enemy occupied without burning through large quantities of ammunition.

But Nathan was well-satisfied with the preparations for his plan. If all went well, they should soon end the stalemate in their favor, and in a most satisfying manner. The plan had a good combination of trickery, added firepower from Stan's trainees, and intimate knowledge of the terrain, thanks to Billy's scouting.

Once the trainees had arrived, Nathan gradually substituted them for the regulars. He instructed them to continue firing with the same general intensity as before, so the enemy wouldn't detect the switch.

He placed Jamie in charge of supervising the trainees on the right side, with Stan doing the same on the left. Their job was to control the overall rate of fire, sporadic for now, but more intense and regular again when called for by the Captain's plan. In addition, he especially wanted to make sure they kept the trainees moving around as they fired. He wanted to avoid anyone getting shot, if possible; continuously firing from the same spot was a good way to take an incoming bullet to one's forehead! And lastly, when the time came, he needed someone to ensure they ceased firing, so they'd not accidentally hit their own men, himself included.

Nathan, Tom, and the two farmhands Joe and Benny carefully and quietly followed Billy. He led them in a circuitous route down the slope and around to a place where they'd be above the enemy to their left, in among the trees up the steep hillside.

At first, Nathan had worried Harry the Dog would make a great deal of noise crashing through the woods. But his fears proved entirely misplaced. Harry was an expert hunter, moving silently when necessary. And somehow Harry's instincts told him the Captain was stalking prey now, so he responded in kind. With four feet to distribute his weight more evenly, Harry actually moved more quietly through the trees than his two-legged companions, despite his great bulk.

They now stood at the point Nathan had envisioned when he'd told Billy the position he had in mind. From here they had an unimpeded view of the enemy soldiers where they crouched behind rocks or lay prone on the ground behind a log or in a ditch or gully. He glanced at his pocket watch and decided to wait five more minutes before giving the signal.

Initially, Nathan's plan called for Tom to move over to the other group and take charge on that side, the same as he'd done back in Texas when the bandit Moat Kangly and his gang had them pinned down in a ditch. Tom was second in command, and the man Nathan trusted most in this type of precision operation.

But Tom surprised him when he said, "I'd rather *not*, sir."

"What's that, Tom?" Nathan was taken aback. Tom had never balked at one of his orders before … well … not *never*, now that he considered it. He faintly recalled *one* other time, though for some reason the memory was foggy.

"But—"

"Sir ... I'd prefer *not*. Why not send Jim instead?"

"Because I had *you* in mind for it, Tom. I—"

"*Nathan*—after all we've been through together since Richmond ... I wish to fight *next to you* from here on, if you don't mind."

Nathan looked Tom in the eye. Suddenly he remembered ... there *had* been one other time Tom had refused his orders. It was also the one other time he'd referred to Nathan by his given name; right after Tom had saved his life from the slavers who were preparing to cut him open.

"Yes, Tom ... I reckon you've more than earned the right. Mr. Wiggins?"

"Captain!"

"Please cross over to the other side and take command of the company. Proceed per the plans we've discussed."

"Sir!" he snapped a salute, then grinned and winked at Tom.

So Jim led the other group of men—Georgie, William, Tony, and Zeke—on a flanking maneuver to the left. Because the slope fell away to the left, they'd work themselves back and around to a position to the right side and slightly downhill of the enemy. Billy had provided Jim with detailed directions on the best way to go, and the best place to position his men. Being downhill from an enemy wasn't ideal, but they hoped the element of surprise and the angle of attack would more than offset that disadvantage.

Nathan looked at his pocket watch again and nodded to Tom, who motioned the others to take aim with their rifles. Nathan pulled out a revolver, pointed it in the air, and fired off three quick rounds. He watched for any reaction from the enemy below, but other than a few confused looks, his shots didn't raise the alarm. He'd worried over it beforehand but could think of no other way to confirm both sets of flankers were in position and ready. He'd decided to chance it—hopefully with all the rifle shots a few pistol shots would cause little concern, if they were noticed at all. He listened a moment and heard the answer from below—again, three quick pistol shots.

He holstered his pistol, picked up a rifle, took aim, and yelled, "Fire!"

Five rifles fired simultaneously with a tooth-rattling blast and thick plume of gun smoke. Jim's left flank below answered in kind with an identical volley of their own. Rifle fire from the men back at the original position on the ridge also picked up in intensity, resuming its earlier steady pace.

The effect on their adversaries was immediate and devastating. Because the flankers had positioned themselves to the exposed sides of the enemy, and had time to take careful aim, each shot was extremely efficacious. More than a half-dozen enemy soldiers went down instantly, and the others began to scramble back to safety in a panic.

But moving suddenly from cover exposed them to the rifles from above. And if the trainees were less than accurate, the same could *not* be said for Stan and Jamie; they worked their neatly arranged stack of pre-loaded rifles to deadly effect.

Then Nathan launched *part two* of his plan. Each flanker slung his rifle onto his back by its strap, unholstered two revolvers and began targeting anyone who moved, and anyone who failed to move and remained exposed to the flankers. The Mountain Meadows fighters were close enough for reasonable accuracy with pistols, especially Nathan's group on the uphill slope.

The previous stalemate had turned into a rout, with many enemy soldiers abandoning their rifles and sprinting back down the hill to escape the sudden onslaught.

The flankers moved forward, Nathan's group coming down off the hill, and Jim's climbing up it. Even as they moved, both groups continued picking off any enemy who offered himself up as a target.

Jamie, looking down from above, noted the pre-planned advance toward the roadway and shouted, "Cease firing! Barrels up! Percussion caps off! Hammers down!" Clearly Stan did likewise, as all gunfire from the ridgeline immediately ceased.

The two flanking groups met on the road and exchanged hearty greetings. The last of the enemy invaders had now made it past the lower pinch point and into the relative safety beyond, and no longer presented any targets.

Nathan hoped they might pursue the invaders and push them all the way back down the hill, retaking the lower pinch point.

But as they tried to press their advantage and moved further down the road, they began taking incoming fire from the lower ridgeline—the same place where they'd held their initial defensive line. The gunfire forced them to take cover and withdraw to a safer position.

This served to confirm Jim's earlier assessment—the leader of the enemy possessed military skill and experience. Even as his men had advanced deliberately up the hill to attack the upper pinch point, he'd reinforced and manned the lower point in the event of a reversal, such as had eventually happened.

Later that day, back on the veranda, Nathan and Tom enjoyed a well-earned cigar and a glass of whiskey as they reflected on the day's momentous events. After the battle was over, they established new defensive positions which now included the positions where the flankers had stood before launching their surprise attack on the enemy. Nathan meant to ensure no one could get past that point again.

They'd only been sitting for half an hour when Jim stepped up to join them. "Late again for whiskey and cigars, Jim?"

"Yes, Captain, but it couldn't be helped this time. Billy was out scouting the enemy to find out what they're up to now we've pushed them further down the hill. I wasn't about to leave until he returned."

"And ... what did he learn?"

"Well, they may have run, but they didn't run far. As I'd originally feared, they have someone in charge who knows a fight. He's recognized he can defend the lower pinch point as good or better from his side as we can from ours. They've set up a solid defensive position there and are digging in. They've also taken those two wagons they'd brought with them and have stretched them across the road at the narrowest point and tipped them over."

"*Clever* ... it serves to prevent us mounting a cavalry charge against him."

"Yep, what I was thinking too, sir. So now we control the upper pinch point, and they the lower, with a few hundred yards in between that none dares enter for fear o' catching a bullet.

"Billy also scouted the Elk Trail that comes down off the backside of your granddaddy's hill. The enemy is digging in there also, at another good defensive point near the bottom. Our Watch men were there keeping an eye on them. But since they never tried to advance further up the hill, they didn't raise the alarm with everything else going on. Now there's no going out that way either, of course. I've positioned a few of our riflemen above theirs on that route, in case they were to try something. It's much narrower and steeper, so it'll be relatively easy for a few of our men to hold off a whole passel of theirs."

"Well done. Thanks, Jim."

Nathan leaned back in his chair and blew a long stream of smoke into the sky, watching it float away on the breeze. "Well, gentlemen … it's safe to say, Mountain Meadows is now officially besieged."

☿☿☿☿☿☿☿☿☿

After the battle they returned to the bunkhouse, and William insisted on examining Stan's injury. Though Stan had shown no sign of discomfort, William winced when he examined the damage, after Stan had peeled off his ragged, bloody shirt.

The wound was roughly six inches across. At least five jagged, bullet-sized rock splinters were embedded well into the muscle below the shoulder, along with numerous smaller pieces.

William looked Stan hard in the eye, "I need to dig these out. Even you, with all your great strength may die if the wound festers."

Stan glanced down at his arm, and shrugged, "Do whatever pleases you, William." Then he smiled.

So William spent the next hour poking, prodding, and cutting the mangled flesh of Stan's arm with a sharp knife. Stan seemed unconcerned, reciting a steady stream of off-color jokes while William worked. Once satisfied he'd extracted every piece of rock he could, William uncorked the whiskey bottle and said, "This is going to sting a bit."

But Stan just smiled and continued the joke he was on. William poured the alcohol into the raw wound, and wiped it out with a clean, white cloth. The swab came away stained a dark red with tiny, black, sand-sized pieces of rock in it.

After a quarter hour of this he was satisfied the wound was clean. William broke out his needle and thread, poured a little whiskey on the needle, and began to stitch up the wound— wounds, actually; there were multiple, varying-sized lacerations from the splinters, expanded by William's cleaning efforts.

William was astounded. He'd always known Stan was tough, never complaining about any sort of hardship or injury, *but this?* Stan never flinched nor displayed any discomfort during the entire excruciatingly painful procedure lasting nearly two hours. And he never stopped his flow of raunchy stories.

The Captain's stoic fortitude is impressive, but Stan is ... well, Stan is Stan, was all William could think to say about that.

ಬಿಎಂಲಜ಼ಬಿಎಂಲಜ಼ಬಿಎಂಲಜ಼

After the heroic service given by Stan's trainees, the Captain called the whole farm together to honor them. He called them out by name: Tony, Johnny, Ned, Phinney, Big George, Will, Sammy, Jimbo, Alex, Jack, and Sid. He stood in front of each man, saluted him, and shook his hand. The men being recognized smiled brightly.

Of course, after that Stan had no difficulty getting the Captain to agree to any additional training he had in mind and in getting more volunteers for the duty.

So he decided to press his luck. He approached the Captain with a proposal to make rifle training mandatory for all men on Mountain Meadows Farm between the ages of thirteen and fifty-five.

"Captain, I know you don't like forcing people do things against free will, but ... there is war on now. And with rifles lying all around after battle, plus those bought at store and Walters' earlier ... *donations* ... we have nearly enough for everyone."

55

Nathan didn't even pause to contemplate his answer, "I agree. We will make the rifle training mandatory, though I will still ask for volunteers when it comes to the actual combat. Please proceed with your plan, Mr. Volkov. I'll let Toby know I've excused the men from regular agricultural duties while you're conducting training. I assume that will be daily and intensive. Time is clearly *not* on our side with our opponent likely to bring in more recruits for another go at us.

"And God only knows if we'll even have a cotton or tobacco harvest this fall. And if we do, who will we sell it to, pray?

"Oh ... and have the other privates assist you ... along with Tony, of course. When you've finished training them up, and the enemy tries it again, we'll not only drive them back, we'll slaughter them!"

After those bold words, accompanied by a fiery look in the Captain's eyes, Stan beamed, a smile that did not entirely fade for the remainder of the day.

But despite his confident words and fiery determination, Nathan was becoming increasingly anxious about their desperate predicament. Though they could defend themselves for the moment, how long before the Confederate States sent a "real" army against them? They might hold off a few hundred men indefinitely, but what about a thousand? Or two thousand, or ... ten?

They were now cut off from the rest of the world, with no end in sight. With no news from the outside, they wouldn't even know what was happening in the looming war, nor if the Western counties were even now splitting off from Richmond and might come to their aid. All the armies on the continent might be poised to sweep right over them and they'd have no warning. It was a precarious situation.

And ... most frustrating and maddening of all for him personally, there'd be no way to communicate with Evelyn. Even the innocuous, "I trust all is well with you and Miss Harriet ..." ridiculously boring letters he'd written thus far would no longer go through, nor would her equally monotonous responses. At least those tepid notes served to confirm they were both still alive, and still willing to take the time to put ink to paper for the other's sake.

And for the thousandth time, the same pleading question went out to her silently from within his mind, now almost unbidden, *And ... what are you thinking right now, Evelyn, my love?*

Then he consciously added the afterthought, *I'd give a fully manned artillery battery to know ... and to hold you close again.*

Chapter 3. Wrath of the Unrighteous

"The belief in a supernatural
source of evil is not necessary;
men alone are quite capable
of every wickedness."
– Joseph Conrad

Monday May 20, 1861 – Greenbrier County, Virginia:

Margaret felt a thrill at the news. By some amazing miracle she could not fathom, Mr. Chambers and his men had defeated Walters once again. This time she'd been sure there was no hope. Walters had more than fifty men for this attack. And several were veteran soldiers, including a former Army officer who'd come out from Richmond to recruit for the new Southern Army.

Apparently, through some argument Margaret hadn't been privy to, Walters had convinced the officer, by the name of Colonel Burns, to attack Mountain Meadows using his new recruits. Maybe he'd argued it'd be a good training exercise for the men. Or perhaps he'd convinced the colonel it'd enhance his reputation back in Richmond. She'd not been able to eavesdrop on their initial conversation because the colonel had brought two men with him who stood in the foyer while they talked, preventing her from taking up her usual listening post.

But she had listened in on their subsequent discussions. They'd spent several evenings in Walters' library planning their attack in great detail.

She'd been terribly frightened for Mr. Chambers and Miss Abbey all this long day knowing the attack was underway. But now, she'd learned it had failed once again.

Colonel Burns had *not* returned to Walters Farm, staying to supervise the troops and lay siege to Mountain Meadows. But Walters had returned with Bob, and they'd sat in the library and discussed the day's events, events that had once again turned out badly for Walters.

From Walters' conversation with Bob, she pieced together what had happened. Walters' initial success—driving Mr. Chambers' men back up the hill toward the farm—soon slowed and finally stopped for several hours in a virtual stalemate. Then a Mountain Meadows counterattack drove Walters' men much of the way back down the hill where a new stalemate was now in progress. And Walters had lost two more of his farmhands, killed during that last action.

She tried to picture the scene in her mind from the one time she'd visited Mountain Meadows—the long, twisting road up the hill to the farm with thick trees lining the sides. She recalled there were places with tall rocks where the narrowed roadway passed between them. This must have been where the fighting took place.

She was absorbed in these thoughts when she suddenly had an uneasy feeling; though at first, she couldn't figure out why. Then she realized she'd heard no voices from the library for several minutes. She listened intently, but the house had gone silent. She felt a sudden fear and strong urge to retreat to her room. But when she turned her head, she suffered a terrible shock. There was Walters, not ten feet away, staring down at her.

"You have been spying on me." It was a statement, not a question, and spoken in the strange, monotone that was particularly frightening, especially when combined with the horrible, bland expression he often showed, as he did now.

"Oh! Elijah ... you have startled me. Spying? Why, no ... it was ... hot in my room, and I stepped into the hallway for a little more air. But I found myself light-headed, so I ... sat for a minute. I was just now preparing to return to my room, and ... well, there you were."

He said nothing for a long moment, just stood where he was, staring at her.

"You're not an especially good liar."

He stepped forward, reached down, grabbed her under the arm, and lifted her roughly to her feet.

"Ow ... you're hurting me ... please stop."

He did not acknowledge her protests, but turned, still clutching her hard by the upper arm and marched her back down the hall toward her room. She went along passively, knowing if she resisted he would only hurt her worse.

When they reached the door to her room, he opened it and pulled her inside. He spun her around, so she was facing him and backhanded her hard across the face. The force of the blow knocked her to the floor and made her head spin as bright lights sparkled before her eyes. She didn't look up but heard his voice say, "Now I must go deal with the maid who was ... *derelict* ... in her duties. Later we shall see to your proper punishment."

She heard the door close—not slammed, but gently, which was even more frightening, somehow. A key turned the lock with a metallic *click*.

She collapsed to the floor, onto the brightly colored braided rug that covered the hardwood, lay her head upon her arms and cried, such as she hadn't cried in a very long time. But the tears were not for herself. Deep down she had always known Walters would hurt her sooner or later—probably even kill her.

She cried because she was almost certain she'd just caused the death of the maid Willona, who was really quite sweet, despite living in Walters' house. She was the same maid Margaret had first intimidated into letting her out of her room. Now Willona would surely pay the ultimate price, and there was nothing Margaret could do about it.

Bob stood in the foyer as Walters walked slowly down the stairs. He gave Walters a questioning look, though he knew better than to ask anything specific. He had a sick feeling in the pit of his stomach and felt badly for the girl Margaret, fearing Walters had finally murdered her.

But when Walters reached the bottom of the steps he said, "Bob, I wish Mrs. Walters to remain locked in her room until I mete out her ... *final* punishment. I find after the long day we've had I am far too tired to ... to properly *enjoy* it."

He turned and walked away down the hall. Bob breathed a sigh of relief. A few moments later he heard a frightened squeal. He assumed Walters had laid his hands on the maid who'd been responsible for watching Margaret's door. He sadly shook his head and said a silent prayer for her soul.

"I can't believe it, Evelyn! What're you thinking? You'll throw away everything we've worked for ... you'll ruin your reputation! And for what? For the sake of a bunch of jungle savages? People who'll never appreciate the sacrifices you're making! Destroying your life ... your opportunity for wealth and happiness—your chance at a proper marriage!"

"Oh, Momma, that's not how it is ..."

"Don't 'oh, Momma' me ... you know perfectly well I'm right!"

"No, Momma ... I *don't* know you're right. In fact, I think you're wrong ... about the black people, about me, and about what'll make me happy. In fact, everything you've just said is wrong." They glared at each, both red in the face.

The argument had started when Harriet unexpectedly returned home early in the middle of the day, finding two strange men in her house, conversing with Evelyn. The men had immediately departed, but Evelyn had been unable to deflect Harriet's interrogation. It was just too strange and incongruous for her to easily explain away or brush off. If it'd been only one man, she might've been able to shrug it off as a moment of weakness and poor judgment—being alone in the house unchaperoned. But *two* men?

Harriet would not give it up, until Evelyn finally confessed the truth, or at least part of it: that the Underground Railroad had recruited her, and she'd been assisting them for several months now.

A part of her had hoped she might sway her mother to her side on it. Or at least convince her to accept it and look the other way. But it was quickly becoming clear neither of those positive outcomes was about to happen.

"Evelyn, I will not have this sort of immoral and illegal activity taking place under my own roof! You will cease and desist from this behavior immediately, young lady!"

"No, Momma ... I can't do that."

"Then ... then you can no longer live in this house."

"What?!"

"This is *my* house … you are an adult woman now … if you will not obey my wishes, you must leave and find your own place to live."

"But … Momma, surely …"

"No, Evelyn. I'll not listen to any more such nonsense! If you'll not do as I say, then go … and be grateful I'm not turning you over to the authorities."

She turned, stomped off to her room, and slammed the door.

ᘓᕹᕹᕹᕹᘓᕹᕹᕹᘓᕹᕹᕹ

Two hours later Evelyn sat in the Hughes' library, sipping tea with Angeline, who was most sympathetic.

"I am so sorry to hear it, my dear. I shall send a carriage around to collect your things whenever you wish, and you shall come live with us until we can find you suitable accommodations."

"Oh, Angeline, you are too kind. I came here because I thought you should know about the … change in my circumstances, and … well, to be honest, I didn't know where else to go. I did not intend to impose on you. How can I ever repay you?"

"Nonsense, Evelyn! We are eternally grateful for everything you've already done for us, and all you intend to do in the future. Think nothing of it! We will be honored to have you as a guest in our home. With our sons off to Boston for the duration of … well, of whatever is going to happen with this whole secession business, this house is practically empty. It will be a pleasure to have someone to talk to."

"Thank you, Angeline. You are most kind, and I must confess it'll be good to speak with you and Jonathan more frequently. My Momma has become … well, difficult for me to converse with, let us say. She has been so singularly focused on finding me a suitable husband that she will hardly speak of anything else. And to tell the truth, with everything that's happening it is the very last thing on my mind. Why, if I'd wanted to be married, I'd have just …"

She was quiet for a moment, and for the thousandth time thought, *Oh Nathan, my love … what have I done?*

Angeline nodded, fairly certain she knew where Evelyn's thoughts were going on the matter.

"Well, anyway, it's not something I want to consider right now."

"I understand, my dear. And you'll have no such talk from me, I promise. As with you, I have many other more important things to occupy my mind, and these are the matters I am most interested in speaking with you about. In fact, only last evening we were discussing a plan Jonathan has come up with, and we were considering you for the task. This break with Miss Harriet, though clearly painful for you—and I am sincerely sorry—may be a blessing in disguise for our scheme, if it works out."

"A blessing? Whatever do you mean?"

"Only that we could not figure a good way for it to work while you were living with ... well, how shall I say it? A person not agreeable to our cause? Someone we could not necessarily trust?"

"Yes, that would describe Miss Harriet, all right."

"Speaking of ... do you think she might make good on her threat of turning you in to the authorities?"

"Oh, *no!* Certainly *not!* If for no other reason than it would also ruin her own reputation, being my mother. In fact, she'll never speak to another soul on the matter, for fear the rumors might spread. No ... she was only angry. I'm positive nothing will come of it."

"Good. But I will say no more about our *other* plan for the moment. Not until I've spoken further with Mr. Hughes and can tell him about your change in living arrangements."

ഇൽൽരുബയൽൽരുബയൽൽരുബ

Later that evening they sat at dinner, and Evelyn was feeling much better about things. It still stung, and was painful to contemplate—no child ever enjoyed disappointing their parents, let alone being thrown out of the house by them.

But she realized she could carry out her activities more easily without the threat of discovery at any moment by someone living with her.

And Angeline and Jonathan were the most pleasant, intelligent, and congenial hosts imaginable. Their conversations ranged across many topics—they exhibited a deep knowledge on a wide variety of subjects. On top of which, they treated Evelyn as if she were their very own daughter.

And they seemed more inclined every day to bring her into their confidence and ask her opinion and advice on their various clandestine activities. It was a good feeling—someone finally believed in her for reasons other than her good looks and ability to attract the proper mate.

After dinner they retired to the veranda, out on the back side of the house. It afforded them a magnificent view of the city, from where the house stood high on a hill down to the river in the distance. Jonathan sipped whiskey, and the ladies enjoyed a splash of warmed brandy.

"Evelyn, earlier today Angeline hinted at an idea we'd been discussing, a new scheme we're trying to hatch."

Evelyn nodded, allowing Jonathan to continue.

"If you're agreeable, we'd like to set you up in a house of your own, here in town. We'll use it to restart the Underground Railroad station disrupted by Dr. Johnson's unfortunate arrest."

"Yes, I'm agreeable to helping in any way I can, but I can't afford rent on a house of my own."

Jonathan waved a hand dismissively, "You needn't concern yourself with that, my dear. This is a house I already own, which I have been keeping for this very purpose. If you would run this house for us, we would be most pleased and grateful."

"Thank you, Jonathan, Angeline. Of course I will do it, without hesitation. But I was just thinking … a single woman, living alone in a … well, I assume it will need to be a fairly *large* house to accommodate the various … *travelers?* Anyway, wouldn't it be suspicious, what with all the strange people coming and going at all hours? Dr. Johnson had the excuse of being a dentist, and one known to legitimately perform dentistry on slaves at the behest of their masters. He could easily explain people visiting at various odd times of day. What possible excuse shall I have?"

Angeline smiled, "Once again you prove yourself most insightful and intelligent. It is a reasonable question but fortunately one for which we have a good answer. You see, this is the main part of the plan we've been considering especially for you."

"Yes," Jonathan said, "and we believe now is the perfect time to try it out, given your circumstances. What we want to do is allow the word to spread of your falling out with Miss Harriet. Only we will make it over something innocuous, such as a disagreement over whom you should consider marrying, or some other mundane matter.

"After a few weeks, we'll spread the word you're in need of an income to live alone outside your Momma's home. And so you've started a business, a business training domestic slaves to serve the very top echelon of society in the formal, traditional manner they so richly deserve!"

Evelyn leaned back in her seat and looked up for a moment. "Yes … yes, I can envision that working. It would explain the need for a large house, and the presence of strange, black faces at odd hours. Yes, that part could very well work. But … if it's to work long term, I believe the business has to be *real*. Otherwise someone will eventually find out."

"Yes, it must be real, like Dr. Johnson's dental practice," Jonathan agreed.

"All right, but there's one major problem with that," Evelyn said, "I've never trained *any* kind of servant, much less a formal, high-society domestic servant."

Angeline smiled, "Never you mind *that*, dear. This very household is fairly bubbling over with such expertise. By the time everything is in place, I promise you will be Richmond's foremost expert on the subject. And we'll start the appropriate rumors to that effect, of course."

"Oh! Well, all right … in that case, I suppose there's no reason it won't work. But … will I actually be collecting money for these … services?"

"Certainly."

"But … won't that make me … well … complicit in the whole slavery system? A part of the problem, so to speak, even if for a good cause?"

Jonathan shared a look with Angeline and smiled. He turned to Evelyn and said, "That is the last, and most important part of this scheme. And the idea I am *most* pleased with, dare I say … *proud of?*

"Yes, you will legitimately train *some* household servants to faithfully serve their masters and mistresses with great skill and expertise. But others … others you will train … to be our *spies!*"

"Spies?! Oh … yes, now I see. Yes … infiltrating our own people into the very upper crust … that would include the highest government officials … governors, senators … generals, even. No one would think to hide anything from such servants and they'd not hesitate to say almost anything in front of them.

"And … if we choose spies who can read and write, and we disguise this from their 'masters,' they'd have unfettered access to confidential government and military documents.

"We can even include a … *'refresher course'* with me, for no additional charge—part of the initial fee. That way, with little risk, I can receive any information they've acquired, and no need for any delivery tricks. Yes … very, very clever, Jonathan. Brilliant, even, I'd have to say!"

Jonathan beamed at the praise, and it occurred to Evelyn he was still a normal man, despite his high status, wealth, and great intelligence.

"Thank you, my dear. Very kindly of you to say. We like it much better than the previous scheme we involved you in. Courting various potentially important men must eventually be curtailed lest you develop a negative reputation harmful to your future. And the time it might take to gain a man's confidence enough to convince him to share state secrets with you, would preclude performing the practice more than a very few times over an extended period. But with this *new* scheme, there's no limit on the activity, and no potential harm to your reputation, short of actually being caught, which is always a risk in whatever we do. And the operation can potentially bear fruit fairly rapidly."

"Yes … I can see that. It makes much more sense than the other scheme, I must agree. And … I feel much better about it, as its success doesn't hinge upon playing false with men's most intimate emotions. Even though it's still false and spying, it somehow feels more ... *ethical* ... if that makes any sense."

"It makes perfect sense to me, dear," Angeline agreed. "I always felt uneasy about the effect it might have on *you*—convincing a man to trust you by preying upon his most natural inclinations and then betraying him. That could not be good for one's *own* emotional state, for one's own *soul*, you might say."

They were quiet for a minute, sipping their drinks, as Evelyn mulled over the scheme, and tried to envision herself in this new role. She'd be taking over the Underground Railroad station Dr. Johnson had been running, from a new location. And at the same time running a business training high-end domestic help. It seemed right, but also sounded extremely demanding, time consuming, and ... overwhelming! When would she sleep?

But before she voiced her concerns, Jonathan seemed to answer the unspoken question, "And you need not do all this alone. I have in mind some good men ... and women, both black and white ... to assist you. They'll be your full-time staff—assistants in the entire operation—doing everything from keeping the books, to cooking and cleaning, to coordinating the conductors of the railroad."

"So ... what do you say, my dear?" Angeline asked, leaning forward expectantly.

"I say ... I say, *I'll do it!*"

ଔଓୖଓଔଓୖଓଔଓୖଓଔଓୖଓ

Henry first heard the screams while he was in the okra field hoeing weeds. He instinctively flinched but resisted the impulse to stop what he was doing and take a look. He knew better than to stop the steady flow of work and risk the sting of the lash on his legs. So he continued to work, and only looked toward the source of the noise in the most discreet and fleeting manner. These quick glances confirmed the noise was coming from the master's house. There was a small group of men gathered near the side of the house on the lawn just past where the gravel drive ended.

As he worked down the row, he came ever closer to the house, and soon he saw a figure tied to one of the hitching posts. It was a black woman. She was kneeling on the ground, her hands tied to the hitching post above her head. Her back had been stripped bare, though she still had clothing below the waist. A large man stepped up with a whip. It was the master, Mr. Walters! He swung the whip, making a distinctive cracking sound, echoed by another scream. Henry cringed but did not pause in his work lest he also feel the lash.

He did not know the woman, nor what indiscretion she had committed, but from the clothing still on her, it appeared she was one of the household slaves. He was *not* one of those who looked down on them or wished them ill. In his mind, a slave was still a slave, and was doing whatever he or she had to do by compulsion, not by choice.

The beating took several minutes, which seemed like hours to those forced to listen. It turned Henry's stomach, imagining the terrible pain the poor woman was suffering. Nothing justified such punishment, no matter how severe the misdeed. The anger boiled in him again. He thought of his own dear wife only a few dozen miles away on the farm where he'd lived before. He imagined her being on the receiving end of that whip. It gave him a moment's gut-wrenching pause.

He glanced up at the house and saw the mistress looking out her usual upstairs window. She stood still and appeared to be watching, though her expression was unreadable from this distance. Once again, he wondered why she always stood looking out the window, but never came out herself.

It was only a moment's hesitation, but it was enough. *Snap!* A sudden, stinging pain burned the back of his right calf.

"Nobody told y'all to pay no mind to whatever's happening over to the house. Unless you be wanting your turn next," the overseer growled.

Chapter 4. A Hawk's Dilemma

"Hunting hawks do not belong in cages,
no matter how much a man covets their grace,
no matter how golden the bars.
They are far more beautiful soaring free.
Heartbreakingly beautiful."
– Lois McMaster Bujold

Thursday May 23, 1861 – Greenbrier County, Virginia:

"Well, Billy, what do you think?" Nathan asked, lowering his spyglass and gazing out over the landscape from the high ridge. The men now referred to the high point as "Granddaddy's Hill," shortened from "The Captain's Granddaddy's Hill" as they'd been calling it.

Below they could see the main road, far down in the valley to the south. Mountain Meadows controlled the high ground and guarded its approaches: the main road up to the farm and the narrower Elk Trail that led up the backside of the hill.

But the enemy controlled the main east-west road and the valley it ran through. And their numbers grew with each passing day as the word spread and more volunteers came to swell their ranks. Mountain Meadows was now effectively cut off from the rest of the world. And of course, there loomed the threat the regular rebel Army might arrive from the east any day.

"A good, defensible position, Captain. Good fighters like ours can hold it for a long time against *many* foes ..."

"Hmm ... why do I feel there is an unspoken *'but'* to your statement?"

Billy turned and looked the Captain in the eye.

"Captain, you remember when I first saw the great ocean?"

"Yes ... you'd had a hard time imagining such a thing, and the sight of it was ... *overwhelming* at first."

"Yes. Though I had been told of it, I could not picture a thing so vast and terrible. The same holds of this war between the white men.

"My whole life, the white soldiers, with great numbers, and powerful guns have been as the ocean. A man may swim against their current for a time, but in the end, he'll go under. So when I hear the white men will make war on each other—two terrible armies with endless men and guns ..." he shook his head.

"Like the ocean, it is great beyond my imagining. It must make our long-ago war with the Comanche seem ... hmm ... no more than one of Big Stan's barroom fights.

"If we stand on this mountain, though we fight with great courage and skill, eventually we will fall. The great ocean of our enemies will sweep over us. We will drown."

Nathan was quiet for a time, staring out at the grand vista in front of them.

"I understand what you're saying, Billy. And I can't say I disagree with it. But what would you have me do? Turn and run, like a whipped cur, with my tail between my legs? Abandoning my family home to the depredations of my enemies?

"It may be wisdom, but ... I tell you, it galls me beyond words! Especially because I know full well the terrible toll we would inflict on them should they try to take this place by force. To turn and run without a *real* fight—to show ourselves nothing but cowards in the eyes of our enemies? A man would almost rather die first."

"I hear you, Captain. I feel the same."

They were silent again for a time, each lost in his own thoughts.

Then Billy spoke again, "Captain, let me tell you a story. It is an ancient story among my people. Maybe you will find it ... *interesting.*"

Nathan raised an eyebrow at Billy. He wasn't really in the mood for a story. But on the other hand, he knew from experience there was great wisdom in this man and in the stories of his people. And right now, he could dearly use some wisdom. So he nodded his head in agreement.

"There was a time when a young red-tailed hawk decided he must find a great tree to build him a nest. He might then seek out a mate and raise a family of nestlings. He searched long and far for the perfect land. Finally, he found it—a mighty pine tree with wide, spreading branches. High upon a wooded hill it stood. With a fine view and good hunting grounds.

"And there he began building his nest. He worked tirelessly as it must be strong and secure against the storms that blow. He meant to live in that place all his days and raise many and many hawk children.

"But when he was almost finished, a wandering group of crows came to the woods. As you know, Captain, crows and hawks are bitter enemies—going back even before The Breaking, maybe. At first the crows were few. And only a nuisance to the hawk, squawking noisily. He was much larger and fiercer than they, so he mostly ignored them. Or chased them off if they came close.

"But one group of crows will follow another, they say. Soon more and more crows had come to the woods. And as their numbers grew, they became ever bolder. Daily they came closer and closer to the nest. And they came in larger groups and pestered him as he hunted.

"But he was young, and brave, and feared no enemies. So he would defend his nest against all foes. It was not in his nature to run. But the fights now came more and more often. Daily his enemies swelled in numbers, and he stood alone against them.

"So finally there came a day. He sat on his nest, looking out across his once proud home. And he saw a large, black cloud of crows rising into the sky. He knew they were coming to make war against him.

"Each crow alone feared the hawk. But together in great numbers nothing could stand against them.

"The hawk saw his own death in the gathering black storm of his enemies."

Nathan was now engrossed in the tale, hanging on Billy's words. "So ... what did he do?"

71

"I believe I said, he was strong and brave, a great fighter. But he knew his home was lost—he must abandon it or die.

"But it was not in him to flee in cowardice. So he flew to the topmost branch of his tree. There he called out in the terrible cry of a hawk preparing for battle, screaming defiance at his enemies."

Nathan smiled. He could almost hear the sound made by that hawk in his mind. The call of a red-tailed hawk in the wild was one of the greatest, most iconic sounds in all of nature. Like a bear's roar, or the bugling of a bull elk. Strong, clear, fiercely proud—unmistakable.

"His call echoed down the valley. For a moment his enemies paused in flight. The challenge struck fear into them.

"And then, before the echoes of his war cry had died out, he launched himself into the air on powerful wings. But not away from his enemies, as in fear, rather he drove with speed and might straight toward the black cloud. And even as he neared his foes, he called his defiant cry again, and swept into them.

"This so shocked and dismayed the crows they parted, making a path for him. He flew straight into the heart of his enemies, but they did not touch him. They backed away in fear.

"But only frightening them did not satisfy the hawk. These were his hated foes. They had stolen his beloved home. So when he reached the center of the cloud, he folded his wings, and dived, straight down through the bottom part of the cloud.

"With sharp claws he struck a crow. Black feathers exploded, the limp form of a crow fell from the sky. Then he struck another. And another, and still another as he fell earthward.

"He dived, like a rock falling from the sky. Surely, he must slam into the ground and end his own life. But just before he hit the earth, he spread his great wings. And he swept up, higher, and higher into the sky with great force and speed. The bodies of his dead foes pounded into the dirt below him. In this way, he was soon above the cloud of crows.

"He screamed his war call again and attacked. This time he came from high above them as if falling out of the sun—the crows were sore afraid.

"He tore through them like a sharp knife through cloth. He ripped their backs with razor-sharp claws. And tore their flesh with a great, hooked beak.

"But he did not fall toward the Earth, as he'd done before. He tipped his wings and flew out the side of the cloud. He turned, screamed again, and came back at them.

"By now the crows were in a panic, their cloud was breaking up. The crows scattered in all directions. They realized their numbers could not save them from their terrible enemy. So each now thought only of protecting his own skin and feathers.

"But the fire in the hawk still burned hot and was not yet quenched. And though he must leave, and never come back, still he wished to go in his own time, in his own way. So he picked out the largest, fiercest looking crow, and followed him as he tried to escape. Though the crow was more nimble, the hawk was a strong, tireless flier. And a fiery wrath still flamed in his breast. So after a long chase, he caught his foe, clutched him in deadly claws, and tore out his throat.

"He carried the carcass back to his nest. There he slowly devoured his enemy to the last feather. And when he had finished his meal, he took a short rest. He put his nest in order and groomed his feathers. Finally, he flew to the very top branch of his tree.

"There, once again, he gave his fierce war cry, defying his enemies. They still occupied the woods in great numbers, despite his deadly attack. But this time, no cloud of foes appeared, and no crow answered his call. A heavy silence had fallen over the hill.

"With one strong stroke of his wings, he lifted into the sky, turned, and slowly flew away, never to return. But it was long, and longer before any crow had the courage to come near the abandoned hawk's nest, for fear of his wrath."

Billy fell silent and looked out over the valley.

But Nathan turned to him, tears in his eyes, and said in a quiet voice, "Thank you, Billy. Thank you."

He was quiet again for a long moment.

"Now I see what I *must* do. Though, like the hawk, it may break my heart to do it. Let's gather the men ... and plan our *attack*. And then ... our *long* retreat, after."

"Yes, Captain."

Later that day, Nathan called a council of war. It included all the old soldiers, plus the farmhands. And to Tony's surprise, the Captain also asked him to attend. Nathan said he was there to represent the "new recruits," as he called the black men Stan was busily training.

"I'll ask y'all to keep what's said in this meeting between us for now until I've told the others later this afternoon. I wanted to lay out my thoughts so y'all can work out the details while I'm taking care of *other* things.

"Gentlemen, as you know I'm a man of action, and not much inclined to sit on this hill waiting for the enemy to attack. I intend to take the battle to *him!* Only this time I don't mean to just drive our foes back down the hill. I mean to destroy them as a fighting force and seize control of the road. And then ... I intend to *kill* Walters, if I can, and rescue Miss Margaret for good measure! The man has attacked this house three times now, bent on destruction and bloody murder. These heinous crimes must *not* go unanswered."

There were wide-eyed looks from several of the men. But Stan and Jim leaned back in their chairs and grinned, exchanging a look between them that said they *liked* where this was going.

Nathan paused in his speech to look each man in the eye, one after the other. He was gratified to see determination, and nervous excitement, but no fear or hesitance.

"Now comes the part I shall ask you to keep to yourselves for the moment. I have come to believe ... though we are more than capable of beating the enemy presently at our gates, our position here is not tenable in the long run. We're too close to the enemy capital in Richmond. It's only a matter of time before they send a whole army here to rid themselves of the nuisance we're causing, once and for all. So I've come to the hard, painful decision that we must abandon the farm and move North. We must be ready to depart immediately after we've secured the road, before the enemy can muster any counter-measures."

The earlier enthusiasm for the Captain's battle plan was suddenly dampened. A somber mood fell over the gathering. Even Big Stan was no longer smiling and gave the Captain a look of sympathy and concern. This didn't surprise William; as fierce and strong as Stan was, he had a soft side that came out from time to time, such as with small children and animals.

"Are you sure there's no other way, sir?" Tom asked. "To abandon Mountain Meadows ... your family home ... to give it over to your enemies? It seems ... unthinkable," he said, looking Nathan hard in the eye.

"Is it worth the lives of these brave young men, Tom? Is it worth the freedom of the hundred and more men, women, and children who are ultimately my responsibility? No! No piece of land is worth *that* sacrifice. In the end it is only a place ... a piece of dirt with some buildings on it, and plants growing from it. It has been a good home to my family—and to all the families who've lived here. But now it's time to go find another, at least for a time.

"If we stay here, our enemies will surround and beset us, entirely cutting us off from the outside world until they finally overthrow us. If we wish to be free, we must flee from those who would enslave us; we must go to the North!"

ಶಿ ಶಿ ೧೩ ೮೪೮ ಶಿ ೮೪೮ ಶಿ ೮೪೮ ಶಿ ೮೪೮

Thursday May 23, 1861 – Greenbrier County, Virginia:

Miss Abbey was shocked. For a moment she stared at Nathan, open-mouthed as if what he had just said made no sense. "But ... Nathan ..."

"I know, Momma ... it's a bitter pill for me, too. It was not always so, but this past year I have come to love this place as no other. But if we try to stay ... eventually they'll send in so many men and guns we can no longer hold them off. And then ... they'll either kill me or throw me in prison. And how many of our good men will die in the process? No, I cannot justify it, Momma.

"I have defied the men who now run the government in Richmond. And I've sworn to fight against them, and *that* they cannot abide. They will continue to send men against us, like waves against the shore, until eventually we're swept under the tide."

"Yes, yes, of course. I recognize you're right, my dear. But … my heart aches at the thought of leaving … this place … *my home,*" her voice choked with emotion, finishing in barely a whisper. Tears filled her eyes.

"Momma, over the years commanding men in the Army I've become over-confident in my abilities—winning every fight, outlasting every enemy, never forced to endure the bitter taste of defeat. It's made me prideful, and cocksure. But Billy has reminded me … I'm still only a man, after all. And if I keep going along the path I'm on, my stubborn pride will destroy everything, and everyone I love. That's not what a *real* man must do … not what a man of God would do, surely. General Washington taught us the wisdom of living to fight another day.

"So that's what I intend to do Momma. Not surrender. Not give in to my hated enemies. But rather to withdraw from an indefensible position and live to fight them again elsewhere. And believe me, Momma, as God is my witness, I *will* fight them! I swear on my sacred honor I will make them rue the day they named me enemy!"

Miss Abbey saw the fire in his eyes, "I believe that's true, Nathan. You make a wonderful son, friend, and leader, but … I believe you would make a terrible enemy."

"I will take that for a compliment, Momma, though I'm not sure it's something one should aspire to.

"In any case, if you will release me from my sacred promise, I will tell the others, so we may start making our preparations straight away."

"Promise? What promise, dear?"

"My promise we would live here together … 'happily ever after,'" he smiled, trying to lighten the mood. But she burst into tears.

"Oh, Nathan … returning to me … you've made me the happiest woman on Earth. I can't tell you how joyful it has been to have you home. But home is *not* a place … it's where your loved ones are. As long as we're together … it doesn't matter where, my dearest."

She leaned forward, and wrapped her arms around his neck, holding him close, weeping.

After she pulled away again, he said, "Thank you for being understanding about it, Momma. I appreciate how much Mountain Meadows means to you. And I promise you this; once this madness is over, we *will* return home, and reclaim our own."

"No one knows what will happen, but I do believe if it can be done by any man, *you* will do it."

"Thank you, Momma. Well, it's settled, then. Please … let's start preparing."

ॐ૭ૡ୪ॐ૭ૡ୪ॐ૭ૡ୪

"The others," Megs and Toby, were just as shocked, but less emotional. Jim and Tom were there as well, though they already knew about it from the earlier soldiers' meeting. They were there to help with the preparations for departure.

Nathan explained to them all the things they needed to do to make ready to depart. Each person should take the bare minimum: a pair of shoes, a hat, coat, and a change of clothes.

They'd take every wagon they had, plus the carriage— basically, anything with wheels that could carry baggage, supplies, or people. The adult men and women would have to walk, other than the soldiers who'd ride the horses and serve as a cavalry force. But very young children, those too old to walk, and women with babes in arms would ride in the wagons.

They'd harvest everything they could of the food crops, plowing under the rest to deprive the enemy of it later.

"What about the cotton and tobacco, Captain?" Toby asked, clearly distressed at the idea of destroying the lush, beautiful plants even as they were nearing fruition.

Nathan thought for a moment then said, "Leave them … just as they are. With the blockade on, the South will have more cotton and tobacco than it can use or sell. Our contribution will be of little matter and will not benefit them at all.

"We'll let these bountiful crops stand as mute testament to what men like us may accomplish when we work together and bury the whip." He looked Toby in the eye and smiled, "Let our enemies gaze upon *that*, and despair!"

Toby returned the smile, and said, "Yes, Captain. As you say."

"And, as for the livestock … let us make cages that will easily fit stacked in the wagons for the smaller animals: chickens, geese, and piglets. The adult cattle we can lash together with leads and take with us. Tie one mature male sheep to a lead and the rest will follow—if we lose one or two along the way it won't matter. Slaughter the rest and salt the meat for the journey: hogs, and calves too young to keep up on the long trek."

Later in private he insisted Miss Abbey fill a traveling trunk with her most treasured articles of clothing. When she objected, he said, "I'll not have my mother going out into the world dressed as a pauper!" The stern look in his eyes stifled further objections.

CHAPTER 5. ACROSS THE RIVER JORDAN

"In spirituals,
the talk of heaven and deliverance
was code for a better life.
'Cross the River Jordan' was code,
of course, for escaping to freedom."
– Kathleen Battle

Friday May 24, 1861 – Greenbrier County, Virginia:

The next morning Nathan sat alone in the library. Before he headed outside to supervise the day's activities, he wanted to make a list of his own personal effects, to make sure he didn't forget something important in his haste to depart. The first thing on the list was the family Bible. He'd written down only a few items when there came a soft knock at the library door.

"Come."

Though he had not been expecting visitors, he was not terribly surprised, given the circumstances, when Megs entered the room, followed by the other slave Elders.

He set down his pen and stood.

"Ladies … and gentlemen … please, make yourselves comfortable. To what do I owe the honor?" he remembered their previous visit to his library distinctly, and fondly. So he genuinely welcomed their visit, though he had no idea what it might be about this time.

They came in and seated themselves, the men once again bringing in their own chairs from the kitchen. Nathan retook his seat.

"Sorry once again, Captain, for disturbing you, sir," Toby said.

Nathan shook his head, and made a dismissive gesture, meaning it was of no matter.

"But it seems we've once again made a decision that needs discussing with you."

The Captain gave him a quizzical look, but said nothing, allowing him to continue at his own pace.

But Toby surprised him, seeming hesitant and looking down at his own feet as if embarrassed somehow. Megs also wouldn't meet his eye, as if she too were embarrassed or ashamed.

"I's truly sorry to say this, sir, after all you done for us all. And … well, it's the first time we done ever disobeyed your wishes, but … we've all agreed to it. No slave will go with you to the North, sir. Not one."

Nathan stared at him, his mouth hanging open in disbelief. "But—" he started to respond, when a sudden notion struck him. He clamped his mouth shut and leaned back in his chair. "Go on …"

"Well, sir, you promised us you'd free us when the time was right. After we done made this farm to prosper without us-all being slaves. But now … now we's leaving this place and … it seems they's a war on, at leastways right around here, anyhow. And, well sir, not to be disrespectful, but … what if something were to happen to *you*, sir? You's talking about fighting and shooting guns and whatnot, and … well, I don't rightly know much about such things, sir. But I reckon one could get hisself kilt doing them things, even you, stout-hearted as you are. Then where would that leave us, sir? No one but *you* ever promised to free us. So if you was suddenly … *gone* … well, we'd be right back where we started, I reckon. So as I said, no *slave* will go north with you, sir. Not a one of us."

Nathan stood from his seat, strode over to the window, and pulled open the drapery. He stared out across the yard. The sky was clear and blue, promising another pleasant day. He stood still for several minutes, and the Elders exchanged worried looks.

He turned to face them, "You're absolutely right! And you humble me once again. I've been so wrapped up in my own plans. And in protecting and taking care of everyone I feel … *responsible for*. I had nearly forgotten the whole reason for all this trouble in the first place, that your people *must be set free!*"

He walked back across the room and sat down. He now had a smile on his face, and was shaking his head, "I … I *sincerely* beg your pardon. You are *absolutely* right. Now that all our plans have come unraveled, there's no reason to wait any longer. Gather your people on the lawn in front of the house at first light, and I shall tell them the good news!"

കരൈൽ

"Tom ... drop whatever you're working on. We have something more important to do."

Tom pushed his chair back from the desk in his office, and looked up, "What is it, Captain ... what has happened?"

"I've decided to free the slaves ... tomorrow if possible, the day after at the latest!"

"Oh! All right. Yes, why not? The world's coming apart at the seams, and now we're getting ready to send them into battle, a battle where some of them may very well be killed. Seems only fair they should die freemen. And after that we're heading north—we can't exactly show up with a hundred slaves in a state where they've outlawed slavery."

"My feelings exactly. So I need you to prepare the proper paperwork ... we'll need ... hmm ... I guess 112 separate manumission documents. It would be perfectly legal for us to list them all in a single, lengthy document and file that with the proper authorities. But we seem to be short on 'proper authorities' at the moment. And besides, I'd prefer they each have a document to keep with them to prove the truth of their freeman status."

"Yes, I agree—but have you then decided to abandon my earlier scheme?"

"Scheme?"

"Yes ... you recall; we would first convert them to indentured servants to skirt the Nat Turner laws?"

"Oh, yes, now I recall; there's no law against turning them all into indentured servants and then they'd be free after a specified period of time."

"Exactly, sir. It seemed a good idea at the time, but with everything falling apart perhaps it no longer matters. Since we're at legal odds with Richmond anyway, one more offense will make little difference."

Nathan thought about this a moment, then said, "No ... it *may* still matter. We don't know what will happen in the wider world. It's still possible there could be a negotiated peace, with Virginia rejoining the Union. If that were to happen, we might suddenly find ourselves on the wrong side of the law in a legitimate state.

"We might be forced to return and answer for our crimes. Of course, we would likely have a lot of other *bigger* crimes to answer for at that point," he gave Tom a rueful grin. "Still, I'd rather not risk freeing our people only to have that freedom stripped away later. With your plan, even a pro-slavery government in Virginia would have to admit—albeit reluctantly—it was all done proper and legal. Yes, let's still go ahead with it, Tom. And, congratulations again for coming up with it."

"Thank you, sir. I was originally planning on making the servitude time period a few months or even a year, for the sake of good form. But now ... well, I guess it will have to be only a single day. Fortunately, there are no restrictions on the length of time one may be bonded. The manumission papers will convert each slave to an indentured servant and specify a date after which he will be a freeman."

"That should be perfect, Tom. Still, it'll be a lot of writing, so we ought to start on it straight away. I'll send for William and Miss Abbey ... hmm ... not sure who else could write this sort of thing and have it legible ... Georgie, maybe?"

"Yes, Georgie, very likely ... perhaps one or two of the farmhands. The other soldiers ... probably *not*. Even Jim, as good as he is at most things, is not much use when it comes to reading and writing. But the good news is, I've been working on these papers for some time now and have a good stack of them already done."

"Have you? But ... how did you know to do it? Even *I* didn't know I was going to free them now, until only a few minutes ago."

"Oh, well ... I didn't know *when* it would happen, but I knew it *would* happen, eventually. When the time came, I didn't want to have to do it all at once. So whenever I've had idle time I've gone ahead and written out one or two more. I've left spaces to fill in the names both as they are now, and any new names they should choose to adopt. And the dates, of course.

"I've made sure the papers include the proper legal wording, but because there were so many to do, I've kept it to a bare minimum. Some people prefer to wax philosophical on such documents, and add all sorts of embellishments, but I have resisted the urge to do so out of necessity.

"I haven't bothered counting, but I'd guess I have several dozen already done."

"Splendid, Tom! Well done, as usual."

"Thank you, sir."

ॐ∞ॐ∞ॐ∞ॐ∞ॐ∞ॐ∞

Nathan stepped onto the veranda as the sun rose above the mountains to the east. It was Saturday morning, not his usual Sunday sermon, so there had been a great deal of curiosity about it around the farm. All the slaves gathered on the lawn before him, even as they'd done on that very first Sunday when he'd addressed them for the first time almost a year ago. The white men, however, were not present this time; they were required to man the defenses of Mountain Meadows, so the black men could be excused to listen to the Captain's talk this morning. This time Miss Abbey stood next to him on the veranda. The great dog laid on the grass next to the veranda, gazing up at his master, tongue hanging out the side of his mouth.

Nathan looked up at the bright rays of the rising sun. Then gazed off into the distance at the beauty of the land surrounding him. He breathed a heavy sigh.

"Good morning," he said in his strong, clear voice.

"Good morning," the gathered people echoed back in a hundred and twelve different voices.

"May God bless y'all on this beautiful day He has made for us.

"I'm sure you will remember the first time I spoke to you, gathered in this very spot nearly a year ago. On that day I told y'all things you'd never expected a white master to say. Most important of which was … I promised to free you, every man, woman, and child."

He looked out and saw the same faces he'd seen on that long-ago Sabbath, only now they were as familiar as the back of his own hand. But unlike that first morning, these faces were relaxed, and generally happy looking, now clearly expecting only *good* things from their master.

"But at the time I said I would not set you free until we all worked together to make this farm prosper without slavery. And not before you'd all learned how to survive on your own out in the world. And ... I asked you to be patient, as it might take several years.

"Well, I'm sure y'all are aware the rest of the world has not stayed as it was, and we can no longer do as we'd planned. The folks over in Richmond have decided they will no longer be part of our great United States of America. They've carried out an act they call 'secession.' They have done this thing mostly so they can continue holding the black people as slaves until the end of time.

"There were good men too—friends of mine—who opposed them and tried to keep the secession from happening. But sadly, we have failed. Now there's a war on, and all our plans are for naught. Those men over in Richmond want to kill me or throw me in prison to make sure y'all will never be free."

"Damn slavers!" someone called out, to which several others said, "Amen, amen ..."

Nathan nodded and smiled but held up his hand for silence.

"Thank you ... yes ... *damn slavers*, indeed!"

There were many smiles, and a few nervous giggles; they were *not* used to hearing the Captain swear, especially not during his sermons.

"So now, as you've heard, we must prepare to leave this place, our beloved home, and travel north to escape the slavers.

"But now we come to the part I have gathered you here to tell y'all. I have decided ... I will take no *slaves* with me when I go north, not a single one."

He said it with a straight face, but he looked at Toby and winked. Toby smiled knowingly in return, but there were many shocked and worried faces in the crowd.

"I say … I'll not take any *slaves* with me … because I will only take *freemen!* So tomorrow, we will hand out manumission papers to each and every one of you. Starting tomorrow … and *forever* after … *you shall all be free!*"

After a momentary shocked silence, the people spontaneously leapt to their feet and began jumping up and down, shouting out, crying, dancing, kissing, and embracing each other.

Nathan took a cigar from his pocket, lit it, and puffed contentedly, a broad smile on his face. Miss Abbey stepped up next to him, grasped his upper arm and leaned her head against his shoulder. She was smiling brightly but had to wipe tears from her eyes. It occurred to Nathan he'd finally received the very satisfying reaction he'd hoped for nearly a year ago—the day he'd told them he planned to free them. The difference was, this time they believed him.

࿊࿌࿉࿌࿊࿌࿉࿌࿊࿌࿉࿌

Sunday May 26, 1861 – Greenbrier County, Virginia:

For the second day in a row, the slaves came together in front of the Big House at daybreak, with Nathan and Miss Abbey standing above them on the veranda.

Strangely there were two small tables set up on the driveway, each with two chairs. At one of the tables sat Tom, and at the other William, a stack of papers and an inkwell in front of each. None of the other white men were present—once again off manning the defenses, or in the case of Jamie and Georgie, maintaining and preparing the weapons for the coming battle.

Nervous excitement pervaded the group. Quiet laughter, boisterous talking, and plenty of smiles. But also tearful, serious looks.

Nathan took it all in as he raised his hands for quiet.

"Good morning, and God bless y'all."

"Good morning," the gathering echoed back.

"Welcome … welcome most happily, to the day you've been awaiting your entire lives. To the day you'll surely remember the *rest* of your lives. The day you'll tell your children about, and your grandchildren. Welcome to *the day of freedom!"*

There were smiles and happy looks exchanged between friends and loved ones, but nobody spoke. No one wanted to interrupt. All wanted to hear what the Captain had to say.

"In the Bible, Exodus chapter twenty, verse two, the Lord God spoke to the Israelites having freed them from slavery under the Egyptian Pharaoh. He said to the people, *'I am the LORD thy God, which have brought thee … out of the house of bondage.'* Today that very same God will take each of you by the hand and lead you out of the house of bondage, into the land of freedom.

"It is a day in which you *should* rightly rejoice and celebrate, a day where there *should be* dancing and singing. Fireworks, and bonfires. But though today is the day you are no longer slaves, alas, it cannot be a day of celebration.

"Even freemen are not free without paying a price. Freemen, even those born free such as I, must fight against those who would take away that freedom. We must ever be vigilant, ever be prepared to defend our freedoms, lest evil, self-serving men come and enslave us.

"So though today is your day of freedom, your work is *not* done. I am sorry it must be so, but though I can grant you freedom today, I cannot *keep* you free. Only *you* can do that … only *we* can do it, all of us *together*. As soon as this freedom ceremony is over, we must go back to work preparing for the fight to come, the young men preparing to meet the enemy in battle, and the rest making ready our escape to the North.

"Make no mistake, we must work together. We must trust each other, and fight for one another, or we will *all* lose our freedom, and likely our very lives.

"But now, in this moment, be light of heart, secure in the knowledge you are held safely the palm of God's gracious hand.

"This morning, we have prepared a special ceremony for y'all. As you can see, the driveway curves in a circle, creating an island of grass. This island will represent the imprisonment of your slavery. The roadway surrounding it, represents the chains of your bondage, which you must cast off to reach freedom on the other side—"

But before he could speak further, Toby stepped forward, "Begging your pardon, Captain, sir. But this here roadway ain't no chains. This here's the River Jordan, sir!" He grinned broadly, and several others nodded in agreement.

Nathan thought for a moment, then smiled, "Ah … yes; I see it now. Right you are, Toby—*the River Jordan*, indeed! In the Bible, the Book of Joshua, chapter three, it tells how the Israelites crossed the River Jordan to reach the promised land. And so, as Toby says, the roadway today will represent that mighty river. And I suppose that means Mr. Tom and Mr. William, who sit in the middle of the roadway, will play the part of the priests of the Israelites—the priests who stopped the river with the Ark of the Covenant, so the people might pass. Only in your case, it will be your manumission papers allowing you to cross over to freedom, rather than the Ark.

"Finally, the wide-open yard of the Big House on the other side of the road will represent the promised land of freedom. The yard has no boundary, no fence. It simply fades off into the woods and from there into the vast, endless expanse of the forest, representing the infinite possibilities a man may pursue in life once he is free.

"So please gather in the island of grass. And when Mr. Tom or Mr. William calls out your name, you will walk to the table and take a seat. There you will tell him the new name you have chosen, if any.

"Though we talked about it yesterday, and several of you have talked with Mr. Tom already, I will remind you again; you may choose a new name if you wish. Your slave name is likely only a shortened form of a longer English name, so you may choose the longer form, like *William* in place of *Will* or *Bill*, or *Elizabeth* in place of *Liz* or *Beth*. Or you may choose something altogether different if you wish, it matters not.

"Many of you have secretly adopted traditional African names, which you use amongst yourselves. I appreciate this tradition and admire your fortitude for keeping it alive against the wishes of the former master. You may use those names, if you wish, although I think it might be best to use names that sound more 'American,' so you'll better fit in and not be set apart and treated differently.

"And you may also choose a *family* name. Again, the name may be whatever you wish—the name of a famous person, such as a president," he smiled at Big George, who'd taken the family name *Washington* at the Great Wedding the year before.

"A name from the Bible, from stories you may have heard, or any other name you fancy. You may even choose *Chambers* if you wish, though it'd be best if not too many of you did that, lest it become confusing concerning which family is which.

"Speaking of ... families will go together to the tables. But each person to the smallest babe will receive his own manumission paper, and each person may select his own given name.

"Miss Abbey and I will wait for you on the lawn there, to welcome you into the promised land of freedom.

"So ... if you will, please ..." he gestured toward the island of grass in the middle of the driveway, and the people turned and moved in that direction.

Nathan and Miss Abbey walked arm in arm down the stairs of the veranda. They moved to a place on the edge of the lawn directly across from where the people were gathering in the driveway island, with Tom and William sitting at their tables in between. Harry the Dog hopped up from where he'd been lying in the shade next to the veranda and followed, plopping back down on the grass a few feet away from Nathan.

When everyone was in place, Nathan once again addressed them.

"Your names will be called in no particular order. They are simply as the papers have ended up arranged, with the exception only of the first and the last, which I have chosen myself.

"The first, is on account of he's been the person most anxious to be free—so much so he started to leave once already."

There was a smattering of laughter, but the people had generally become solemn and serious, recognizing the significance of the moment. Tony looked down at his feet, but the sides of his mouth betrayed the hint of a grin.

"But also because he was the first man among you to step up and fight back against the slavers. Tony, please step forward to Mr. Tom's table, and receive your freedom papers, the first slave of Mountain Meadows to do so!"

Johnny and Ned slapped Tony on the back, grabbed him by the arms and shook him good naturedly, before freeing him. All three friends beamed from ear to ear.

Tony walked over and sat opposite Tom at the small table.

"Tony, this paper in front of me says as of today you are a freeman. Have you decided if you will choose a new name?"

"I ... I been thinking on it, Mr. Tom, but I ain't come up with nothing. Can you ... *help* me?"

Tom looked at him for a moment, then said, "Well ... Tony is actually short for Anthony. The name belonged to a famous Roman general back in the great Caesar's time—in fact, Caesar's good friend. They call him Marcus Antonius in the Latin, but in English we say Mark Anthony."

"Mark Anthony. I likes the sound of that. Would that make a good name, do you reckon, Mr. Tom?"

"Yes, certainly, Tony! And you can still have people call you Tony if you wish, but your 'real' name from now on would be 'Mark Anthony.' Would you like to make it so?"

"Yes, please, sir."

So Tom added the name to Tony's paper. Blotted it and handed the paper to him. Tom extended his hand, "Congratulations, *Mark Anthony*. You are now a freeman."

Tony gazed at him, then down at the paper, and finally to the extended hand. He looked shocked, like he couldn't believe what was happening. Then a bright smile lit his features, and he reached out and firmly shook Tom's hand. "Thank you, sir. Thank you most kindly!"

He stood and looked back toward where the others waited on the island. Johnny and Ned smiled at him but gestured for him to go on across to the yard ... on over to freedom.

He turned and walked across the drive to where the Captain stood, smiling at him as he approached, hand outstretched.

"Congratulations, Tony. Welcome to freedom."

They shook hands and exchanged a smile. "Thank you kindly, sir. I ... I don't know what to say to you ... I don't feel I rightly deserve this."

"Nonsense, Tony. You've earned it better'n most of the others. It's why I chose you to go first. You're a good man, and a brave fighter. I *need* you fighting on my side and am damned lucky to have you."

A sense of pride welled up inside Tony. He'd never felt this good before, and nobody'd ever talked to him the way the Captain had just now. He finally understood why the soldiers said they'd gladly lay down their lives for him.

"George, Babs, Annie, and Lucy Washington," William called out.

Twenty minutes later the lawn was becoming more populated, while the island was quickly shrinking. Nathan and Miss Abbey had taken turns welcoming the newly freed men, women, and children.

When Rosa crossed over it happened to be Nathan's turn. It suddenly struck him he'd not thought about her, and the potential problem she represented, for a long time. He still wasn't certain she was harboring romantic feelings toward him, but he feared it might be so. He *was* certain, however, that Tony would be watching every move and every look, listening to every word. To make matters worse, the new name she'd chosen was telling: Rosanna *Chambers!* He cringed when she said it. Now he wondered if he should've told them they *couldn't* use his family name.

Before she arrived, he located Tony and gave him a hard look. Tony returned the look. Nathan nodded to him. Tony returned the nod.

Nathan turned toward Rosa, and embraced her, welcoming her to the land of freedom. But before he could step away, she reached up and kissed him on the cheek, then smiled up at him.

He returned her smile briefly, then turned to greet the next person coming across.

He wondered if this was only the beginning of more troubles to come with her. Now that she was no longer his slave, she might assume the rules had changed. He couldn't think of how to resolve it, short of hurting her feelings or discovering the truth about her mother. And now, with the impending war, he could no longer visit the mother and ask her.

An hour later, one person stood alone on the island. It wasn't a surprise to the former slave Elders, nor to the person standing there alone. In fact, had they called her name earlier, she certainly would've refused to cross.

Nathan stepped up onto the road, and turned to face the newly freed black men, women, and children standing on the lawn.

"And now ... we have come to the last slave to receive her freedom. We all know her as *Megs*, but I understand she has chosen the name *Magdalena Chambers* to use from this day forward. She wouldn't care, but I want y'all to know ... Miss Abbey offered Megs her freedom on three separate occasions over the years. But each time freedom was offered, Megs answered, 'Not until I am *the very last slave on this farm*.'"

He turned toward Megs, who now had tears streaming down her face. "Megs ... now you *are* the very last slave of Mountain Meadows. Will you *finally* come across to freedom?"

She covered her face in her hands and wept. The people gathered on the lawn laughed and cried, and many called out to her, "Come on across, Megs ... come across to freedom."

She finally pulled her hands down, nodded, and ran across the drive, not bothering to stop at Tom's table. He smiled, set down his pen, and shook his head in amusement as she hurried past. This time Nathan and Miss Abbey greeted her together, and she immediately wrapped her arms around both of them, her head buried between theirs. All three of them embraced as they shed happy tears.

After a minute, Nathan pushed her back to arm's length, looked her in the eye and said, "Welcome to freedom ... *mother*."

And Miss Abbey added, "Welcome to freedom ... *sister*."

Megs looked back and forth between the two loving, smiling faces and was overcome, collapsing to her knees and sobbing. Miss Abbey and Nathan knelt with her and resumed the embrace as Megs continued to sob.

After a few moments, Nathan stood and faced the people. Raising his hands above his head, he declared, "And the Lord God said, *'I have brought thee … out of the house of bondage'*!"

Then they all wept, laughed, shouted, danced, and sang, with a hundred and twelve different joyous voices.

ಐಐಐ⅃ᘓ♄ಐಐᘓ⅃ᘓ♄ಐಐᘓ⅃♄

Sunday May 26, 1861 – Greenbrier County, Virginia:

Margaret heard a key turn in the lock. After nearly a week of being locked in, she'd begun to think Walters wasn't going to beat her or kill her, after all. That things had returned to "normal" to some extent—normal, except now her door was always locked. One of the white overseers was always there to unlock it and let the maids in with meals, or to clean the room, after which they'd lock it again. But despite her status as no better than a prisoner, the men still knocked politely before unlocking and opening the door.

But she'd always known that when Walters decided to come, he would *not* knock; he would simply come in. He *owned* her, like his slaves, or his horses—he had no need to be polite. And this time, as the key turned in the lock, she was certain it was him— there'd been no knock.

But when the door opened, and a man stepped in, quickly closing the door behind him and locking it, she was surprised it wasn't Walters, rather the head overseer, Bob Hill. Despite him being Walters' right-hand man, and coconspirator in his nefarious activities, Bob had never treated her unkindly. Was he being sent to do Walters' dirty work for him, she wondered? But she decided, no. It wasn't Walters' way. If he wanted someone whipped, he was only too eager to do it himself.

"Hello, Bob."

"Miss Margaret. May I?" he gestured toward a chair.

"Please," she said, seating herself on the bed opposite where Bob sat.

"I'm here because I'm leaving Walters Farm ... I'm fixing to ride over to Richmond and volunteer with the new Confederate Army. I figure with my experience leading men and whatnot, they might make me an officer."

Margaret didn't know how to respond. Though he'd always been polite, she'd never been close to him. Why would he tell her his plans before he departed?

"You're probably wondering why I should tell you these things, or why you should care. Or perhaps you're even wondering why I would leave Walters after all we've been through. I'll answer the last question first ... it's partly because of *you* I'm leaving.

"You see ... I wasn't always ... well, whatever it is I am now. I was once a hard-working young farmhand, who'd never gotten into any trouble, nor ever done anything wrong. But I was ambitious and had a burning desire to be the boss, the head man of a large plantation like this one. I was sure I'd excel at it. So when Mr. Walters offered me the job, I was thrilled and set out to prove his faith in me was justified.

"Then ... it started with little things, really: an undeserved beating here ... a scheme to get the better of a neighbor there. An unethical business transaction ... a bribe paid to a law officer. As the years went by Walters seemed less interested in what other people thought of him or his actions. And I ... I never stopped to consider what *I* was becoming by doing his bidding.

"This past year I've found myself wound up in his plots against the Chambers. It became so bad I finally started wondering what I had become. I was now plotting murder against a family that was upstanding, law-abiding, and perfectly innocent," he shook his head sadly.

"But then there was *you*. Somehow it was worse with you. You're smart, and kindly, and well ... unlike Mr. Chambers, or even Miss Abbey ... you're all alone—totally helpless and completely at his mercy. It ... well, it touched me somehow, and I just couldn't let it happen."

"Let *what* happen, Bob?"

"He means to murder you, Miss Margaret. Right here in this room with his bare hands. I'm not sure why he hasn't done it already. Except maybe ... I hesitate to say it ... it is too horrible speak of. But ... I think he's waiting so he can *savor* it, somehow, if you understand what I mean."

She didn't answer, but her face whitened, and tears began to well in her eyes.

"I have heard this from his own mouth, Miss Margaret. He plans to tell everyone you have died from your delicate constitution and bury you out in the woods. Then he intends to go back to Richmond and marry another woman, starting the whole thing all over again."

"Why ... why are you telling me this, Bob?" she said in a voice choked with emotion such that it came out in barely a whisper.

He stood up, and walked toward the window, gazing out before turning quickly away from it, realizing someone passing by outside might see him in the mistress's bedroom.

"Because I mean to prevent it from happening, if I can."

"Oh! God bless you, Bob; and thank you! But ... how will you help me?"

"I'd considered killing him myself, but ... well, I can't bring myself to do it, somehow. Perhaps after all these years serving him loyally I just can't ...

"Anyway, I'd also considered taking you with me when I rode off to Richmond, while he was off at church, as he is now."

Margaret silently chastised herself; she'd forgotten it was Sunday morning, or she'd have had no fear of Walters being at her door. Except for the time he traveled to Richmond he had never missed church, being a man of very strict habits. But locked in her room, one day was the same as the next, and she'd lost track of which it was.

"But ... in the end, I'm only a coward, I suppose. I'm afraid of Walters, you see. If I were to take you away, he would hunt me down and ... well, I haven't the stomach to face him."

"So then ... how *will* you help me?"

He held up a cloth sack he'd been carrying with him. It appeared to have some heft to it.

"May I?" he asked, gesturing toward a place on the bed next to her.

She gestured for him to come and sit next to her.

He moved over and sat on the bed, holding the cloth sack between them.

"I have arranged for your escape. It won't be easy once you've left this house as you must travel by foot. But I'm confident you can do it."

Margaret said nothing, only gazed at him as he explained his scheme.

"You see, I have arranged for a hole in the watch. For a half hour, starting at midnight, no one will guard your door, nor will there be anyone between your room and the front door."

"All right, but … they lock my bedroom door, as you know. So how —"

Before she could complete the question, he stretched out his hand, palm up. In it was …

"The key!"

"Yes, I'm giving you my key. It will also unlock the front door. Once you're out in the woods, I would appreciate if you would toss it away where it'll never be found. I'll be long gone by then, but still … I'd rather he not know it was me who gave it to you."

"All right, but —"

"This sack is mostly filled with food for the journey, along with a bottle of water. If you're careful, the food should last you two or three days. Hopefully by then you can find something on your own. Wear comfortable shoes you can walk in, and clothing that's sturdy, with subdued colors if you have them. The weather's good right now, but take something to cover yourself if it turns cool or rains. Travel by night if you can, and hide during the day. Avoid everyone and trust no one, *especially* law men. Most around here are paid to do Walters' bidding. I should know, I'm the one who pays them.

"Head west through Lewisburg and out the far side, following the main road. About twenty-five miles from town you will come to a major fork in the road. Here you must decide to either continue west toward Kentucky or turn on the right-hand fork and head north toward Wheeling. Either way, if I were you, I would keep going until I was out of Virginia entirely. But you'll have to see how far you can go before you're too tired to continue. Wherever you end up, I would recommend changing your name, so he will never find you."

"All right ... but surely Walters will set his dogs on my trail come morning. I'll never outrun them, and with their keen sense of smell there is no hiding either. How ever shall I escape *them*?"

"Your intelligent questions do you credit, Miss Margaret. I agree the hounds *would have been* an obstacle you could never have defeated. As you say, no matter where you ran, or where you hid, they would certainly have found and caught you, eventually. But ... I have considered that as well, of course. I have put arsenic in their food this morning, enough to kill a horse. By nightfall they will be too sick to move and by morning they will all be dead."

She gasped, "Oh, no ... you didn't! The poor things ..."

"Miss Margaret, I appreciate the sentiment, and typically I am also fond of dogs, horses, and other innocent creatures. But these particular animals ... well, they're a perfect reflection of their master, either by chance or design. They are vicious brutes who seem to revel in the pain and suffering of other creatures, including the slaves, if they can get at them. Believe me, if you'd seen them chew a man's arm off, as I have, you'd have no sympathy for them. They are no loss to the world, I can assure you."

"Oh ... very well. I suppose you're right, and I certainly owe you my undying gratitude for your help, and your advice but ... midnight? What if Walters decides today is *the day* ... he'd surely come to this room well before midnight?"

"Yes, of course, that would be a problem. But ... I have allowed for that contingency as well. He reached into the bag and pulled out a small, single shot pistol. He turned the handle toward her and held it out.

"Have you ever used one before?"

She looked at the pistol, wide-eyed, afraid to even touch it.

"No! No, never ... I am afraid."

"Nonsense, Miss Margaret. You are an intelligent, competent woman. It is truly child's play to use it. I have already loaded it for you. All you have to do is pull the hammer back until it clicks, like so ... and then ... squeeze the trigger and it will fire."

"Oh ... I don't know if I could ..."

Bob was quiet for a moment and gazed at her gravely. "Miss Margaret ... if Walters comes to this room today, he *will* murder you, as sure as the sun rises in the East. But he will hurt you first. You will suffer great pain, and when he has tired of the sport, you will die.

"Or ... when he walks in that door, you will stand up, pull back the hammer, point it at the center of his chest and pull the trigger. Then *you* will live, and *he* will die. It's as simple as that. One or the other. It's *your* choice."

She thought on this a moment, then reached out her hand, and took the pistol, "I will do it."

"Good. Again, you do yourself credit."

"No ... I'm just more afraid of Walters than I am of this ... *thing.*"

"As you should be."

"But Bob ... I have one more question, and it is the most important of all, in my mind. *Why?* Why are you doing this for me? You could have just ridden away and been done with this place, off to the war. And never thought of me, or Walters again."

He was quiet and thoughtful for a moment before answering.

"Miss Margaret ... I'm not proud of the things I've done the last few years. I've lost my way. I'm joining the Army to serve a greater cause. Maybe this way I can make amends. Perhaps if I give unselfishly of myself, God will forgive me. And then maybe ... maybe I will even forgive myself.

"But as for *you* ... well ... when I thought of riding off to war and leaving you to your fate, helpless; that can't be the way to seek redemption.

"But ... also ... selfishly I wished ... well, I wished when I was out in battle somewhere, there might be ... maybe ... someone in the world who cared whether I lived or died. God knows I have done nothing up 'til now to give anyone cause. And I hoped if I helped you, you might … think of me sometimes. And maybe think of something *good* I have done, not just the wicked things."

She could see this meant a lot to him, and it had been difficult to say. She reached out and held his hand.

"Thank you for all you've done to save me, Bob. If I live, and find my way to safety, I shall pray every day for God to keep you safe during the terrible war to come. And I will remember the wonderful, honorable things you have done for me tonight. And if I die, I will watch over you from heaven, if I can."

She could see there were now tears in his eyes, "Thank you, Miss Margaret. That means more to me than … well, than you can imagine. Thank you. Like I said before, if I had any courage, I would take you with me."

"Never you mind *that*. You have plenty of courage, but you're not *foolish*. That is *not* the way. It must be done as you've planned it for me, or it won't work, and we both know it. If I were to ride away with you, we'd have to run the rest of our lives. And we'd always be looking back to see if *he* was following. That's no way to live. This is the only way, Bob.

"But perhaps one day … if we both survive all this … *maybe* …"

She gave his hand a squeeze and smiled at him. His eyes widened, and his face turned red. He returned the smile and the squeeze. Then he stood, turned, and walked to the door.

"Come, Miss Margaret, unlock the door for me, and lock it after. Remember … if Walters enters this room, you *must* kill him, or you will surely die. Don't let him close enough to grab the pistol. Then after you've shot him, run out the door and don't stop. Hopefully if he's dead, no one will bother to pursue you."

"I will remember, thank you. Goodbye. And Bob … we *will* see each other again, either here on Earth … or in heaven!"

He blushed again and smiled. She unlocked the door, and he was gone.

⁊⁂⁃

An hour after the freedom ceremony, Nathan stepped into the smithing shed to check on the work Jamie and Georgie were doing. He'd heard they'd gathered every spare rifle that wasn't actively being used on the defensive lines. Nathan appreciated their thoroughness—cleaning and oiling the guns, fixing any damaged or malfunctioning parts. It was a time-consuming and tedious task, but critical to the proper functioning of the weapon; it could spell the difference between life and death for the person wielding the rifle. He wanted to offer them praise and encouragement.

But when he stepped into the room it surprised him to see the forge fired up to red-hot. Georgie pounded a piece of metal with a hammer on top of the anvil, sparks flying. These were *not* typical gunsmithing tools or activities.

Jamie saw the Captain first and swatted Georgie's arm to get his attention, so he'd leave off the hammering.

He turned to see why Jamie had interrupted him, "Oh! Hello, Captain. How was the big ceremony?"

"It was … *very moving* … it was … just the right thing."

"Now you are for making me sorry I missed it, sir," Jamie said, looking wistful.

"But we been busy, sir. Look what we been doing!" Georgie's enthusiasm for whatever they'd been doing was obvious.

Nathan looked at the anvil, and saw a long, thin piece of metal, the glowing-hot point being hammered flat.

"What is it?"

"Lookie over here, sir," Jamie said, pointing to a row of rifles leaning up against the side of the shed. Nathan had seen them as he'd walked in the door. But the light was dim, and he'd paid them little mind. He'd assumed they were stacked there either because they'd already been worked on or were about to be.

Now he examined the weapons more closely and experienced a sudden, excited gasp, "Why … they've got *bayonets!* The whole lot of 'em! Honest-to-God, eighteen-inch, socket-type military bayonets!"

He gave them a look of amazement … "What a beautiful sight! Have you made them all yourselves? And how ever have you attached them to ordinary hunting rifles such as we have here?"

Not waiting for the answers, he reached out and picked up a rifle, examining the end of the barrel where the offset bayonet was attached. He could see they'd cut back the wood of the stock to expose enough of the metal barrel to accommodate attaching the bayonet.

"You've welded on a bayonet lug!" He grabbed the base of the bayonet and gave it a hard twist. The bayonet came loose, and he easily slipped it off the barrel of the gun. "*Damn!* Fine work, gentlemen. Fine work, indeed! But … how? How did you think of it and … how have you *done* all this?"

"Well, once we learned we was abandoning the farm, Jamie and I got to talking about what we should do with all the scrap metal lying about. Not to mention a large pile of horseshoes, too heavy to take along with us. We figured on digging a hole and burying all the stuff to keep the enemy from using it."

"But then I wondered … why not make some good use of all that metal ourselves before we go?" Jamie added.

"Yep. Only we couldn't come up with anything, lest we was to try and forge a cannon! But that requires a whole other knowledge and skill beyond a gunsmith or a blacksmith!

"But that got us to talking about the guns, and the battle to come. And Jamie was lamenting the loss of them two Springfields we had to leave behind back at the boarding house when we rode out of Richmond, duckin' enemy gunfire all the way."

"Yes, and I says, 'Georgie lad, the worst shame of it is, we got these here two perfectly beautiful bayonets, and no gun to mount 'em on.' To which he says, '*Bayonets!* That's it, Jamie my brother; we'll use the scrap metal to make *bayonets* … and lugs to attach 'em … for all these here hunting rifles.' So … well, we been at it for pretty much two solid days now, and up all night … but, as you can see, we're nearly finished."

Nathan examined their handiwork on the rifle he was holding. Simple, efficient and sturdy, they'd fashioned them in the offset style, allowing the soldier to fire and reload the rifle with the bayonet fixed. They were of rough metal, unpolished. They'd sharpened each bayonet's end into a wedge shape, like a turnscrew, rather than down to a point like a needle, as was more typical.

Georgie saw him examining the point, and said, "We figured it'd be easier and quicker to build them that way. And likely they'd be sturdier than a needle point."

"Right, laddie. And they're for killing a man every bit as dead as the other kind," Jamie added with a grin.

Nathan touched the sharp end with his finger and felt the edge begin to bite. "Yes, I reckon you've got something there ... these ought to work perfectly well, and as you say, may be sturdier — less likely to bend or snap off."

Nathan pushed the bayonet back on. He grasped the rifle with both hands, turned and thrust it hard into the wall of the shed. It punched through the wall, embedding itself a good ten inches of its length. Nathan turned to the men and smiled, before pulling it back out of the wall, and setting it back next to the others.

His mind was racing with the possibilities. The bayonet was rarely used in combat and was strategically insignificant; a Minni ball fired from a rifle could kill a man hundreds of yards away, while a bayonet required the enemy to be within a single rifle's length. But there was something about a well-organized and bravely fought bayonet charge that had an unnerving effect on even the most battle-hardened veteran soldier. Men who'll stand all day under heavy rifle fire will wilt at the sight of foes charging at them with eighteen-inch knife blades sticking out of their rifles.

And ... Nathan grinned at the thought, *the enemy soldiers at the bottom of this hill are, for the most part, anything but battle-hardened veterans.*

"Excellent work, gentlemen!" he said, and strode out of the shed still beaming, "Yes ... very excellent work!"

Jamie and Georgie shared a happy look, smiling brightly, before congratulating each other with an enthusiastic handshake, and a firm pat on the back.

In the late afternoon Nathan gave another speech. But this time there were only men standing before him. Strong, young men, with determined faces, both black and white. Georgie and Jamie stood there, and Tom and William; the rest of the white men were off manning the front lines. No smiles, no laughter, but a nervous, excited energy pervaded the group that was almost palpable.

"Men ... tomorrow we go into battle. For most of you it will be the very first time. But this morning you became *freemen*, so I can no longer *order* you to do it. Each of you must now decide for himself: fight or don't fight. Stand up and risk all for love of family and freedom or shrink away in fear. Step up and be a man, or wilt and slink away like a fearful cur.

"I've looked in your eyes ... each of you, and I've seen a determination and fire there. A look to put fear into your enemies and courage into the hearts of your fellows.

"You black men whose forefathers were once mighty warriors in old Africa ... you've been as men asleep these past years. But now, you've awakened! Even as the Christ, you have arisen! From a dark dream of bondage, fear, and death, you've come back into the light of the waking world ... and you've discovered you're *strong!* You're alive and free! Woe be unto any man who would put you back in chains!"

Nathan was now nearly shouting, and he shook his fist above his head to emphasize the words.

"Amen to that, Captain!" Georgie shouted, raising his rifle, pumping it up and down, turning toward the former slaves gathered in front of the Captain.

"Amen!" Jamie, William, and Tom echoed. The four of them started chanting, "Amen, amen ... amen ..." pumping their rifles in the air. The black men looked startled at first, staring at their white counterparts, not knowing what was the expected of them. But they soon caught on to it and joined in the chant, raising rifles high, shouting, "Amen, amen, amen ..."

This brought a smile to Nathan's lips. But not a pleasant, friendly smile, rather the fierce, killer smile of a warrior contemplating battle. A smile that presaged death and destruction to his enemies.

After a few seconds he held up his hands for silence.

"Men ... there is never any lasting freedom without fighting for it. Though there are many good-hearted men in the world, there are still too many evil ones. Men who care only for themselves, their own wealth, their own wellbeing.

"These men will gladly enslave us—black or white—if they can. Or kill us if they can't.

"In fact, when I was over in Richmond, these same evil slavers tried to force me to join with them and fight against my own country—to fight for slavery, else they'd throw me in chains or kill me. When I refused, they tried their best to murder me, and nearly succeeded.

"If not for the selfless courage of the men standing beside you, who risked their very lives to save me, I'd be a dead man now, not standing before you.

"But I must warn you, this will be a fight to the death. Some of us, or even all of us, may die or suffer grievous wounds. War is at our very gates—a war between slavers and freemen. I want each one of you to go into this with eyes wide open, knowing what may happen.

"But this one truth I know for sure ... any man who dies tomorrow will have died a *freeman*, fighting for his own freedom, for his family, and for his friends. Any man who falls tomorrow will die a *hero*; he will be honored always, and he will never be forgotten to the end of days. This is the way a freeman *should* die, a weapon in his hands and a curse for his wicked enemy upon his lips—not shackled in chains, whimpering, with whip marks across his back!

"But lest you feel downhearted and fearful, let me also say this: I am a man used to *winning* battles, and *I mean to win this one!* I intend to drive the foe before us, to slaughter all who stand in our way. To clear a path to the North and freedom, for ourselves, our friends, and our families.

"I can't promise you this will happen, but I *believe* it will! So what I *can* promise you is this: we will fight *together* every step of the way and with the last measure of our strength and courage!"

He paused for a moment, gazing across the crowd, making eye contact with every man. He was gratified to see hard, determined looks staring back at him: Big George, Tony, Ned, Johnny; even easy-going Cobb, who typically sported a jovial grin, looked ready to fight.

"Who will fight with me?" Nathan shouted, raising a bayoneted rifle above his head.

"Huzzah!" Georgie shouted, again raising his rifle high overhead. His fellow white soldiers echoed him, "Huzzah!" This time the black men joined in without hesitation, "Huzzah! Huzzah! Huzzah!" And the sound of strong male voices joined together echoed throughout the farm, bringing a thrill to all who heard it.

Nathan shouted with them, raising the rifle high in his right fist with every chant. This continued for several minutes before he finally lowered the rifle and held up his left hand for silence.

"You make me proud, gentlemen. Prouder than I've ever been in front of a group of fighting men; and that's saying a lot.

"In a moment your officers will lead you out into the practice field to teach you how to use a new weapon: *the bayonet!* This is a weapon the enemy will not expect, and I promise you it will strike fear into his heart like nothing else!

"But before I dismiss you to your training, I want you to remember these things. If you do, then we will surely prevail.

"Listen to your officers and do as they say without question or hesitation. These men have fought many battles and understand how best to defeat the enemy and yet preserve your life, if both can possibly be done.

"Whenever you move, move quickly—a man moving is a difficult target for the enemy, who will soon become confused and disheartened.

"Most of you have never killed a man, but tomorrow you must not hesitate to kill. These men would take away your freedom, your very lives, and the lives of your loved ones. They deserve nothing less than *death* at your hands!

"But when you kill, don't kill out of anger or hatred, but rather because they would enslave or murder you; for this they deserve the answer you will give them. If they don't drop their weapons and stand still with their hands raised in the air … shoot them! If they run, if they hide, if they point a gun at you, if they do *anything at all* other than *clearly* surrender … *kill them!* Whenever your rifle isn't loaded, use the bayonet. They deserve no less."

He bowed his head and was silent for a long moment. Finally, he looked up, and there were clearly tears welling in eyes, "Tomorrow we march into battle, to conquer our enemies and *kick open* the door to freedom, or die trying. And remember this; in the *Good Book*, Deuteronomy chapter three, verse twenty-two it says, *'Ye shall not fear them: for the LORD your God He shall fight for you'*!"

☙ℰℛℭℬ☙ℰℛℭℬ☙ℰℛℭℬ

For the next two hours, Tom, Georgie, William, and Jamie drilled the men on the proper use of the bayonet. How to put it on and take it off. How to march without accidentally impaling your fellows, and how to charge as one with a fearsome shout. And finally, how to kill the enemy with it.

Nathan walked around the field observing, giving pointers here and there, and generally offering words of encouragement to the trainees, his large, four-legged shadow always close behind. In the end he was well satisfied with the men and with the new weapon at his disposal—his mind was spinning with the possibilities, and how best to use them come the morning.

As they walked from the practice field, heading toward a well-earned meal and rest, Nathan pulled William aside.

"William, I hope you understand how grateful I am about all you did to save my life on the way home from Richmond. Though I can remember but little of it, Tom has told me how handsomely you conducted yourself."

"Thank you, sir. But you've thanked me already before, and there's no need to say it again. I agree with Tom when he says he'd rather die himself than allow *you* to be killed, sir."

Nathan smiled at William and reached over to pat him affectionately on the back.

"Thank you, William. I can never repay you for what you've done. So I want to make sure you appreciate in what high regard I hold you.

"When I first arrived at Fort Davis, I thought … well, I thought you weren't much of a soldier. But you proved me wrong … in spades! I've learned you're every bit as tough and courageous as you are smart."

William blushed. "Very kind of you to say, sir. But I expect nobody else ever has thought so."

"Nonsense, William! Before we left Texas, you'd gained the respect of every soldier there … including Big Stan, which I can tell you, was no mean feat! Do you truly believe Stan would've befriended you as he did if he'd considered you some wilting violet? I can promise you he wouldn't have. He understood deep down inside you were as strong as he."

"Thank you for saying so, sir."

Nathan waved his hand dismissively.

"William … the reason I say these things now is … I want to ask you to hang back when we launch our attack tomorrow."

"Hang back, sir?"

"William … I fear … I am almost certain, in fact … we will take casualties tomorrow. Despite my brave speech earlier, I'm afraid many of our fine young men may not survive the morrow. And we may have many wounded. They'll desperately need medical help, and you're the only one who can provide it. If you're in the front lines of the battle, you'll not be able to help them. You might even be wounded yourself, and then where would we be?

"I don't say this because you're a less capable fighter than the rest of us, rather because you're the one person we can least afford to lose!"

William was quiet for a long moment. Tears began to form in his eyes and his voice was choked with emotion, "Thank you, sir. That was the kindest thing anyone ever said to me. I'll do my best to keep our men alive … so long as you understand I'd rather be up front fighting next to you … and Stan."

"Of course, William, of course. That goes without saying. And thank you. Thank you most sincerely!"

Margaret spent the day either sitting on the bed or standing at the window. She gazed out over the farm imagining what it would be like walking away in the dark. Wherever she stood, and whatever she was contemplating, a part of her was constantly listening, dreading the sound of a key turning the lock of the door. But she'd taken Bob's advice to heart; she either carried the loaded pistol in her hand, or had it sitting next to her on the bed the entire day.

But now she sat on the bed and watched the clock tick to midnight. Walters had *not* come, and the only time the door had opened, to serve her lunch and dinner, it'd been preceded by a polite knock, so she'd known it wasn't him.

She stood from the bed, pulled on a light jacket she'd chosen to take with her, and shouldered the small cloth bag Bob had brought her earlier. It contained the food and water he'd supplied, and now a few articles of clothing she'd added. She pulled the key out of her pocket and picked up the pistol with her other hand. She'd debated leaving the gun behind if Walters failed to appear; it still frightened her to touch it. But in the end, she took it with her. For one, if Walters caught her, she'd either shoot him, or take her own life depending on the circumstances. And for another, it would surely incriminate Bob if she left it behind.

She unlocked the door, quietly opened it, and peered out. As Bob had promised, no one was there. She stepped out and pulled the door closed. As an afterthought she reached back and locked it. *Let Walters chew on that little mystery*, she thought and grinned. She stuck the key back into her pocket and switched the pistol to her right hand.

If anyone tried to stop her, she'd threaten them with it, and if Walters himself appeared she'd shoot him!

She moved quietly to the end of the hall and down the stairway to the foyer. Moving quickly to the front door, she reached out and turned the knob. But the knob didn't move and made a rattling sound when she tried turning it. Locked! She cringed at the sound it had made and stood still, listening for a response.

She remembered Bob had said his key also unlocked the front door and silently scolded herself for not remembering before. Nobody she knew ever locked their front door except when leaving on an extended trip if they had no servants to tend the house. So when Bob had mentioned it, she'd assumed it was general information, never imagining Walters was so odd and mistrusting he'd lock his own front door each night!

She reached into her pocket and pulled out the key with her left hand. But when she tried to put it into the lock, she missed the opening in the dark. The key fell from her hand and hit the floor with a clatter. Again, she froze, cringing at the noise, listening for a reaction in the house. But after a moment, and no response, she reached down, picked up the key, and unlocked the door. She opened it carefully and stepped out. Again, she turned and re-locked the door.

She hurried down the stairs and onto the gravel drive. She'd decided to stick to the road while it was dark. It would allow her to move much more easily than trying to go cross-country through the woods. And she could walk without tripping or getting tangled, even in almost total darkness. It was a cloudless night with a nearly full moon, so she had no trouble seeing where she was going.

Though she didn't expect to meet anyone, she was ready to bolt off the road and into the ditch at a moment's notice. She stopped regularly to listen for any sounds of pursuit from behind. But after nearly an hour seeing and hearing nothing threatening, she began to relax and contemplate the road ahead.

When she approached the edge of Walters Farm, she encountered her first natural obstacle: Howard Creek. It'd been so long since she'd been on the road, she'd forgotten about the ford. The road intersected the creek just before it joined the main east-west road from Richmond. She stopped at the edge for a few moments and contemplated the obstacle.

In the dark moonlit night, the stream was black with sparkly ridges, flowing from east to west where it eventually joined the

Greenbrier River. She had a sudden fear of being swept away in the darkness and drowning.

But she calmed herself and forced her rational mind to take over. This was a ford; they'd made the road cross at this specific point for good reason. Both shallowness and lack of current were likely. And she could be certain they'd long since removed any underwater obstacles, such as large, slippery rocks. Very likely they'd also laid down gravel to prevent the feet of horses and men slipping or sinking into the mud. And Walters pulled heavily laden wagons across year-round, so the bottom must be smooth, flat, and hard.

With this image of a safe, easy crossing held firmly in mind, she sat in the road and untied her shoes. In a few minutes she was barefoot, her shoes dangling around her neck; tied together by the laces. She'd tucked her stockings safely inside the shoes.

She gripped the sides of her skirts, pulled them up to her waist, and carefully stepped out into the stream. As she'd suspected, the bottom was smooth and covered in gravel—rough on her bare feet, but not painful. The water felt cold against her legs. And though the water reached nearly to her knees when she was midway across, the current wasn't strong. She had no trouble crossing.

She was soon re-shod and on her way. In a few moments she arrived at the main east-west road where she stopped, gazing along it in both directions, listening for any sound of movement. Hearing none, she turned to the east, though Bob had advised her to head west toward Lewisburg. Bob had meant well, she was certain, but there was something he hadn't known—that Margaret had previously visited Nathan Chambers, and he'd offered her refuge. It was time to accept his offer.

ৠৡৣ৳ৠৡৣ৳ৠৡৣ৳ৠৡৣ৳

"I tell you, they won't touch their food, and mostly they can't hardly move. And they's puked all over their pen and shat themselves."

"Ewww ... what d'ya reckon it is?"

"I figure they got the consumptions, or some such. Whatever it is hounds gets."

"What we gonna do for them?"

"Nothing. I reckon they've bought it."

"Holy Jesus! Who's gonna tell the master? He gonna be some kind of furious mad about it. I ain't telling him!"

"Well, I sure ain't. And us already bein' shorthanded after them two fellas got theyselves kilt today up at the Chambers' place. Let's pray the darkies don't get wind of it, or there'll be no end of trouble!"

Henry's heart skipped a beat. It was pitch dark, the moon not yet risen. He'd been settled into his bed, such as it was, when he'd suddenly had the most inconvenient call of nature. But when he'd gone outside to relieve himself, he'd heard voices over around the corner of the barn next door. So he quietly crept forward to listen. It was two white farmhands, clearly coming back from feeding the master's hounds.

Now his mind raced. The hounds were sick, unable to move, and likely dying. And two white farmhands had been killed today, so they were also shorthanded there. If ever there were a time to run, this was it!

He crept back toward the cabin, his heart beating so fast he was nearly out of breath. *Relax, Henry. Think. Where will you go ... what can you take with you?* It took only a second to decide he'd head east, back toward where his wife still lived on the farm he'd come from. If he could evade capture long enough to get there, he was sure he could figure a way to get her out. Then they could head out west into the woods ... and turn north through the mountains. To the North, where people like them could be free. It was a dream almost beyond his imagining. He shook his head to clear away the image, *One thing at a time, Henry!*

So with his general course of action decided ... what to take with him? He slipped back into the cabin and quietly closed the door behind him. He weaved his way over to the place where he slept—a man-sized plank of wood on the dirt floor up next to one wall. A dozen other such "beds" surrounded it, their occupants already stretched out asleep on the floor.

He looked over the few things he had stashed between his bed board and the log wall. He had no food; whatever they'd cooked up for that evening's dinner had been eaten to the last black-eyed pea. He had a nicely shaped piece of wood, which he had a mind to carve it into a pipe-like instrument someday, if he ever came upon something sharp enough to carve it; a rag he always carried with him, so he could wipe his brow when the sweat started running into his eyes; and a smooth round stone that felt good in his hand when he rolled it around, along with a few other such worthless items. It occurred to him these things were still where he'd left them this morning because they weren't worth stealing. He had no water bottle. Not even a straw hat to keep off the sun.

He shrugged. It didn't matter. He'd have to take his chances on finding the things he needed along the way. He'd long ago decided a quick death was preferable to living a long life at Walters Farm. So he was not averse to taking serious risks to get away. And this seemed a most fortuitous, God-given event—too good to pass up.

He snatched up the rag, leaving the other odds and ends, and started back toward the door.

Then a sudden idea struck him. He'd initially planned to keep quiet and make his escape alone, the others be damned. He'd never become close to anyone here, and in fact had a strong hatred for several of them who'd treated him harshly when he first arrived. So he had no desire to help them in any way.

But it occurred to him if several slaves tried to escape at the same time, going in different directions, it would help his odds of getting away. If the master's hands were already spread thin, a large breakout would spread them even thinner.

"Hey! Wake up, y'all! I got a thing to say. Could be something y'all want to know!"

There were general grumblings, and one of the surlier ones sat up and said, "What're you waking us up for, stupid shit? I's tired and only done got myself to sleep."

"Maybe when you hear what I says you not think it stupid. Came in from outside after hearing two white masters talking 'bout how the hounds is all too sick to eat or stand, and likely's dying o' some sickness. And that ain't all … they be saying two of the white hands done got theyselves kilt today over in a fight."

There was a shocked silence for a moment. Then someone said, "Is it true? The hounds can't track us?"

"I was out fixing to relieve myself and they was talking, not knowing I was there. Heard it plain as day. Hounds is all puking sick, and likely dead soon. I for one am fixing to run now, 'fore master can get more hounds and more men. Y'all can do as you will."

Henry'd said all he intended to say, and headed toward the door, when he heard a familiar voice.

"What if the stupid shit's wrong and we all gets caught. Master gonna whip the hide clean off us."

It was a voice he knew well … and *hated*. Andy … a mean-mouthed young tough, the very same who'd punched Henry and taken his shirt on that first night at Walters Farm. Henry had eventually gotten another, but he hadn't forgotten.

He stepped over to where Andy stood talking to two other young men. Henry stood staring at him a moment, until Andy turned to look at him, and said, "What?"

"I'll take my shirt back now."

"Shirt? What—"

Henry punched him hard in the stomach with his left fist. When Andy bent over to grasp his aching middle Henry swung hard at his face with his right. Andy fell hard backward onto the floor. Henry glared at the other two men. Their eyes widened as they backed away. He bent down, grabbed the shirtsleeve of the fallen man, and yanked, rolling him over hard onto his stomach. In a few seconds he'd stripped the shirt off, flipped it over his shoulder, and headed for the door.

For months he'd been repeating to himself, *Maybe tomorrow I'll get even … maybe tomorrow I'll fight back, maybe tomorrow I'll escape.* But now he chuckled, and thought, *Guess tomorrow's finally today!*

He reached out to open the door and had another notion. He turned and faced the room. About half the people were scrambling to gather whatever they could, clearly preparing to follow Henry's example. The rest huddled to the sides, too afraid or too beaten down to take the risk.

"Don't nobody figure on followin' me ... I's goin' *alone*. If you follow me, I swear by God I'll kill you," and he meant it.

He turned, opened the door and peered out. It was pitch black. He stepped out and moved along the path to the road. Once on the road, he turned and headed north at a trot.

Chapter 6. Breakout

"A soldier surrounded by enemies,
if he is to cut his way out,
needs to combine a strong desire for living
with a strange carelessness about dying.
He must not merely cling to life,
for then he will be a coward,
and will not escape.
He must not merely wait for death,
for then he will be a suicide,
and will not escape.
He must seek his life
in a spirit of furious indifference to it;
he must desire life like water
and yet drink death like wine."
- John Eldredge

Monday May 27, 1861 – Greenbrier County, Virginia:

Damn it, Margaret! Should have done as Bob advised and headed west—you'd be safely away by now! Not nearly so clever as you thought you were! Margaret silently scolded herself.

She crouched behind a bush, gazing out along the road toward Mountain Meadows Farm. Though it was not yet dawn, the sky was lightening, enough so she clearly saw the impassible object blocking her from her destination. Less than a hundred yards ahead the road passed through a narrow, steep-sided ravine. And they'd blocked the road at that strategic spot by what appeared to be wagons tipped on their sides. Men with rifles paced back and forth on her side of the barricade.

Though she'd known there'd been fighting around Mr. Chambers' farm, she'd naively assumed there'd be little activity in the dead of night; she might slip past the warring factions in the dark without being seen.

When she'd seen the size of the encampment, she realized her journey would be more difficult than she'd assumed. They'd erected dozens upon dozens of neatly aligned white tents in the field next to the Mountain Meadows' road. And despite the late hour, somewhere between three and four in the morning she guessed, there were plenty of men awake and moving about in and around the camp.

She'd had to pick her way carefully forward avoiding these men, so what should have taken minutes had taken hours. All that fearful, anxious hiding and running, only to get to the place she now crouched—where she could go no further.

She briefly considered abandoning the road and climbing up the hill through the woods. But she abandoned this idea almost immediately; the slope was extremely steep, and the woods an almost impassible tangle of branches and undergrowth. Besides, if it were possible to do so, wouldn't Nathan's enemies have already done it rather than forcing their way up the strongly defended road?

Now she wished she'd spent more library time studying military strategies and less time studying constitutional law! If she had, she might've better understood siege tactics. Now she understood it was nearly impossible to slip past the alert and watchful men on Walters' side. And even if she somehow accomplished that miraculous feat, likely Chambers' side would shoot her before they knew who she was.

No, not a good idea at all. She sighed and turned around, intending to make her way back the way she'd come, abandoning her attempt to link up with Nathan Chambers and Miss Abbey.

But as she stood, she gasped, "Oh!" Directly in front of her stood two men pointing rifles at her!

"Well, lookie what we got here, Herbert!" the one on the right said.

"Not the most fearsome looking spy, I reckon," Herbert answered.

"Spy? Oh … come now, gentlemen! Surely you jest. I'm no spy, as you can clearly see."

"Well, not exactly what we was expecting, I'll admit. But if you ain't a spy, then what're you doin' out here sneaking around in the darkness by our camp?"

She had, of course, gone over in her mind what she'd say if caught, so was not completely unprepared.

"I live in a nearby farmhouse, and … couldn't sleep on account of all the noise and excitement of the day … and the heat. Figured I'd come see how y'all brave soldiers were getting along, and if there was anything I might do to help. Like fixing a warm meal come morning, or some such."

"Hmm … but the camp's over yonder ma'am. Why ain't you over there speaking with our officers? What're you doing over here by the road and looking up toward our barricade?"

"Oh … I was only curious is all. Never seen any real fighting or soldiers before. I wanted to see for myself what the front lines really looked like. You know?"

The two men exchanged a look, and then incongruously shared a smile.

"You know what I believe, ma'am?" the one who'd first spoken asked.

"What's that, sir?"

"I figure you're that runaway wife of Mr. Walters."

She gasped, then realized she'd just given herself away.

"That's right … *Mrs. Walters* … word came down a few hours ago that Mr. Walters wife had run off after helping several slaves escape. Apparently, her having secret abolitionist sympathies or some such. Anyway, we was told to be on the lookout for runaway slaves and … a woman matching your description out by herself in the dark or with slaves. And … we heard Mr. Walters was offering a sizable reward for either. Well, some other men done caught one of your runaways a short time ago. Now I reckon we've copped you."

He smiled a wicked smile echoed by his partner — anticipating the reward money, she assumed. Her mind went blank. She could think of nothing to say or do to save herself.

Ira Cooper strained to see anything in front of him in the pre-dawn darkness. He sat behind a ridgeline of rock looking out over no-man's-land. It ran along the road from his present position up to where Chambers' men were likewise dug in, several hundred yards up the hill. After the initial excitement of the back-and-forth battle a week ago, things had settled down to a tedious routine of watching with no action. Neither side seemed inclined to risk exposing themselves to the deadly rifle fire that would greet anyone trying to move forward on the road.

He was fairly sure the officers were planning some new action, but he was only a new recruit, and not privy to any such discussions. In the past week he'd taken his turn at sentry duty up on the ridgeline, along with a dozen other men at a time. He scolded himself for being stupid enough to brag about his shooting skills, his daddy having taken him hunting ever since he was old enough to walk. This unfortunate running of the mouth had earned him his unenviable spot up on a rock in the dark, the rest of the men comfortably back in camp below, many still asleep.

He stretched himself up onto the top of the rock to have a peek out along the roadway ahead. He gripped the rock with both hands to steady himself as he looked over. His rifle lay propped against a tree stump below where he'd set it. He'd had little enough use for it in recent days, and it was tiresome holding it while trying to balance himself as he peered out.

Though the sky was lightening, the sun was not yet above the horizon, so there was little enough to see. He began to lower himself back down off the rock when suddenly he was lifted bodily from the ground, smothered by something firmly planted across his nose and mouth. He tried to shout, but with his air cut off no noise came out. Iron-hard resistance met his attempts to squirm free. The last thing he felt in life before all went dark was a hard, sharp, intense burning pain up through the center of his chest.

Stan continued holding the man, his knife embedded to the hilt in his chest, until all movement ceased, and the body went limp.

Then he set the form gently on the ground, rolling it over to extract the knife. He wiped the blade on the man's shirt before slipping it back into the knife sheath on his belt.

Three down, and three to go on his side. He was confident Billy was doing his part on the other side. Stan knew he must hurry to stay even. He couldn't allow Billy to kill his sentries quicker than he killed his!

Like a great prowling cat in the darkness, Stan moved stealthily up the ridgeline to find the next sentry.

೮೮೨)ೞ೮೮೮೨೨)ೞ೮೮೮೨೨)ೞ೮೮

"Just put her in here with the runaway slave. We'll keep watch on her from here."

"But, sir … we're the ones done caught her. We wants to make sure we get that reward money."

"Don't worry, Benton; I'll make sure Walters knows it's you and Sims as should get the reward. Now, get back to your posts. The night ain't over yet."

"Yes, sir."

The men who'd caught her turned and left, back the way they'd come. It was an older man in his thirties and clearly a superior officer who now took charge of her. He pulled back the flap of a tent and ushered her in, "Ma'am … if you please."

She ducked into the tent. A younger man with a rifle sat in a chair watching a black man sitting on the ground opposite him in the tent. The runaway slave, she assumed.

He briefly glanced up at her and looked surprised. But he quickly looked down again. She was sure she recognized him—a slave she'd seen working the okra field outside her bedroom window. They'd shackled his hands together in front—rusty steel cuffs connected by a short, thick chain little more than a foot long.

"You may sit on the cot while you wait, ma'am. Sleep if you wish. I understand your husband will be here at first light. He'll take you home."

"Thank you, sir, but please … you don't understand … he means to *kill* me."

"Kill you? Who means to kill you, ma'am?"

118

"Mr. Walters."

"Your *own* husband? Oh, I'm sure he's terribly angry with you at the moment, but I very much doubt he'll commit murder over it, ma'am."

"I know it sounds incredible, but it's true."

"What makes you think so, if I may ask?"

"Someone told me—one of his men—who'd heard it with his own ears."

"Humph! I'm sure there's plenty of times I've said the same about my wife in a fit of anger. But I ain't kilt her yet!" he laughed and exited the tent.

She sat on the cot. Perhaps the younger soldier would be more receptive.

"It's true, you know."

"What's true, ma'am?"

"My husband will kill me once he gets me home."

The man gave her a hard look. "I'd kill you too, ma'am, if you was my wife and done run off in the middle of the night with a bunch o' damned darkies."

She was shocked, "But I ... didn't ..."

"You're wasting your breath on me, ma'am. I ain't in no mood to listen to a string o' lies. May as well lie down and rest until your husband gets here. Then he can do with you as he will."

No help there, she realized. But she remembered the loaded pistol she still had in her pack. The men who'd captured her hadn't bothered searching it, assuming she was harmless. *Hmm ... maybe not so harmless after all*, she thought.

She lay on the cot, closed her eyes and began pondering how best to save her own life. And with a sudden chill she realized dawn was only an hour or two away, then Walters would arrive.

☙₰Ↄ☜☞₰₰Ↄ☜☞₰₰Ↄ☜☞

Daniel Lewis and Isaac Kelly stood together behind the tipped-over wagons that served as a barricade blocking the road leading to the Chambers' farm. Isaac heard a strange bird call from the ridgeline off to his left. He didn't recognize the bird, but another of the same kind answered back off to his right.

He looked up at the sky. Almost dawn. He shivered and reached into his pocket, pulling out the last of his cigars. *Damn*, he thought, *who'd have figured we'd be out here so long?*

He felt in his pockets for a match. But finding none, he looked over at Daniel who was gazing out toward the enemy position. "Hey, Daniel … you got a match?"

"A match? Sure thing, Isaac," he turned and stepped forward, reaching into his jacket pocket and pulling out a match. But as he stretched out his hand offering the match, something strange happened. Daniel's whole body twitched, and he stopped still where he was. Isaac looked from the extended hand holding the match up to Daniel's face and suffered a terrible shock. Daniel's eyes were wide open, as was his mouth, but no sound came out, and there was no recognition in the eyes. The pointy, blood-covered head of an arrow protruded from the left side of his head, with the feathered shaft sticking out on the right side.

Before Isaac could react, Daniel crumpled to the ground.

John Simmers, who'd been standing next to Daniel on the other side stepped up to see what had happened. But he stopped, clutching his chest. Isaac saw the shaft of an arrow sticking out between John's hands. His eyes widened, and he too slumped to the earth.

Isaac dropped face down, covering his head and screaming, "We're being attacked! We're being attacked!"

The other men standing by the wagons looked at him and the others lying on the ground in startled confusion. Isaac glanced up to witness another man take an arrow through his right eye.

Someone shouted, "It's Indians! It's Indians shooting arrows!"

Men began to scramble back away from the wagons in a panic, trying to get away from the deadly rain of arrows. Another man fell to the ground with an arrow in his back. Isaac scrambled to his feet and ran with the rest, heading down the hill toward the camp below.

Just before the road turned a sharp corner to the right, Isaac risked a glance back. He saw men on horseback next to the wagons. They'd attached ropes and had righted the wagons and were now pulling them clear of the road. Isaac watched in horror as the wagons parted and a whole troop of heavily armed cavalry came down the road at full gallop.

He immediately thought better of returning to camp; he'd never make it before they ran him down. Scrambling off the road, he crawled between thick bushes into the woods. There he shamelessly hid the rest of the day, likely saving his life.

ༀ๖ঞෆ๖ঞෆ๖ঞෆ

Once they'd cleared the wagons, Nathan led the Mountain Meadows cavalry at a gallop down the road. Besides Nathan, Tom, and Jamie, the troopers included, Zeke, Joe, and Benny, the original farmhands. And now Billy and Stan joined them, having completed their clandestine assignment.

They'd brought two extra horses, including Stan's great stallion, Groz. Harry the Dog followed closely on Millie's heels, tongue hanging out.

Billy had come up with the plan while they were discussing how to clear the wagons from the roadway. Jim had suggested Billy shoot fire arrows and light the wagons afire. But when he asked Billy if he could do it, he shrugged, "Sure, Sergeant Jim. But ... why waste perfectly good wagons?"

He told them he'd already scouted each enemy sentry's location. There were a dozen spread out along the ridgeline at any given time. But foolishly the enemy hadn't paired them up. So each man was isolated and alone—easy prey for someone with Billy's skills.

"But what about the men behind the barricade?" Nathan had asked, "You'll not be able to sneak up on them."

Jim answered this time, "Well, hell, sir. Once we've eliminated the sentries from the ridgeline, alls Billy's gotta do is feather a few of them with arrows. The rest'll run screaming like babies for their mommas!"

Nathan considered that a moment and decided it was likely so. "But ... the road divides the ridgeline sentries, with half on each side. It'd take all night for Billy to take out those on one side, then work his way all the way around to the other without being seen. Before he could do it, they might have a change of guard,

121

and then the whole effort would have been for naught. It'll take at least two men to clear the sentries, and we've only got one Billy. None of the rest of us can sneak up a hill in the dark and kill men stealthily like that."

But Billy surprised them again, "Stan can do it."

"What? Big Stan?"

"Yes, Captain."

"Surely, you're joking, Billy. He's so huge. I can't imagine how he could possibly sneak up on anyone."

"He may be a giant man, Captain, but he is a skilled killer. I have watched him strangle a great Comanche warrior with only his bare hands. And I have seen him move through the woods quietly as a cat, when he wants to. Stan can kill sentries silently. Good as I can, maybe better."

Nathan looked over at Jim with incredulity, expecting the sergeant to share his skepticism. But Jim surprised him, nodding, "I think he's right, sir. Stan is ... *something special* ... extraordinary even. I agree with Billy. I reckon he can do it."

And so it was decided. And thus far everything had gone perfectly and according to plan. Now the cavalry troop raced down the road, hoping to reach the camp and wreak as much havoc and destruction as possible before the enemy sounded the alarm.

Each man was armed to the teeth with four loaded pistols— two in holsters at the hip, and two more up under their shoulders. Their successful escape from Richmond on horseback with no rifles had been an epiphany for Nathan. He'd become convinced skilled men on horseback with revolvers were a deadly combination of speed and rate of fire that was hard for a stationary enemy to counter.

Besides the pistols, Nathan and Tom carried their Army sabers, which they now carried unsheathed. Nathan had ordered no shots fired until they were fired upon, or he gave the order. He wanted to keep the element of surprise as long as possible, and though the barricade guards were yelling and screaming, none had fired off a shot. Nathan knew nothing would rouse a drowsy armed camp quicker than the sound of gunfire. So as they charged down the hill, overrunning the fleeing guards, Nathan and Tom cut them down with their sabers. Billy continued felling them with arrows, though he had few left, having had no time to retrieve the ones he'd used back at the wagons.

No barricade guard survived the attack, save the one who'd escaped into the woods. But they had made enough noise to prevent the camp being taken completely by surprise. Nathan returned the saber to its scabbard before they rounded the last bend in the road above the camp. As Billy had reported, the enemy camp was past the bottom of the hill in a wide, grassy field. The field occupied the flat ground between the main east-west road intersection and the place where the Mountain Meadows' road began its ascent.

They came down off the slope onto the flat section, leaving the road and heading across the field straight toward the camp, about five hundred yards away. The sun crept over the horizon in the east, lighting the waist-high grass in front of them with a golden-green glow.

Nathan spurred Millie into a hard gallop, dropping her reins and pulling out two pistols. The other riders did likewise. The Army-trained horses needed no guidance; when their rider dropped the reins they'd run straight ahead at full speed. Besides, if in doubt they'd all follow Millie.

Nathan's heart leapt in his chest as the horses' hooves pounded the turf at full gallop, racing to battle.

They saw the enemy camp beginning to rouse. Men were yelling, scrambling from tents, grabbing up rifles from stacks, and frantically loading them. As they closed to within fifty yards, they encountered scattered incoming fire. It was wild and erratic, fired in panic.

They were within thirty yards of the tents when Nathan finally fired the first shot, signaling the start of a ferocious pistol volley from his men. Without pause the Mountain Meadows' cavalry swept into the camp, charging between rows of white canvas tents at a gallop. They cut down dozens of enemy soldiers with pistol fire before passing through and coming out into the field on the other side.

Nathan holstered his right-hand pistol, grabbed Millie's reins on that side, and turned her sharply back toward the tents. But this time, instead of charging back through the middle, he led them around the outside of the encampment. Again, they peppered the enemy with pistol fire, though by now few risked exposing themselves to the attackers—most ducked behind any cover available.

By the time they'd circled back around to their starting point they were down to the last of their loaded bullets. So Nathan led their withdrawal, steering Millie back toward the point across the field where they'd begun their charge.

They reined in at the base of the hill and turned once again to face the enemy camp. They were out of range of the enemy's rifles, so each man reloaded his four pistols. Harry the Dog dropped heavily onto the ground, panting hard. With his long legs and broad chest, he kept up with the horses, even at a full gallop. But he tired more easily and was now nearly done in after following closely at Millie's heels the entire run.

Nathan pulled the spy glass from his saddle bag and raised it to his eye. He saw they'd stirred the enemy camp like a stick in a beehive. Men ran in every direction, shouting and gesturing wildly, desperate to organize a response amid the chaos.

Though it'd been a good start and as heady a cavalry charge as Nathan could remember, he knew the battle was far from over. The enemy would soon be ready to fight in earnest. When he'd finished reloading his last pistol, Nathan pulled out his pocket watch, then looked over at Tom. "They should be here soon."

Tom nodded agreement but said nothing. Nathan noticed he was breathing heavily and was red in the face with exhilaration. Looking around, he saw the others were similarly affected. They'd just survived an experience as thrilling and dangerous as anything a man might do on this Earth. And it wasn't over yet!

Five minutes passed, and then another five, but still the Mountain Meadows men sat their horses, gazing across at the enemy. They saw rows of men formed up into companies armed with rifles. Nathan looked through the spy glass again, making a quick count. Still nearly a hundred, despite the dozen or more they'd taken out with their cavalry charge. *Damn! Still so many …* he thought. For a moment he'd held out some hope their foes might simply panic and run away. But clearly that was *not* going to happen. *It's that damned Army officer they've got with them,* he decided, *he knows how to hold them together and prevent a rout. Well … let's see how he handles our little surprise.*

Billy called out, "They come, Captain."

"Good. Then we can finish this …"

ᏘᏋᏋᏗᏋᏗᏘᏋᏗᏘᏋᏗᏘᏋᏗᏘᏋᏗᏗ

Margaret's thoughts kept going around in circles. But, always coming around to the same conclusion: she had no solution.

Her pistol was the old-fashioned, single-shot kind, and she had no gunpowder or lead to reload it. So she had only one shot. She might shoot the guard and try to sneak out of camp. But the sound of a gunshot would certainly bring others running. Or, she could wait until Walters arrived, then step up and shoot him right in the chest as Bob had instructed. But she knew now they'd never believe her story about Walters' intentions—they'd surely hang her for a murderess.

She was becoming more anxious and frustrated with herself for not figuring out an answer. And to top it off, the camp had become very noisy—so loud she could barely think. She assumed it was the men rousing for the morning routine. But then she realized *this* was something more.

Men were shouting and running through camp. There was great excitement and also … *fear?* … in those voices.

She sat up and looked over at their guard. He'd heard it too and sat on the edge of his seat, the rifle gripped tight across his lap. His head cocked to the side, he listened with a worried expression. He stood and moved over to the tent flap, glancing back at the slave and Margaret every few seconds as he peeked out.

Margaret noticed, despite the noise, the slave had apparently fallen asleep on the ground where he sat. His chin was against his chest, his eyes were closed, and he breathed in the slow, even rhythm of sleep.

She nearly jumped from her seat; sudden gunfire echoed through the camp. She'd watched men hunting birds and such, so recognized the sound. But this was a *whole* other thing! A thunderous sound—many shots going off at once, the likes of which she'd never imagined possible.

The unmistakable sound of horses galloping followed the gunfire, pounding between the tents. And the gunshots continued, though more sporadic now. But the sounds were much louder, coming ever closer.

Their guard looked over at the slave, still sleeping on the floor, then raised his rifle and leaned out the tent flap, as if trying to get a shot at whoever was riding through the camp.

A sudden motion from the corner of her eye caught Margaret's attention. She glanced over and was surprised to see the slave on his feet and moving forward, wide awake. He glanced at her with a hard, determined look in his eyes. He held a finger up in front of his mouth. She nodded.

He moved up behind the guard with a stealthy grace that nearly took Margaret's breath away. He stretched the chain between shackled hands out over the man's head and jerked back. Both men fell backward into the tent, hitting hard on the ground. Margaret jumped to her feet and out of the way to avoid being crushed.

The slave was on his back with the guard on top of him, facing away. Strong legs wrapped firmly around the guard's waist as the shackle's chain squeezed his neck. The soldier's face turned a dark red as he strained for air, hands grasping in vain at the chain digging into his throat.

The muscles of the black man's arms bulged with the force of his exertions. His cheeks puffed out with the strain and his breath came in great gasps.

The guard realized his only hope was the rifle he'd dropped when first seized. It lay on the ground next to the two struggling men, only a few feet away. He reached out for it with his right hand.

Margaret watched the whole event in silence, mesmerized by the sudden brutality of it. But she realized with a shock, the guard *would* soon reach the rifle and then …

Without conscious thought, Margaret was on her feet scooping up the gun. The soldier looked up at her beseechingly, reaching for the weapon. But his expression turned to shock when she stepped back and held the weapon up out of his reach. She would never forget the desperate, pleading look on his face in those last moments of his life.

And then it was over. The man's body turned rigid. He twitched and shook violently. His eyes bulged from their sockets. His face was a dark, purple color.

Margaret felt she'd be sick. It was the most horrifying sight she'd ever seen, except when Walters had beaten the slaves. But she'd seen that only from a distance and had been able to look away. *This …*

The guard went limp. But the black man continued to hold the chain tight for another full minute before finally relaxing his grip. He released the man, unwrapped the chain from his neck and pushed him off. He sat up, still breathing hard, unable to speak.

After a few minutes, he looked up at her, reached out his hand and said, "Give me the gun."

She handed it to him—it never occurred to her to do otherwise, though she now felt a certain healthy fear of the man.

He knelt on the ground and grasped the rifle by the stock with the barrel pointing up. She wondered what he was up to. He slammed the butt hard against the ground. She noticed he'd looped the chain around the butt of the rifle. Of course! He was trying to break the shackles.

"I'll not run far with hands chained together," he said, and repeated the action again and again. As impressive as his strength and the force of his blows were, still the chain held.

"Damn! Ground's too soft. Can't break it."

She felt his growing anxiety and frustration. She'd been so caught up in the drama playing out before her she'd almost forgotten her own predicament. Like being in a dream … *Wake up, Margaret! Do something!*

"Does he have the key?"

"No. The other fella has it. Seen him stick it in his pocket 'fore he left the tent."

"Then use the gun to shoot off the chain."

He looked at her questioningly.

"He never got off a shot, so the rifle's still loaded. The gunfire continues out there, so likely no one will notice one more shot. If you put the barrel against the chain and pull the trigger, it should break the chain."

"Yeah … could be. But I can't pull the trigger … chain ain't long enough."

"I'll do it. Put your hands on the ground and spread the chain between them. You'll need to make sure the barrel is right over the chain; we'll only have one chance at this."

"All right," he said, and handed her the rifle. She took it and noticed the hammer was back and the percussion cap in place. Lucky it hadn't gone off while he was banging the stock into the ground!

He did as she bid, spreading the chain out in the dirt. She held the rifle barrel down on the chain. He moved it slightly to make sure it was well-placed, then stretched the chain tight.

"Okay, *now*, missus."

But she hesitated, and he looked up at her questioningly. "Ain't never fired a gun before ma'am?"

"Well, yes, that's true enough. But that's not why I hesitate. It occurred to me right now we both need each other; you need me to pull this trigger, and I need you … to help me get out of here and hide. But once I pull this trigger, you no longer need me."

"Yeah … I reckon so. But if we don't get out of here quick, it ain't gonna matter what either one of us does."

"Promise me you'll take me with you … only 'til we're safely out of this camp and have found a good hiding place."

He looked up at her a moment as if considering it, then said, "Okay, missus. My name's Henry. And since my name's all I own, I swear on my good name I'll take you with me. Now … *please* … pull that trigger!"

128

Tony trotted down the road directly behind Sergeant Jim, followed by a row of more than thirty men. To his left, Cobb led the other column, directly behind Mr. Georgie. The pre-dawn sky was light enough to see the road in front of them. Despite the intensive training they'd had in the past week, the rifle slung on his back still felt awkward, uncomfortably bouncing up and down on his back as he ran.

And the bayonet dangled behind his back, held in place by a thin rope wrapped around his waist. The rope belt also held a small cloth sack with a gunpowder flask and a handful of lead bullets. The Captain insisted they keep the bayonets hidden behind their backs until called for … *'our secret weapon'* he'd called them. Tony knew he'd not want to be on the receiving end of the thing! For safety's sake each man had embedded the tip of the weapon into a piece of corn cob, or a chunk of wood — something to cover the point as he jogged along. Otherwise he'd risk a serious gash from the sharp end as it bounced around.

They'd formed up and started their run above the upper pinch point, the place from which they'd watched the enemy for more than a week now. He was nervous about trotting out into the open road beyond; it'd been a place they'd avoided at extreme peril ever since the present standoff started. But the officers assured them there'd be no response from the enemy *this* time, that the Captain "would see to it," whatever that meant. From stories he'd heard the white soldiers tell, the Captain somehow always had his way on a battlefield. Maybe God really was on his side, or he was more than an ordinary man after all.

They kept a steady pace as they jogged toward the lower pinch point, and as promised, there was nothing but darkness and silence to greet them. As they passed through, he saw two wagons, one on each side of the road. Something resembling sacks of potatoes lay on the ground near the wagons and out in the middle of the road. As he got closer, he realized they were bodies. Arrows stuck out of several. He shuddered. Clearly the Indian Billy had killed them with his frightful, ancient weapon.

The officers led them past several other bodies lying in the road. As he passed the first one, he couldn't tell what had felled him in the dim light. But as he trotted past the next, he noticed a deep gash at the point where the neck joined the body. The man's head lay at an odd angle, as if he'd been struck by an ax. Tony felt bile rising in his mouth, but he forced it back down. *Not going to be sick ... not now!*

He nearly jumped at a gunshot ahead in the distance. An eruption of noise followed the single shot. He imagined a furious battle raging just out of sight down the hill.

He knew he ought to be tiring by now, after running such a distance with a heavy rifle and ammunition. But his heart raced with excitement, or maybe fear, so he paid little attention to his complaining legs. He took a quick glance over at the men in the other column; their eyes were wide with anticipation.

They turned a corner and had now nearly reached the bottom of the hill. A wide field of tall grass spread out before them, and the light of dawn was now shining on it, turning it to a field of gold.

Far out across the field, Tony saw rows of white tents, and men moving around in front of them. A thin wisp of smoke floated in the air above the tents. At first, he'd assumed it must be from campfires. But he realized it was gun smoke from the brief battle they'd heard moments earlier.

Ahead, a group of horsemen gathered on the road. They'd been warned if they saw horsemen it was likely their own men, so not to shoot at them.

As the road leveled out Sergeant Jim called a halt. Tony was surprised at a feeling of disappointment at stopping. For some reason he'd imagined they'd keep running all the way to the fight with the enemy.

Now he stood in place, breathing heavily. He was so filled with nervous energy he could hardly keep from moving around, like his skin was crawling with bugs. He looked around and realized the others felt the same.

He looked forward and saw a single horseman walking slowly toward them. It was still dark where they stood, the light of dawn had not yet touched this part of the road, so he couldn't make out who it was.

But the man struck a match and lit a cigar. The light of the match illuminated his face—the Captain!

ༀೠ୨ฦ୰ปༀೠ୨ฦ୰ปༀೠ୨ฦ

Nathan turned Millie and trotted back up to the bend in the road where Billy sat on his horse. He pulled up next to Billy and looked up the road. Two columns of men trotted down the hill toward them. Each man shouldered a rifle. Jim led the column on his left, and Georgie the one on his right. More than thirty black men followed each. And behind the columns came William riding his horse. He carried no rifle, but Nathan noticed he had two Colt revolvers at his waist. Not quite ready to bow completely out of the fight, apparently!

Nathan pulled a cigar from his pocket, lit it and walked Millie toward the newcomers. Jim and Georgie called the men to a halt just short of the Captain. They both snapped him a salute which he returned crisply.

"Gentlemen … good of you to join us. Sergeant Wiggins … stop for a game of cards along the way?"

Jim smiled good naturedly, "No sir, but now you mention it, it sounds like a good idea."

But Georgie chimed in, "No disrespect, sir, but it's a bit of a hike when you ain't sitting a horse! We done come along as quick as we could, still bein' able to fight at the end of it."

But Nathan smiled at him, "Take no offense, Mr. Thompson; you've done well and have arrived timely. Mr. Wiggins would be disappointed, is all, if I weren't to give him a little grief from time to time."

"Yes, sir … sorry. Thank you, sir."

"We'll give the men a couple minutes rest, then move out. Looks like the camp's laid out even as Billy reported. The enemy's all lined up in front of the tents now, expecting another cavalry charge. We'll play it like we planned."

"Yes, sir," they both said, almost simultaneously. Jim beamed. Nathan looked at him and shook his head in amusement, *The man loves nothing better'n a good fight.*

Nathan moved toward the columns of men, knowing how important it was at a time like this for the men to see a calm, confident leader. He walked his horse slowly along the columns, meeting eyes, and exchanging friendly greetings. He was on the outside of the left-hand column, so greeted Cobb first. Then he looked over, spotted Tony and smiled, "Good morning, Tony. Had a nice run?"

Tony couldn't help smiling, despite the circumstances, "Yes, sir. I reckon it was ... mighty *wakesome,* at least."

The Captain chuckled, tipped his hat, and moved further down the line, continuing the warm greetings, puffing on his cigar.

Tony shook his head in wonder. The man had just come back from shooting it out with the enemy from atop his charging horse. But he acted as if he'd only been over to church on the Sabbath!

When he was past the end of the line, he rode up next to William. They exchanged a quick salute and a warm smile before reaching out to shake hands.

"William."

"Good morning, Captain, sir."

Nathan turned Millie around and walked slowly back toward the front, this time speaking loudly to the whole group.

"Gentlemen ... you'll be pleased to know—in addition to the bodies you saw for yourselves back there on the road—we've already killed several dozen down at their camp. Now it's your turn. Remember what you've been taught, do as your officers say, and we *will* win our freedom today!

"Men ... I know you are likely nervous, or even a little afraid. So allow me to give you few words from the Good Book to lift your spirits. Deuteronomy chapter twenty, verse one, *'When thou goest out to battle against thine enemies, and seest horses, and chariots, and a people more than thou, be not afraid of them; for the LORD thy God is with thee, which brought thee up out of the land of Egypt.'*"

When he reached the front of the line again, he turned and said, "Make me proud out there today, men. Sergeant ... let's move out!"

He was gratified by two columns of grim, determined faces staring back at him. No smiles, but no fearful looks either. *Good,* he thought.

He turned Millie back toward the enemy camp, beginning a slow walk, the two columns of men moving out behind him. William brought up the rear.

As they moved toward the camp, the other riders fell in next to the Captain, lined up in a broad row, side to side. In this way, sight of the infantry, moving in two long files behind, would be obscured from those in the camp. Nathan meant to disguise his intentions and the numbers in his force from the enemy as long as possible.

They marched steadily across the field and soon were within the outer limits of rifle range. But Nathan counted on the enemy commander holding fire until they were within a hundred yards or so. He had mostly raw recruits whose ability to shoot accurately at any distance was highly questionable, which was why Nathan intended to form up his line at 150 yards, under the assumption his men might be slightly better shots having had rigorous, if hurried, recent training. And that might give them a chance to form up without first coming under fire.

But he knew it was a big gamble. If the enemy opened fire on them before they were properly deployed, it might be a disaster. Infantry orthodoxy said to form up the men now, then march them across the field in one or two wide rows, the men already aligned for firing upon the enemy.

But he'd never been a big believer in doing things the way they were *supposed* to be done, the way it had *always* been done. Despite what Mr. Wiggins believed, he *was* inclined to gamble, just not at cards.

Once they were well within rifle range, at around two hundred yards, it required nerves of steel to continue marching steadily toward the enemy line. If their foe opened fire now, several of his riders would likely be killed, and probably a few of the men marching behind as well.

But he counted on his opponent holding fire until the range was so diminished, they'd not miss. This was the advantage of having a relatively strong cavalry force; the enemy commander knew he'd only have one shot at them. There'd never be enough time to reload before the cavalry would be amongst them, sabers slashing and pistols hammering, decimating defenseless soldiers trying to reload.

When they reached the desired position, he breathed a sigh of relief and said a silent prayer of thanks; the enemy commander still held his fire. While the men on horseback continued their slow walk, Nathan gave Jim and Georgie the prearranged hand signal, and they shouted an order to their men.

The two columns began pivoting; the first man stopped where he was, and the man behind him sprinted up next to him on his outside shoulder, followed by the next man, and so on. In this way, the man last in line ended up in the position farthest out from the center. The men in the right column moved out to the right of center while those on the left did likewise to the left.

They'd practiced it so many times the day before, Tony figured they could do it with their eyes closed. Soon they were all spread out, shoulder to shoulder in a wide row, each spaced about three feet apart.

Tony was the 'anchor man' on the right side, standing a few feet behind and to the right of Sergeant Jim. To his left, Cobb anchored the left side, behind Mr. Georgie. And to Tony's immediate right was Johnny, then Big George, then Ned, and then … a whole row of others, looking wide-eyed and anxious.

Tony had unslung his rifle as soon as he'd stopped, and the others had done likewise even as they were moving into position. He now stood up straight and still, his rifle butt planted on the ground, barrel up at his side.

Once again, he experienced the odd sensation of not wanting to be still, his skin crawling and his heart pounding in his ears.

Looking out across the field he saw a row of white men likewise standing with rifles. There appeared to be a lot more of them than there were on his side. But he remembered the Bible quote from the Captain and felt better. If ever there was a time God ought to help good men outnumbered in a righteous fight, surely this was it! He waited anxiously for the orders he knew were coming ... the orders to fight and kill, and maybe to die.

As the infantry deployed, Nathan looked out across the field and was gratified by the shocked surprise on the faces of the enemy. He looked over at Tom and they met eyes, exchanging a warm smile, knowing it might be their last, but never once thinking it *would* be so.

Nathan pulled his two pistols and spurred Millie forward. His other horsemen did likewise. But this time it was only a feint, meant to distract the enemy from the real danger forming up behind the horsemen. After only a few yards Nathan fired a single shot from both pistols, as did the rest of the riders. He grabbed Millie's reins, peeling her off to the right. Tom did likewise, peeling off to the left, the others following one or the other. They galloped to the sides, so they'd no longer be in front of their own line of men. Even as they spurred across the front of their line, Jim called out *"Present Arms!"*

Tony lifted the rifle up to his chest. He was only vaguely aware of the others on either side of him doing the same, along with the two officers.

And as Nathan reached the end of the row, and began to turn Millie back behind, Jim called, *"Aim!"*

Tony lifted the rifle to his shoulder, pulled back the hammer, and looked down the sights. He pointed the rifle directly at a man standing across the field in front of him. He aimed at the man's head, as he'd been taught, knowing the bullet would drop to chest level from this distance. He didn't know the man he targeted, nor did he hate him especially, but he was the enemy, among those who would take away his new freedom. The man had to die.

And as the last of the horses cleared the row of Mountain Meadows men, *"Fire!"*

Tony squeezed the trigger. There followed a thunderous noise and thick smoke all around him.

Nathan was pleased; the volley felled dozens of enemy soldiers. He pivoted Millie. This time the cavalry charged in earnest, peeling off at about seventy-five yards distance before unloading pistols at the rows of enemy.

This assault was met with a smattering of rifle fire that spontaneously escalated into a thunderous response before the enemy officers could put a stop to it. The enemy gunfire hadn't hit any of the fast-moving riders, but Nathan turned to see the effect on his long row of men. He grimaced; more than a half-dozen had fallen.

But the enemy had taken the bait and stuck both feet into his trap; they'd fired their whole row at once, in response to Nathan's own total volley, and cavalry charge. This meant they were effectively disarmed for the half minute it would take to reload.

Sergeant Jim knew what to do now without being told, and wasted no time, shouting out, *"Prepare to Fix Bayonets!"*

Tony reached behind his back and grabbed the bayonet. He jerked it free from the rope holding it and pulled off the corn cob he'd rammed onto the end. Next, he held the base of it up onto the end of his rifle barrel as he'd been taught.

"Fix ... Bayonets!"

He slid the bayonet shaft onto the barrel, and gave it a twist to secure it, as he'd practiced doing a hundred times before. He heard the clattering of metal on down the row, as bayonets were mounted on nearly sixty rifles, including those of Sergeant Jim and Mr. Georgie.

But something was wrong with Johnny. He'd not reached for his bayonet and now leaned heavily on his rifle. Tony turned to scold him. But Johnny slumped to the ground before Tony could reach out to catch him.

"Johnny! What's wrong?" Tony knelt in the grass next to him. He'd curled up into a ball, rifle cast aside. His hands gripped his mid-section. Blood oozed out between his fingers.

Tony leaned closer ... to help ... somehow. But he felt a strong grip on his right arm and was fairly yanked to his feet. He looked up into the face of Big George.

"We gots to *go*, Tony! Can't help him none now. Mr. William'll be along shortly for doctoring. Come … let's go kill them that's done this to him!"

Tony's head was swimming. He began tearing up making it hard to think or see clearly. But when he looked into the hard, determined eyes of Big George he knew he was right. They'd been warned some men might go down. But they had to keep fighting or all would be lost. But *Johnny* …?

He straightened up. "You just lays still there now, Johnny. Mr. William will be along shortly to help you."

Tony looked across the field toward the enemy. Men were frantically working to load their rifles.

"Charge!"

Tony surged forward, yelling as loudly as he could, bayonet thrust out in front of him. His mind went blank as he ran. The enemy soldiers, wide-eyed, loomed closer with each stride. All around him he felt the noise from his own men as they ran and shouted as one.

As planned, the cavalry led the charge, ranging ahead of the infantry to attack specific enemy soldiers. Any soldier who'd managed to reload, or any officer with a pistol or a saber were immediately targeted. With little fear from enemy guns, they rode directly in front of their lines, firing from point-blank range.

The effect of the combined cavalry assault and the oncoming bayonet charge on the unprepared enemy was unnerving. Many enemy soldiers threw down their rifles, turned, and ran back through the tents. Others dropped their weapons and held up their hands in surrender. The rest stood their ground, bravely attempting to reload. But Nathan's cavalry ranged back and forth in front of their lines, shooting anyone attempting to raise a loaded rifle.

As Nathan trotted down the line, something caught his eye. He turned and saw an older man aiming a pistol at him. The pistol fired. Nathan heard the bullet zip past his right ear. He returned fire, dropping the man like a stone.

The bayonet charge hit the enemy as a wave crashing into the shore. Tony would later recall but little of it. Only a dream-like vision of stabbing at men trying to fend him off with rifle butts or bare arms and hands. But he was strong and quick, and a fire burned in him; these men were trying to take away his freedom and kill him and his friends. He punched the bayonet into a man over and over until he no longer moved. He moved on to the next, battering aside a rifle, and slashing the man across the face. Blood splattered everywhere, but he never stopped. Jumping on top of the man, he plunged the bayonet down, through the man, pinning him to the Earth underneath. He had to plant his foot on the dead man's chest to pull the blade free.

There were several more furious moments of the same. He killed at least one more man and wounded several others. Then he looked around and saw no more enemy soldiers standing between him and the row of white tents a few yards away.

To his left, Cobb and several others held a group of enemy soldiers at bayonet point. They held their hands high in the air, fear on their faces.

He turned to his right and saw Big George striding toward him, rifle still gripped in his hands, followed closely by Ned. Both still held a smoldering fire in their eyes. George appeared untouched, though his shirt was splattered with blood. But Ned was holding his left arm which had blood on it.

"You okay, Tony?" George asked.

At first Tony couldn't answer. He'd yelled so long and hard and his throat was so dry he'd lost his voice. Aside from which, after the experience he'd just had, talking seemed a strange thing to do.

He looked down at himself and saw blood everywhere. But he felt about, and it seemed like none of it was his own.

"Yeah ... guess so, George," he managed with a croak. "Ned ... they get your arm?"

But Ned smiled and shook his head, "Ain't no great thing, Tony. No more'n a scratch. But I reckon I repaid some o' these-here whip marks on my back today."

Tony realized it was one of the few times he'd seen Ned smile since he'd suffered his bad whipping a few years back.

"Yeah ... reckon so, Ned. I reckon so."

The enemy resistance had completely buckled. It was a bloody, brutal business. Nathan assumed his men were taking out years of anger and frustration on their unfortunate foes. But he never attempted to stop them; they were only doing as he'd instructed. And he was pleased to note, they did *not* kill the men who'd thrown down their weapons in surrender. They only cut down those who continued to resist. Soon his men were running through the camp, routing out any remaining enemy soldiers trying to hide or attempting to run away.

With the battle now winding down, he placed Tom in command, and turned Millie around. He hurried back to the place out in the field where the Mountain Meadows' line had stood when they first took enemy fire. He headed straight toward where William's horse stood, cropping grass.

William knelt on the ground nearby, tending a wounded man. He was pressing a cloth—already soaked red—into the man's abdomen.

Nathan dismounted and came over, removing his hat and kneeling next to the man on the grass. Harry padded up behind and flopped heavily to the ground, panting hard.

It was Tony's friend Johnny. He was conscious, but obviously in great pain, sweat streaming from his brow.

Nathan met eyes with William, who shook his head sadly.

"Hello, Johnny."

"Huh? Oh … hello, Captain, sir. Did we whup 'em, sir?"

"Yes, we did that, Johnny. I'm sorry to see you hurting, but I'm proud of how you stood up to those damned slavers, showed them you were a man. That was handsomely done, son, and I'll not forget it."

"Thank you, Captain. Hey … how come it's so dark and cold today?"

But Nathan didn't bother answering. He knew from the look in Johnny's eyes he was already gone. He felt a lump forming in his own throat. *No time for that now, Nathaniel,* he scolded himself.

He gave William a questioning look.

"Four dead ... oh, five now, counting Johnny here. Four wounded, but they should live, the good Lord willing—though one may lose an arm."

Nathan looked over to where William had gestured and saw the wounded men sitting or lying on the ground a few yards away. They were talking quietly amongst themselves. He walked over and greeted them, asking after their health, congratulating them on their victory, and wishing them well before striding back to his horse.

"When you've secured these men's wounds, you'd best ride over to where the other fighting was, William. Likely there're more casualties over that way."

"Yes, sir, I'll only be another moment here. Then I'll check on the others and send a few men back here to help these fellows. I figure we can load them up in those wagons the enemy provided us and take them back up to the farm. There I'll be able to do a bit more for them."

"Good idea, William."

"And ... then I suppose I should see what I can do for the enemy wounded."

"Yes ... that would be good of you William. Certainly the Christian thing to do, thank you."

ഇന്ദ്രന്ദ്രന്ദ്രന്ദ്രന്ദ്ര

They secured the enemy camp and rounded up the surrendered and wounded soldiers, placing them under guard. Nathan left Georgie in charge, along with William, and gathered the rest of the white men together on horseback. Jim grabbed a horse that had belonged to the enemy and climbed into the saddle, insisting on riding along with the Captain this time.

They reloaded their pistols and rode out at a trot toward the base of the Elk Trail that led up the backside of Granddaddy's Hill. Nathan wanted to get there before the enemy soldiers dug in at the bottom learned their side had lost the battle. It was only a couple of miles between the two points, so they'd clearly have heard gunfire in the distance. But they wouldn't yet know the outcome.

When they arrived, they found the enemy still dug in, but facing away from them with their backs exposed. Nathan opened fire without warning, not wanting to risk the enemy turning and putting up a fight. He'd have no more casualties among his men if he could help it. After several fell, the others threw down their rifles and surrendered. Nathan called to the Mountain Meadows men dug in above on the trail. They came out and took the prisoners in hand, marching them off at gunpoint toward the other camp to join their fellows.

The men on horseback came together again for a quick conference. Jim smiled at Nathan, an unlit cigar clenched between his teeth, and said, "Well, I'd say that was a *mighty* good day, sir. I reckon that's the best operation we've had since … well *ever*, one might say! Even that time we rousted out old Moat Kangly and his gang of bushwhackers can't compare."

"I agree, Mr. Wiggins … though we suffered more casualties than I'd hoped."

"Yes, sir … the *butcher's bill* must be paid, sadly."

"Well, can't be helped, I suppose, and it could have been much worse."

"Yes, sir."

"But … gentlemen, I'm not done yet."

"Not done, sir? I doubt there's any more enemy left in all Greenbrier County after *that* battle. Hell, I think you even shot their officer right before the bayonet charge. I seen a man strutting back and forth, shouting orders before we charged. So I'd decided I'd have a go at sticking him. Only you rode up and shot him dead before I could get there, more's the pity."

"Well, if it makes you feel better, the fellow nearly shot my ear off first."

"Oh, did he now? Well, that does make it better somehow, though I can't tell you why."

"Anyway, Mr. Wiggins, you're forgetting our old friend Elijah Walters."

"Oh! Yeah … *him!* I was hoping to see him at the battle so's I could poke him with my little stick pin. But I never seen him."

"Neither did I. So I expect he's lurking back at his house. Gentlemen ... I mean to go there and kill him before this day is done."

They rode at a fast trot to Walters Farm. Nathan was sorely tempted to go at the gallop, but he knew the horses had already been used hard this day and he didn't want to risk injuring them. And he didn't want to rush headlong into an ambush, which was always a possibility. So he asked Billy to ride a few dozen yards ahead with Jim. Close enough to keep in visual contact, but far enough it'd be impossible to net them all in the same trap. Besides which, Billy was extremely difficult to catch by surprise.

But when they reached the farm, only two of Walters' hands offered any resistance. One was hiding up in the loft of a barn and fired at them from out a window. But he was a poor rifle shot, and with only their pistols they quickly brought him down.

Then when Nathan climbed the steps up to the front door, a man stepped out, pistol in hand. But the Mountain Meadows men had pistols drawn, expecting trouble. The man never fired his pistol. He was nearly cut in half; six bullets tore through his chest almost simultaneously.

Nathan continued to the front entrance, revolver in hand. He tried the door, but it was locked; so he stepped back and planted his boot in the center of it. The door cracked and shuddered but held. He tried again with the same result.

Stan stepped up, "Is thing for big stupid private, not small, prissy captain," he said with a grin. No one had ever called Nathan "small and prissy" before. But coming from Stan it seemed almost reasonable. Nathan scowled, but stepped back with a bow, gesturing him forward.

Stan looked at the door a moment, seeming to examine its thickness and strength. He looked back at the men, shrugged his shoulders, then turned and slammed into the door with his shoulder. The door crashed inward. A window in the adjacent room shattered from the force of the blow.

Nathan turned and glared at his men, "If Walters is here, he's *mine*."

No one argued. Nathan led the men inside, pistol held out front. Harry the Dog followed him inside, though he normally stayed out of buildings.

A white-coated male slave greeted them, groveling on the floor.

"Please don't kill us, masters!" he howled.

"Where's Walters?" Nathan demanded.

"He gone, master. Some men came and said they was a great battle and his side done lost. He got on his horse and rode outta here an hour or so back."

"Which direction did he go?"

"South, master. Down into the wild lands to the south of this-here farm. He done locked the door and said don't let no one in."

Nathan scowled, "Damned, insufferable man! Slipped away again. *Damn him!*"

"Shall we go after him, sir?" Jim asked, clearly hoping he'd say yes.

"No ... no, he was only a target of opportunity, not our primary mission. We must go back and secure the road, so we can safely evacuate the farm."

He turned back toward the butler, still prone on the floor.

"All right ... stand up now ... I'll not hurt you. I'm no monster like your *accursed* master. What's your name?"

"Josiah, master," he said, rising slowly to his feet.

"Well, Josiah, if Walters isn't here, you can at least lead me to your mistress, Miss Margaret. Where is she kept?"

"Miss Margaret, sir? Why ... she ain't here, sir."

Nathan growled, "Don't play me false, Josiah ... I've killed any number of men today, and I'm in no mood for games."

"No, sir, no, sir! I tell it true. Miss Margaret done disappeared right outta this house in the middle of last night. Nobody seen her go, and nobody knows where she went. Master was powerful angry ... like thunder and lightning in this house last night. I figured he gonna skin us all, sir."

Nathan scowled. "Tom, Jim … search this house. Every room, every closet. Tear the place apart if you have to. From the attic to the cellar. If she's still in this house, I want her found. *Damn it! Hellfire and damnation!* After all these months of worry, we finally come to fetch her, and she's gone! And gone only last night! Curse the bad luck!"

He briefly considered encouraging Walters slaves to run away. He assumed they suffered terribly under Walters' severe regime. And it would clearly be in his own self-interest, forcing Walters to waste time rounding up his own fleeing slaves would keep him well occupied for some time. But in the end, he thought better of it. He had no way to ensure their safety once they left this place, and likely Walters punishment if and when he caught them later would be swift and extreme.

After they'd come up empty in the house, he had his men search every barn and outbuilding on the farm. He felt in no particular hurry to get back to Mountain Meadows. After all, the enemy was now well in hand, either dead, captured, or scattered in fear. And he wanted to make sure Margaret wasn't hiding somewhere close by. It occurred to him it would be the kind of clever thing she might do to throw any pursuers off her track. Despite it being unlikely she was nearby, Nathan insisted his men continue the search, which ultimately turned up nothing; it was a decision he would soon regret.

☙❧☙❧☙❧☙❧☙❧☙❧

"Only a little further, Miss Abbey."

"But Megs, you still haven't told me why we're here," Abbey pushed aside another thorny branch that'd attached itself to her dress.

"You'll see, we're almost there."

They'd been packing Miss Abbey's traveling trunk before Megs had asked her to step outside to see something "interesting."

When Megs had entered the room, Miss Abbey had paused in her packing and sat on the bed with a heavy sigh.

She gazed around the room at the furniture and furnishings. An elegant, brass-framed looking glass mounted atop a beautifully carved dresser, with multi-colored wood inlays—Nathan's grandmother had purchased it in Richmond and had it carted over the mountains at great expense. The bed, with its delicately carved posts, worn smooth in spots by the touch of the occupant's hands over uncounted years of getting in and out of bed. There were many other precious and meaningful items she hated to part with in this room.

And every room had more of the same. She shuddered at the thought of leaving so many beautiful things behind ... free for the taking ... or destroying ... for anyone who came along. And there was nothing she could do about it.

As she sat on the bed, she began to tear up, and a growing feeling of despair threatened to overwhelm her.

Megs came over and sat next to her, wrapping an arm around her shoulders. "I have a pretty good notion what you're thinking on, Miss Abbey."

She sighed again, and sniffed back a tear, "It breaks my heart, Megs. All these wonderful things ... every one carried here at great cost ... and now ... all will be lost."

"Maybe ... but still, to my way of thinking people's more important than *things*. And if the Captain can get us all outta here still in our skins, that'll be a right fine thing."

"Yes ... of course, you're right. I'm just being ... *nostalgic* ... is all. These things have been part of my life for so many years now it's hard to leave them behind."

"Well, I ain't entirely sure what that word *nost ... whatever ...* means, but I get your meaning."

They sat still for several minutes, arm in arm, there on the bed looking around at the room.

Then Megs stood up and held out her hands, "Will you come with me for a few minutes? I'd like to show you something."

"Show me? Show me *what*, dear?"

"Something that's been a secret since ... well since before I was born, I reckon. And I've been sworn to secrecy on it myself, ever since I was a young girl. But now … well, now the time for secrets is past. Will you come?"

"All right, Megs, if you wish." She reached up and took Megs hands, and they left the room arm in arm.

Megs had led her out through the flower garden, and on toward the duck pond. They'd circled around the pond into the field on the far side. Past the field was a thicket of bushes that tangled their skirts and scratched their arms as they pushed their way through.

Abbey gingerly pulled another prickly branch off her sleeve and nearly ran into Megs' back in the process, not noticing she'd stopped.

She stood up next to Megs and looked ahead. The bushes had thinned a bit, giving way to huge rocks that covered the landscape in the area stretching out in front of them. She'd known they'd never used this part of the property for farming, and now she saw why. There was no soil at all, only bedrock humped up in odd shapes, spreading off into the distance.

"Come, Miss Abbey … let me show you what I came to show you."

Megs led her a twisty route around rocks, and through more bushes, then stopped and held out her hand, "What do you see?"

Abbey looked where Megs gestured, "More of these damned prickly bushes."

Megs laughed, then stepped up and pulled back a large branch in front of her, "Now look!"

Abbey stepped up and looked into … darkness. She gasped, "Why … it's a cave … a great, large one from the looks of that darkness. They'd always said the caves here-abouts were up in the hills on the east side of the property, that there were none over here to the west."

"Yep, that's what everyone always believed, until one of us found this-here place long ago. No one remembers now who it was, but it happened some years before I ever arrived on this farm. We've kept it a sworn secret ever since. Runaways have hidden here when they've strayed onto the farm from time to time. And folks have stored various things they wanted kept from the master. But ... like I said back at the house, there's no need for secrets no more."

"Well, this is ... *interesting*, Megs ... and I'm honored you've entrusted me with this secret, but ..."

Megs scowled at her, "It ain't about honor or any other nonsense ... ain't you heard what I said? They's no more need to keep this-here cave a secret now we're all freemen! No ... *think*, Miss Abbey! Though it were a twisty hike for us women afoot, it's fairly flat all the way from here to the house. Only these last few steps have been rough. And there're no trees to speak of, only these prickly bushes. Why ... it'd be little trouble at all clearing a way for a wagon ... or two ..."

Abbey thought about that a moment, then her mouth dropped open, and she looked over at Megs, "You mean ... you mean we might hide things here? Things from the house? And they'd be safe from ... *others?*"

Megs had a self-satisfied grin, "Yes, ma'am, that's exactly what I'm saying. And there's no time to waste if we're gonna get it done 'fore the Captain means to leave."

"But ... all the men're off fighting ... how'll we possibly move all that heavy furniture?"

"The men may be gone, but there's still plenty o' us women folk. And I heard it said, 'many hands make light work.' I expect if there's enough of us, we could even lift that old piano of yours outta the house and onto a wagon."

Abbeys eyes widened, and tears started welling, "Oh Megs ... do you really think so?"

"Of course, Miss Abbey ... there really ain't nothing men can do that women can't do also, if we sets our minds ... and our muscles ... to it! And ... if we work together!"

₧₧₧₧₧₧₧₧₧

Evelyn arrived back at her new house as the sun was setting. A cool breeze had accompanied scudding clouds across the sky, making her shiver as she'd walked the mile or more from a secret meeting place. The meeting had been with one of Jonathan Hughes' "observers"—a euphemistic term for a freeman spy, whose job was to slip into large plantations posing as a slave. He'd learn the routine of the farm and encourage slaves to escape, providing them with the information they needed to do so—where to "board" the Underground Railroad.

Evelyn had met with this observer, who went by "Nat" on this occasion, to learn the results of his latest assignment, the expansive Miller plantation several miles out to the southwest of Richmond near Amelia.

He'd explained how it'd been an especially difficult mission for him. Many of the slaves he'd met were fearful and did not want to associate with him for fear he'd be caught, and they'd be punished. Nat encountered little enthusiasm for the information he tried to give the slaves about how to escape and where to go after doing so. He'd also had several close calls when white farmhands had questioned who he was. But fortunately, they'd been relatively new hands and fell for his pre-planned tale.

To make matters worse, he'd had a difficult time escaping. The farmer's dogs had pursued him, and he'd only eluded them by diving into the river and letting it wash him several miles downstream. He eventually dragged himself out on the riverbank, half drowned. It'd been a harrowing tale, and Evelyn had become anxious and fearful just listening to it.

And after they'd parted, the anxiety had dogged her footsteps all the way home. She'd taken a circuitous route, as was her habit after such meetings. But though she'd watched for anyone following, and had seen nothing, she couldn't shake the itchy feeling of being watched.

When she stepped up to her front door, an especially strong gust of wind buffeted her. She wrapped her shawl more tightly around her neck and shivered. But before she opened the door to step inside, she turned and took one last look back along the road and around the neighborhood. Nothing. She shrugged her shoulders, turned and entered the house.

A few moments later, two men stepped out from behind a hedge row on the opposite side of the street one house down from Evelyn's. They'd dressed neatly, though not elegantly, in gray suits and hats of the kind worn by gentlemen on a casual outing.

A closer inspection might have noticed each man wore a leather gun belt at his hip, covered by his jacket.

The men looked around furtively before hurriedly crossing the road and moving up the street toward Evelyn's house. They paused at the edge of her property, looking up and down the street once again as the light of day faded with the setting sun, but they saw no traffic, either by horse or afoot. They pushed through a hedgerow, behind which was the back yard of Evelyn's house. In moments they were at her back basement door. One of them carefully turned the doorknob, and found it unlocked. He looked up and met eyes with the other man. They shared a grin as they unholstered their pistols.

Chapter 7. Chess Moves

*"Some people think if their opponent plays
a beautiful game, it's OK to lose.
I don't. You have to be merciless."*
– Magnus Carlsen, World Chess Champion

Monday May 27, 1861 – Greenbrier County, Virginia:

When he was only halfway across the ford at Howard Creek, Nathan saw a dark cloud of smoke off to the east. He knew it was coming from the defeated enemy's camp. He spurred Millie forward and was already at the gallop when she reached dry land. Harry was hard on Millie's heels, not even taking time to shake the water from his fur.

Nathan hadn't said a word, but the others had seen it as well. They all moved up the road at full speed. Something had happened back where they'd left their men.

As they came up the road to the field where the battle had taken place, they saw several tents had burned to the ground and were still smoldering. No one was anywhere in sight. Nathan slowed to a trot and grabbed the pistol from his hip. But as they approached the camp four black men rose up out of the grass near the burning tents. They held rifles and waved at the riders as they approached. Nathan pulled up to a stop in front of them. He recognized Cobb, Phinney, Matt, and Eddie.

Cobb stepped up next to Nathan's horse, "Hello, Captain! Lordie, we's happy to see you, sir!"

"Cobb. What's happened here?"

"Don't rightly know, sir. We was back yonder guarding them fellas that'd surrendered, when someone calls out there's a fire. Mr. Georgie points to a dozen or so of us and says, 'Come with me, lads!'

"And when we get here, we see these-here tents ablaze, but not knowing the why-for of it. Well, we's standing around looking when we hear gunshots back up where we come from. Mr.

Georgie, he says, 'Goddamn it! It's a trick, and we fell for it! Cobb, you and these fellas stay here. Hide in the grass and wait for the Captain to come. Anyone else comes, shoot 'em.'

"Then he runs off with the rest of the fellas, and we stays here doing as we was told. And we heard a whole lot more gunshots back yonder, though it's been quiet now for a spell. We ain't seen a soul 'til you rode up just now, sir."

"You did well, Cobb. Stay here and continue doing as Georgie ordered. I'll send someone to relieve you as soon as may be."

"Yes, sir!" Cobb snapped Nathan a salute, as neat as any done by the veteran soldiers.

Nathan returned it sharply and spurred Millie ahead. They rode away from the burned tents up along the west edge of the camp toward the north side where they'd last seen Georgie and William. When they rounded the northwest corner of the camp, they were relieved to see Georgie standing there with several of their men. William was there too, but he was kneeling on the ground, apparently tending to someone lying there.

As they approached, Georgie looked up and saw them, waved, and trotted in their direction. Nathan took the scene in with a quick glance. He saw seven bodies that hadn't been there when they'd left. He cringed when as he noted four of the seven had black skin. The living black men were spread out in an arc facing southeast, kneeling in the grass, rifles in hand pointing outward.

As they came to a stop next to Georgie, he snapped a salute at Nathan but had a serious look on his face.

"It was a sneak attack, sir. They drew a bunch of us off by setting some tents afire. They attacked the others without warning, shooting down several of our men before William could rally them in a counterattack, driving the enemy off. By the time I got back here with my men it was all but over. I'm afraid the prisoners done run off during the scuffle ... as they'd planned, no doubt."

"Yes, that seems likely. How many casualties this time?"

"Four more of ours killed, sir, and seven wounded. That brings our total count to ten killed and twelve wounded."

"Damn it! Too high by a wide margin. We should've never lost these men. If only …"

"There's more to it, sir … William says it was Walters led them."

"Walters?! We were told he'd run away to the south, tail between his legs."

"*Told*, sir? Told by whom?"

"We were told by … *damn!* Told by his own butler. And I was foolish and prideful enough to believe it! I never thought a slave would side with him and do his bidding when he didn't have to. And Walters knew full well I'd be cock-sure enough to believe he'd run from me in fear. *Damn it!*"

"Likely the butler was afraid to do anything else," Tom said quietly, well aware how the preventable loss of men would affect Nathan.

Nathan hopped down from the saddle, stuck a cigar in his mouth and chewed it vigorously while striding toward where William continued to kneel on the grass.

"William. It seems I am in your debt again. Georgie says you have acquitted yourself most handsomely once more. And here I'd tried keeping you from the fight!"

William finished tying off the bandage he'd been working on and stood up. Nathan noticed he was blushing, "Happy to help, sir, but to tell the truth I had little choice in the matter.

"After Georgie headed off to check on the fire, I went back to tending the wounded. Next thing I knew gunshots were going off all around us, coming from the bushes just outside the camp over yonder. They'd already hit several of our men. The others were scrambling to get out of the way, and … well, it was near a panic, to my thinking. So I yelled at them to stop and face the enemy like men. And I pulled my pistols, rushing forward, firing both barrels.

"Just … trying to set the example, you know … doing what I thought *you* would've done in the same circumstances, sir. Only … well, I wasn't sure anyone would follow. But to their credit, next thing I knew the men were coming along with me, firing their rifles, and rushing forward with bayonets and a shout.

That *Big George* fellow was soon outrunning me, along with Tony and Ned. But the enemy pulled back and melted away into the woods, so I called a halt. But before they left, I got a clear look at their leader, yelling orders—Walters, for sure.

"When Georgie got back with his men, we set up a defensive perimeter and started counting our losses and tending our wounded. It was then we realized the prisoners had escaped. No one had thought to watch them, what with all that was going on. I'm very sorry about *that*, sir."

"You have nothing to be sorry for, William. Sounds like you saved our fellows from a rout and turned the tables on the enemy. Losing a few prisoners was a small price to pay. We'd have had to cut them loose eventually, anyway—we could hardly have taken them with us. I'm proud of you William, and much obliged."

"Never mention it, sir. Happy I was here to help."

But Stan strode up, scooped William off his feet and embraced him before setting him down and planting a kiss on each cheek.

"The men are telling me you are regular *hero*, William. I am being very proud of knowing you!"

William blushed. "It was ... nothing, really. Any of us would have done the same."

"Nonsense, William! You are born leader ... and *pretty good fighter* ... for little scrawny guy!"

Nathan exchanged a knowing look with William and smiled.

He turned toward Georgie and said, "Don't forget to send some men to relieve Cobb and his crew. They've been back by those burned-out tents for some time, wondering what in blazes is going on."

Georgie put his hand to his forehead, "Oh! Blazes is right, sir. In all the excitement I plumb forgot all about them. Guess I still have a lot to learn about being an officer, sir. I'll send a relief guard straightaway."

"Don't be too hard on yourself, Georgie. You've also performed most admirably today ... and you make a very *fine* officer!"

Georgie beamed, "Thank you, sir! Very kindly of you to say!"

Margaret's anxiety increased with every mile. It was now bright daylight. The long walk, and the long day and night of fear and stress before that had exhausted her. But she knew they couldn't stop, not until they found a safe place to hide for the rest of the daylight hours.

They'd been lucky so far, scrambling for cover off the road several times just when men on horseback were about to spot them. She had no delusions their luck would hold as they became more tired and less alert.

Even Henry, who'd proved his great strength in the struggle with the guard, was showing signs of fatigue. She wasn't the only one who'd had a long, frightful night of it.

The original plan Bob had laid out had her sneaking through Lewisburg in the dark pre-dawn hours when no one would be up and alert. That wouldn't be possible during the day, so she'd have to find shelter somewhere short of town and try passing through when it got dark again. What Henry would do and which direction he would take were still a mystery to her; they'd had little time to converse about anything that didn't involve running and hiding.

At the moment, they were heading west to get away from the fighting, which worked for her. After her failed attempt to reach Mountain Meadows, she'd decided to follow Bob's plan, albeit a day late.

About an hour ago, they'd passed by the road branching off to Walters Farm to their left. She'd lost track of where they were, and the sudden sight of it struck such fear and anxiety in her that for a minute she couldn't move.

But Henry had looked at her, then over at the road. He seemed to understand, "Come, missus … we gots to keep movin'. And don't you worry yourself none, we ain't goin' *that a-way* no-how!"

She'd gazed at him, and he'd smiled at her reassuringly. It was the first time she'd seen him smile, and it helped snap her out of her malaise.

But now they faced a major obstacle. They'd snuck past what appeared to be an inn off to the left of the road. But ahead the road crossed a great river over a long, covered bridge.

She looked over at Henry, but he shook his head, "River's too wide to swim, missus, and likely too deep to wade."

"We'd be out in the open a long time if we crossed over the bridge," she said, "and nowhere to hide if someone came."

He nodded but said nothing, continuing to gaze out at the bridge from where they crouched behind some brush on the north side of the road.

The south side of the road appeared to be farm country, likely the pastures and subsistence crops belonging to the inn. Other than the high weeds in the ditch bank, there'd be no place to hide or take shelter on that side.

The north side was heavily wooded, which would at least provide cover. But it would be a long, cold wait if it started to rain. Though the day had dawned clear and sunny, clouds had formed as they'd progressed, threatening a downpour.

She was about to resign herself to curling up among the trees back from the road when she noticed something she'd previously overlooked. She nudged Henry with her elbow and pointed. He looked toward where she'd indicated, up toward the bridge along the north side of the road. At first, he couldn't figure what she meant. But then he saw it too.

"A trail?"

"Looks like. I say we go see where it leads. At least it may get us back off the road a ways without having to push through these trees. And if we're lucky, maybe we'll find some sort of shelter."

"All right, missus. Let's try it."

They hurried to where the trail started, then followed it north. It seemed to parallel the river and appeared man-made—wider and straighter than she imagined a game trail might be. And even more hopeful, tall grass and weeds grew thickly on it. Whatever its original purpose, it had long since been abandoned.

They followed the trail through the woods for a few hundred yards when it suddenly opened up into a wedge-shaped clearing several acres in size. The field was relatively flat and contained the same tall grass and weeds that grew on the path.

A small building stood on the far side of the clearing. As they got closer, they decided it had been a farm building, a small barn or tool shed. But it was dilapidated and abandoned. There were gaps in the siding and holes in the roof.

Oh well ... any port in a storm, she thought. They cautiously moved around the building to find a door. They found it on the side facing the river. Two doors, in fact, double doors originally designed to admit something wide like a wagon. One door was fairly intact, but the other hung crookedly, one large hinge having rusted through.

It was then she noticed the burned-out remains of a house a few hundred feet further over toward the river. She wondered if whoever had originally lived here had abandoned the small farm after the fire had destroyed the house. Or they'd died in the fire ... she shuddered at the horrible image that conjured in her mind.

They peered inside, straining to make out anything in the nearly complete darkness. The only light not coming in at the door was that coming in from the holes in the roof. She pulled the pack from her back for the first time and laid it down on the ground in front of her. Henry looked on, clearly curious, but he said nothing.

She reached in and quickly retrieved a candle and a match. As was her habit, she'd considered and planned her packing of the simple bag as logically as possible. And something she'd decided should be readily accessible and easy to locate, even in complete darkness, was the candle and match! She re-shouldered the pack and lit the candle. Holding the light out in front of her, she stepped into the barn. Henry followed right behind her.

It had a musty smell, with old straw strewn across the floor. A broken-down wagon sagged on three wheels along the left side, covered in spider webs and dust. Beyond that, there was a storage area with a half-height wall running partway across the back wall, and shelves running up the wall behind it. She looked up and immediately saw the holes in the roof she'd seen from outside. There were three large holes and numerous smaller ones. Though it would likely not be an ideal shelter in a rainstorm, it did not appear to be at risk of imminent collapse. It was a relatively low ceiling, with no hay loft, so clearly a storage building for farm equipment and vehicles rather than a stable for animals.

There was nothing else. So she decided the storage area back behind the wagon would be the best place to shelter and get some rest. She prayed there were no rats in the building, but then scolded herself; it was a trivial concern with everything else to worry about.

She moved past the wagon and stepped toward the opening in the half-height wall. Peering cautiously around the corner, she was relieved to find it relatively clean and dry, with solid-looking floorboards. She motioned Henry to join her and again removed her pack.

They settled down on the floor, their backs against the barn wall, grateful to be able to relax and rest. After all they'd been through, this simple shelter was a great relief, despite its decrepit condition.

She set the candle on the floor between them and reached back into her pack.

"You bring any food with you?"

"No, missus. There was none in the cabin when I ran."

"Henry, my name is Margaret. I'd appreciate if you'd *only* call me that. Clearly, I am no longer the Missus at Walters Farm.

"Yes, ma'am ... Miss Margaret. Is it true then, ma'am?"

"Is what true?"

"That Walters meant to murder *you* ma'am? His own wife?"

"Yes, it's true."

"What kind of man would *do* such a thing?"

"The wicked kind; the same kind that beats innocent slaves to death."

"Yes, ma'am ... I reckon so. That's why I ran. Walters Farm was the cruelest most frightful place I ever been. So when I heard them white overseers say the hounds was sick and dying, I ran."

"Oh! So, Bob was right."

"Bob, ma'am?"

"Never mind. Anyway ... it seems we're both trying to escape Walters, Henry."

He nodded his agreement but said nothing more.

Then she said, "When I first saw you in the tent, I thought I recognized you. Did we meet eyes once, out my window, when you were hoeing weeds in the fields?"

"Yes, Missus ... I mean ... *Miss Margaret*. I seen you from time to time looking out your window up in the house when I was in the fields. Wondered why you was always up in that room looking out and never was outside the house."

"Because I was a prisoner in my own room, in my own house. I wasn't a slave like you were, Henry, but I was never free."

His eyes widened, and he slowly shook his head. "The man is ... something that ain't quite *human*, ma'am."

"True ... Walters is evil, which you know something about, I'm sure. But not just evil to his slaves; the white men suffer as well, though not nearly as badly, as a rule."

"'Cept maybe you," he said with a serious look.

She shrugged.

As they talked, she pulled food from her pack and shared it out: a slice of bread each, a hunk of hard cheese, and a small water bottle.

Henry thanked her kindly, and for a while there was no more talk as they broke their fast.

When she'd finished her meager meal, Margaret leaned back against the wall. After a moment she turned to her companion and said, "Henry ... when you left Walters Farm, did you have any idea where you would go?"

"Yes, ma'am."

He went quiet, staring at the floorboards in front of him. She wondered if that was all she would get from him. But after a moment he looked over at her with a serious expression and said, "I was fixin' to go fetch my wife."

"Your wife?"

"She's back on the farm I came from before Walters bought me."

"Oh! And ... do you know where that is? What town it's close to, I mean?"

"It's near a town called Lynchburg, ma'am."

She recalled looking at a map of this part of Virginia just before her wedding to get an idea of where she'd be living. She concentrated and after a moment remembered where Lynchburg was. "But ... Henry, that's got to be ... I don't know, likely more than a hundred miles from here. And up over the mountains to the other side."

"Yes, I know ma'am. I done walked all that way, up and over them mountains ... with a metal ring 'round my neck, dragging a heavy chain attached to other men."

"Oh ... how dreadful, Henry. But ... however did you expect to get back there without being caught? And if you were to make it there, how would you possibly get your wife out?"

He looked down at the floorboards again and shook his head. "Guess I didn't think it out too well, did I ma'am? 'Specially seein's how I never even made it a day before they done caught me again."

"Well ... as for that ... you shouldn't be too hard on yourself. You had no way of knowing there was a battle brewing, with hundreds of alert men who wouldn't normally be out watching the road."

He nodded his head but said nothing.

"But I agree ... you didn't think it out very well, Henry. Though nothing is impossible, getting your wife out *that* way is as close to it as I can imagine."

"Yes, ma'am. But what was I to do? Save myself and live the rest of my life trying to forget about her? The woman I love more'n anything else in the world? More'n my own life ..." he finished softly.

He was quiet and had tears in his eyes.

She sat back and considered his problem. How would *she* go about it?

After a few moments, she sat up. "Henry, I'm alone in the world, and terribly afraid—a young woman from the city who has done nothing of this kind before. And if Walters catches me, he *will* kill me. If you'll help me escape, all the way to a safe place, I'll help you get your wife back."

He looked over at her, eyes wide. "How would you do *that*, ma'am?"

"Henry, such is the world we now live in. What is impossible for a black man such as yourself, as strong and brave as you are, is simple child's play for a small, frightened white woman, such as me."

He didn't seem to understand what she was getting at, so she explained, "Henry, once we get someplace safe, I will get a job, as a teacher, librarian, or something ... I don't know. Anyway, as soon as I'm able to make a little money, I'll hire an agent to ride to Lynchburg. There he can simply buy your wife all proper and legal and return with her to wherever we are."

"It's simple as that?"

"Yes ... simple as that."

"And ... you would do that for me? Spend your own hard-earned money to buy her."

"Of course! But don't consider it *my* money ... you will have earned it helping me escape from Walters."

"Oh, *no* ma'am. A proper man ought to do a thing like that out of his own goodness, not for pay."

"Well, then think of it as one good turn deserving another."

Henry considered what she was suggesting. Although she'd done well so far, she was a petite young thing, with likely little strength or endurance. And she admitted she had no skills to speak of outside a house or a city. She'd probably slow him down and become a burden later on. Likely get him killed if Walters ever caught them.

But then he shrugged; Walters would probably kill him anyway if he caught him, and besides ... she *had* spotted the trail that led to this shelter, hadn't she? And she'd been resourceful enough to bring along food and water before running. And kindly enough to share it.

Also ... there was something about her that reminded him of his own wife. He hoped someday someone might help her in need. And ... if she could truly help him get his wife back ...

"All right, Miss Margaret. I reckon we can help each other escape."

"*Good!* And thank you, Henry. I mean to make sure you'll not regret it. I'll do my best to keep up, and not to make things more difficult for you. It may also be if folks see us together, I can claim you're my servant and they'll not suspect you're a runaway. That may be a help to you."

"Yes, ma'am ... I reckon that's true enough."

"And if we ever make it to freedom, in addition to getting your wife back, I will do ... well, anything else I can to help you *stay* free."

"Thank you, Miss Margaret. I'm sure I's gonna need all the help I can get out amongst the white folks if ever we do get up North." He thought of his wife back on the farm to the east, and though it galled him to head in the other direction, he knew Margaret was right. Her way made a lot more sense and might actually work.

They each found a comfortable spot to lie down. Margaret considered taking turns sleeping, with one keeping a watch. But she quickly discarded the idea. If someone came looking for them, there'd be little enough they could do about it, anyway. They would just have to trust to luck and providence to keep them safe and see them through. She did, however, sleep with the loaded pistol in her right hand.

ದುಜಾಂಞಿಜುೞುಜಾಂಞಿಜುೞುಜಾಂಞಿಜ

Tuesday May 28, 1861 – Lewisburg, Virginia:

Once they'd established a defensive perimeter and organized a cavalry patrol of the road, Nathan dispatched more than a dozen young men back up to the farm. There they'd help load the wagons and assist Miss Abbey in any other way she might require. He sent strict orders the wagons were to depart at first light the following morning.

The remaining men formed a somber burial detail overseen by Nathan himself. He ordered the Mountain Meadows men buried back in the woods in hopes the enemy might not desecrate their gravesite.

They would not bury the enemy soldiers; instead, he ordered them laid out in a neat row, side by side. They were treated respectfully—their belongings, except for weapons, left with them—in the hopes their families might come to reclaim their bodies and personal effects later.

When they were laying them out, Georgie noticed something odd about one of the dead men. He'd not been shot, nor bayonetted, but appeared to have been strangled. "Hey Stan! This some o' your handiwork?"

Stan walked over and looked, "Nyet. Not mine, neck's not even broken. And look, they used rope ... or chain. Dug into flesh. I've no need of such toys." He sniffed and walked away, indignant Georgie would accuse him of such sloppy, amateurish work.

No one else claimed to know anything about it either, so it remained a mystery.

Nathan ordered a common grave for the Mountain Meadows men. But he laid the men out, side to side and recorded the relative position of each on a piece of paper. He intended to transcribe this list into the back of the Chambers family Bible when time allowed. It was his plan, should they return in happier times, to exhume these heroes, and bury them with proper headstones in full honor in the Chambers family plot back at the farm. He told the men his intentions, for which he received several nods of approval, and "thank you, sir"s.

Before they filled the dirt back in, he stepped up to the edge of the grave and removed his hat. The others did likewise. Tony was there and couldn't stop a steady flow of tears as he looked upon on the form of his lifelong friend, Johnny, for the last time.

"'I have fought the good fight, I have finished my course ... I have kept the faith,' second book of Timothy, chapter four, verse seven."

Nathan stood another minute with his head bowed, then looked up, wiped back a tear, replaced his hat, turned on his heels and strode back toward camp. The men began shoveling earth back into the grave.

That evening the men helped themselves to a dinner cooked from the abundant supplies the enemy had abandoned. Later they also made use of their tents, alternating the watch such that everyone got at least a few hours of sleep under cover.

Nathan had contemplated setting the enemy's remaining supplies, tents and all, to the torch before they departed. But then he thought better of it, holding out at least a slim hope the enemy might refrain from likewise burning down the Big House and all the Mountain Meadows outbuildings. But he was philosophical about it; it was out of his hands once he departed. At least he could set the example for civility.

For the same reason, he'd turned down Billy's earlier offer to set deadly traps around the Big House once everyone was clear. "These traps would kill anyone coming close to the house, or trying to enter," Billy explained.

"Would these traps know the difference between enemy soldiers and innocent women or children coming here seeking shelter in the coming war?"

"Hmm ... no. Traps don't know the difference and don't care."

Nathan didn't want to risk harming someone innocent. And it also occurred to him if the enemy couldn't come into the house and make use of it, they'd be more inclined to burn it down. So he not only declined Billy's offer, he also ordered the doors be left unlocked. If someone wanted to come in, they would; why force them to break down the door?

The only thing he confiscated from the enemy camp was food they could take along with them, and the weapons and ammunition, of course. This was simple common sense, and common practice in warfare, after all.

But despite his firm orders to Miss Abbey, dawn had come and gone with no sign of the wagons and their precious cargo. So Nathan had sent Cobb back on horseback to check on the status. He'd returned a little more than an hour later, shrugging his shoulders and apologizing.

"Did you ask Miss Abbey why they've not yet departed?"

"Yes, Captain."

"And?"

"Well, sir ... I may be a freeman now, and a blooded fighter and all, but ... to tell it true, crossing Miss Abbey ... well, *it just ain't in me!* When I pressed her, she only scowled at me. Then she said, 'You ride on back and tell the Captain we'll be there when we're good and ready, and not a moment before!' I looks over to Megs for to appeal-like, and she also scowls. So I reckoned there weren't much more I could do. But it looked like the wagons was mostly loaded and folks was gathered round, so I don't rightly know what she was waiting on."

Nathan fumed and paced about, looking at his pocket watch every five minutes, as if that might make them arrive sooner. It was now nearly noon, and no sign of the wagons.

Jamie came riding back from the highway patrol to give a report. He pulled up his horse neatly in front of Nathan and snapped a salute. "Sergeant Jim sends his compliments, sir. He says to report the road is clear back to the east all the way to White Sulphur Springs, and over to the bridge across the Greenbrier by the Caldwell Place to the west. No sign of the enemy. The sergeant plans to wait 'til the wagons are on the road to send anyone on ahead to scout over beyond the bridge to town."

Then Jamie looked around in puzzlement, "Speaking of which, sir …"

"Yes, yes, I *know*. Not here yet, *damn it!* I'm about to ride back there myself and light a fire under some backsides …"

"Yes, sir. Seems like such a thing may be in order … *oh!* There they be now, sir!"

Nathan looked back toward the hill and saw a horse-drawn wagon appear, followed by a line of others. A large group of people walked along beside them.

"Finally! Georgie, form up the men and let's get ready to move out."

"Sir!"

When the lead wagon pulled to a stop, Nathan was already mounted and waiting. Miss Abbey sat next to Phinney, who was driving. She looked up at Nathan and smiled pleasantly, ignoring his frown.

"Momma. I sincerely hope whatever has caused this delay was worth the time it has cost us."

But she appeared not to take offense only smiled more brightly. "Oh, *yes*, dear. It was most *certainly* worth the delay!"

He gazed at her another moment, then shook his head in puzzlement and frustration. He snapped Millie around with the reins and kicked her into motion.

Jamie turned his horse to follow, and Georgie ordered the foot soldiers to move out as well, him leading the column on foot. By Captain's earlier orders, Tony would wait and lead a smaller group of men taking up positions behind the wagons to serve as rearguard during their march. Of course, the mounted riders out patrolling the road would shadow the whole caravan, like watchful guardian angels.

When they reached the road, Tom met them and dispatched Benny to ride back east along the road to tell the rearguard the column was finally on the move. Jim had ridden ahead with Billy. They waited before the next bend in the road, about a half-mile distant. When the wagons appeared, Jim waved a broad salute at Nathan then turned and headed off west with Billy. They'd now scout beyond the bridge, making sure the road was clear all the way to Lewisburg.

It made Nathan anxious to have his men spread so far afield, but it was necessary. It wouldn't do to march right into an ambush with a whole column of noncombatants, nor to be taken unawares from behind. Besides, they were likely close enough to hear gunshots in the distance, should their scouts come under fire.

Benny soon rejoined them, reporting the rearguard was moving forward. So Nathan sent him off with Jamie to ride along the edge of the woods to the left of the road, and he ordered the column to move out.

As they rolled west, the Mountain Meadows order of battle comprised Stan, Zeke, and Joe as mounted rearguard, Jim and Billy riding out front, with Benny and Jamie taking the left side of the roadway. Georgie took the right side along with Cobb, who'd volunteered to ride as a cavalry scout when Nathan had declared they were short-handed in that regard, with William riding in a wagon so he might look after the wounded.

Though Cobb was an excellent rider, being a groom, he had no experience with a pistol. So Georgie had given him a quick five-minute lesson on the Colt revolver—mostly intended to keep him from accidentally shooting himself or someone else—and then off they rode.

Nathan had also made two field promotions appointing Tony and Big George as corporals to lead two columns of foot soldiers—Big George in front of the wagons, and Tony to the rear. They'd long since reloaded the rifles, and he ordered they keep the bayonets on this time, figuring anyone spying on them might have second thoughts about attacking men wielding the wicked looking spears.

Tom and Nathan rode next to the wagons, so they'd be in the center of the column, able to issue orders and react in any direction as needed.

The first several miles along the road were uneventful. They quickly passed the turn off to Walters Farm. Nathan gazed down it for a long time, puffing on a cigar, as they moved past. Tom could guess the thoughts going through Nathan's mind at that moment.

Shortly after, they passed the turn off to the community church. It sat a short distance from the main road back in the woods, reached by its own narrow gravel driveway.

They soon passed in front of the Caldwell Place, the inn just this side of the Greenbrier River Bridge. The inn was on their left, so it fell to Jamie and Benny to scout it out. They pulled up in front of the veranda and dismounted, unceremoniously striding inside, pistols drawn. They searched every room, both public and private, locked or not, kicking in doors when necessary, despite the stormy objections of Mrs. Caldwell.

Surprisingly, they found no men at all in the building, which they found odd. Only women and children. Even Mr. Caldwell, who was almost always holding forth in the common room, was missing. When they quizzed Mrs. Caldwell about it, she shrugged and said, "I reckon the men are off on business of their own. It's none of my concern, and I can't see how it's any of your'n!"

While still within sight of the inn they crossed the long, covered bridge over the Greenbrier River. Their horses' hooves echoed loudly inside the wooden enclosure, and the wagon wheels made a roaring sound like a train on the wood planks.

When they'd gone about a mile past the bridge Nathan raised his hand and called a halt. He wanted to make sure the rearguard was on *this* side of the river before the column proceeded further. If the enemy tried to come at them from that direction, the three men might keep an entire army from crossing the narrow bridge for a very long time.

He also wanted to wait for Jim and Billy to return from their scouting mission out to the edge of town.

They discussed what to do next. Moving through the town was infinitely more dangerous than being out in the open countryside. Enemy riflemen might be hiding on top of any building. The enemy might position whole companies of armed men in alleyways, behind doorways, inside buildings, or up on rooftops.

They'd only been stationary a few minutes before Jim and Billy came up at a gallop. They pulled up by Nathan and Tom, snapping quick salutes.

"Sir ... all's clear between here and the town."

"And after that?"

Well, sir ... we crept up close enough for a peek, but it's pretty hard to tell. One good sign was things seemed fairly normal, women and children going about their usual business. To my way of thinking that indicates the enemy's not planning on attacking us as we cross through town."

"Hmm ... maybe ... but Walters has already outsmarted me once this campaign, and I don't intend to let it happen again. Would he be clever enough to parade women and children around on the streets where he knew we'd see them? We have to at least consider the possibility."

"True, sir."

They were quiet for a moment, contemplating how to make their way safely through the town, avoiding a bloodbath, should they find their passage opposed.

"Billy ... have you seen any way around the town?"

"No, Captain. I have gone around it in the woods other times, but there's no path a wagon can use. The only road big enough goes right through the town and out the other side to the west."

"Hmm ... that's what I feared."

"Tom ... any suggestions?"

"Nothing very useful, sir. I'm afraid we're going to have to bear up and bluff our way through, hoping for the best."

"Bluff?" Jim's eyes lit up, "That gives me an idea, gentlemen. I think I know a way we can force our way through without a fight. Allow me to borrow Big Stan, and the two of us will ride into the middle of town ... with a white flag!"

ജഈരജ୪ଔഈവജୠୠ

As Jim and Stan rode slowly through town to the wide square in front of the courthouse, they drew startled looks from the people on the street. People began to follow along, at a safe distance. It was a sight not seen every day in Lewisburg, Virginia: a very large man on an even larger horse, armed to the teeth with four pistols, a rifle, and a white cloth tied to the end of a bayonet! Jim was likewise armed, though he'd not brought along a rifle. Instead he'd borrowed Tom's cavalry saber, strapped to his side for effect. He smoked calmly on a cigar as they rode along.

When they reached the middle of the town square they stopped. Some people stopped and stared. Others walked past, doing their best to act nonchalant, despite the odd occurrence.

But nonchalance was not an option for long. As soon as they came to a halt, Stan stood up in his stirrups and waved the white flag vigorously above his head. He called out in his loudest voice, "People of Lewisburg! My name is *Stanislav Ivanovich Volkov*. I am Russian, and soldier. Is not of my liking to wave white flag of parley, I rather *fight!* But Captain says talk first before the killing! So ... if you wish for still breathing on the morrow, come listen to my sergeant." He gestured for the people to gather about them, then sat back down in his saddle.

And his presence was so compelling, and their curiosity so piqued, a large crowd was soon gathered around them, men, women, and children. It didn't surprise Jim the looks he and Stan received were unfriendly; after all, they'd doubtless already killed several men from the town during the recent fighting. Jim suspected some men in the crowd were armed, but none openly. Good, it meant they were at least nominally intimidated. Everything depended on him playing off that.

"My name is Sergeant Wiggins. I served under Captain Chambers out West in Texas, fighting the savage Comanche Indians. As Stan here says, we are soldiers, so if our Captain says fight, we fight. And if he says kill, we kill. And y'all already know there's been plenty of fighting out east of town over on the road to Mountain Meadows. Y'all also heard we already done killed plenty of those men who attacked us ... *unprovoked!*"

He nearly shouted that last word, and pointed with his cigar for emphasis, before spitting to the side.

Someone in the crowd had the courage to shout out, "Chambers is a traitor!" But Stan pointedly put his hand on the pistol at his hip and glared in the general direction, and there were no more catcalls.

Jim did not acknowledge the shout, but continued, "Listen up, y'all! Captain Chambers intends to pass through this town today with all his men and goods one hour from now. He'd prefer to pass through peacefully, but that's entirely up to y'all. Because peacefully or not, he *will* pass through!

"So ... here's how it's going to be. Anyone appearing on the street armed will be shot on sight. Anyone tries to impede or delay us, will be shot. Anyone shoots at us, he'll be shot ... then bayoneted, along with any man found near him. If we meet any sort of organized, armed resistance, we'll hunt down and kill every man in town above the age of ... *thirteen*.

"Oh, and in case anyone has a mind to take out his displeasure on us *messengers*, the Captain has instructed me to say; if the two of us don't return within the hour, he will ride in here and burn the entire town to the ground, barn, rick, and cot!"

He looked about the crowd and found the serious looks returned most satisfying. So he tipped his hat to his audience, turned his horse and walked it through the crowd, which parted to make way. Stan followed behind him, still holding the rifle barrel with white flag in the air, glaring around him — a gaze no man there had the courage to meet.

They continued their slow walk to the edge of town, then kicked their horses into a trot.

When they rejoined Nathan he asked, "Well?"

Stan just shrugged, but Jim said, "I predict they'll part like the Red Sea in front of old Moses," and grinned broadly, a cigar clenched between his teeth.

"Well, that sounds encouraging, at least," Tom said, "But what'd you tell them?"

Jim put on his most pious look, "I just appealed to their better nature, and their good, Christian charity. Asking them most kindly to allow us poor, helpless souls to pass through in peace."

Nathan scowled at him, rolled his eyes, and shook his head, "Yes ... I'm sure that's *exactly* how it went. If I know you, Mr. Wiggins, you've once again besmirched my good name and reputation. This time with all my neighbors, such that I'll likely *never* be welcomed back, regardless of what happens out in the wider world!"

"Oh, no, sir! I'd never do *that!* I just told them if they didn't allow you to pass, you'd kill them all and burn their town to the ground. There's no *besmirching* in that!" he laughed at his own grim humor, slapping his thigh.

Before the hour was up, seven horses thundered through the mostly empty streets of Lewisburg: Jim, Billy, Stan, Zeke, Joe, Benny, and Jamie. They held pistols in their hands and took turns leaping from the saddle in front of buildings at random, stopping long enough to kick in a door here, smash out a window there, looking inside for anyone acting suspiciously. Stan was especially good at this exercise, though normally he only needed his strong right arm for the job rather than his boot.

Following closely behind the horsemen were the wagons and the men walking beside them. Despite protests from his two sergeants, Nathan had decided to disarm his black soldiers for the march through town. No need to provoke the townspeople needlessly. He envisioned his enemies making all kinds of wild-eyed claims about him arming a slave insurrection, so they might

170

recruit more men for the fight. He truly hoped once he was clear of Lewisburg his enemies might give it up and let him leave Virginia in peace. Better not to give them any reason to do otherwise. So they'd hidden the rifles in the wagons, covered with blankets or tarps. But the men marched alongside the wagons with the rifles, ready to distribute them quickly should trouble break out.

Nathan even made Cobb dismount and walk, as William took over scouting for him. William and Georgie rode rearguard.

As they passed through the town square, Nathan felt a nervous twitch between his shoulder blades, as if someone were targeting him with a rifle from one of the surrounding buildings. But nothing happened, and no enemy was visible. In fact, they saw very few people at all, and these were women and children, or very old men. Tom turned to Nathan to mention that fact, but Nathan nodded, "Yes, I've noticed. And it makes me wonder ... *where are all the men?"*

⁖⁐⁐⁐⁐⁐⁐⁐⁐⁐

Henry had to admit the escape to freedom had been more difficult and dangerous than he'd ever imagined it would be. And not because of Margaret, as he'd earlier feared. She'd turned out to be more stout-hearted than most men he'd known. Never complaining, despite long, hot days of hiding in uncomfortable thickets, and long, hard nights of walking, and scrambling through ditches and into woods at the first sound of anyone on the road. And all this on very short rations.

No, it wasn't Margaret that was the problem; the battle that'd nearly caught them up that first night seemed to have spread. The whole countryside appeared to be roused, literally up in arms. Groups of white men with rifles, both mounted and afoot appeared everywhere on the roads, coming and going to God knows where. Henry was convinced something big was going on ... perhaps Mr. Lincoln had arrived with his soldiers? That might account for it ...

But whatever it was, it had made their situation extremely dicey. The farms they'd passed at night were on high alert; men with rifles and torches moving about at all hours, dogs constantly barking at the slightest noise, scent, or movement. So he'd been unable to obtain any food—something that should've been relatively easy. And yesterday they'd eaten the last of the food Miss Margaret had brought with her.

He could go the better part of a week with no food—he'd done it before on several occasions. On the first farm he'd worked it was a standard punishment, the master thinking it made the point without damaging his valuable property like a whipping might.

But he wasn't sure how long Miss Margaret could hold up without eating. Aside from the fact she'd never had to endure it, she was already of a very slight build, so would feel the sting of hunger quicker.

But so far, she hadn't complained, and trudged along gamely behind him on the road, mile after mile in almost complete darkness.

They'd been walking half the night when Henry suddenly came to a stop. Margaret stepped up beside him, "What is it, Henry?"

"It's the road ahead, ma'am. Look!"

She squinted ahead into the moonlit darkness, trying to see what had caught his attention. At first, she couldn't make out anything unusual. Finally, she saw it, "The road forks."

"Yes, ma'am. Which way you think we oughtta go?"

She looked from one branch to the other, "The one on the left is the main road; it's wider and looks like it's had more heavy traffic. Perhaps we should stick with that. But ..." her voice trailed off. Henry was afraid she was succumbing to her hunger and exhaustion. But then he realized she was lost in deep thought.

"Henry ... do you have any idea how many miles we've come since Lewisburg?"

"No, ma'am. I ain't never had much reason to figure exactly what a mile looked like, though I heard the white men speak of it plenty."

"Oh ... yes, of course, sorry. Let me ask it differently; how many hours you reckon we've walked, *altogether*, since we left the town."

He considered that a moment and said, "Well ... I figure we done walked most of the darkness for one whole night and parts of another. And they's about ten hours of darkness during the summertime. But we wasted several hours trying to get food, and in and out of hiding places, so ..."

"So around twelve hours, give or take," Margaret said, "and a person walks on average two miles in an hour, which would make it about twenty-four miles. Henry, I was told there was a fork in the road at around twenty-five miles from Lewisburg. This must be it."

"Well ... how about that! I guess we got this far all right."

But even before he'd finished his sentence, she grabbed his arm, "Shhh ... listen."

He did as she bid, "Horses coming along behind us. Come, Miss Margaret, let's get off the road. Only ... this time I want to stay close enough to see which way they take. And maybe see who they are, and what they's up to."

"All right ..."

After a quick look around, Henry grabbed her hand and led her at a trot toward the angle where the two roads came together. There was a large, thick bush growing there that hung down close to the roadway. They scrambled up the embankment and crawled in under the bush, facing out toward the road. The moonlight lit the roadway, so they'd be able to get a good idea of the riders' features. But it was dark enough there was little risk of them being seen where they hid under the bush.

They didn't have long to wait. In a few minutes they could clearly make out the silhouette of two riders, coming up the road. When they reached the fork they stopped, not ten feet from where Margaret and Henry crouched under the bush. One of the men reached inside his jacket for something, and there was a small flash of light. He'd struck a match and was lighting a cigar. The other pulled up next to him, and leaned over, using the match to light his cigar as well.

In the match's glow Margaret caught a glint of something shiny on the second man's chest. She recognized what it was and nearly gasped aloud—a lawman's badge! Bob had specifically

The plan had been to flank the enemy from two directions and drive them down into their own trap. The black soldiers quickly uncovered the rifles and distributed them, preparing to charge forward and seal the western entrance to the ravine, closing the trap from that end. After driving the enemy from the ridge, Jim's scouts would return to the road and block the eastern entrance, effectively trapping the enemy.

But the hillside had been steep and heavily wooded; it'd slowed the horses, preventing them from flanking the enemy. There was a brief, heavy firefight in the four places where Nathan's cavalry strove to get up and behind the enemy. But the fighting was indecisive, with neither side able to gain any real advantage amongst the thick undergrowth. Eventually the enemy fighters simply melted back into the woods. Nathan's riders returned to the roadway, having accomplished nothing more than spoiling the enemy's trap. Fortunately, there'd been no casualties; the thick woods had prevented either side from effective targeting.

The black soldiers had taken up position on the road at the entrance to the ravine, as ordered, led by Tony and Big George. But they'd never even fired a shot. None of the enemy had come down to the roadway level. When they saw their own riders returning, Tony looked over at Big George with a questioning look. But George shrugged and shook his head. He had no idea what had happened either. So they marched their men back to the wagons to await further orders.

Once they'd regrouped on the road, Nathan ordered an advance through the ravine, after deciding he'd keep the foot soldiers armed for the rest of the journey.

The riders continued to range ahead and behind, but now the trees pushed in so close to the road there was no way to effectively scout in that direction. So they had a constant fear of attack from the sides. And, sure enough, at several points along the way gunfire broke out from the surrounding woods. The Mountain Meadows freemen gamely returned fire until the cavalry showed up to rout the enemy out of their hiding places. But this occurred multiple times throughout the day, and casualties were mounting, with several more men going down wounded, even one woman who'd been walking along with the men. Thankfully no one had been killed ... so far.

It was an exhausted group that finally made camp that evening. But they got very little sleep that night. The enemy had dogged their steps all the way to their eventual campsite and continued intermittent sniper fire at the caravan throughout the night, though Nathan's people took no further casualties.

Βŋ)ĆŖℬΒŋ)ĆŖℬΒℬΒŋ)ĆŖℬ

Elijah Walters sat at the small table in his command tent. Unlike the previous camp captured by Chambers, this camp was temporary and extremely mobile. Most men simply slept out in the open with nothing more than a blanket over them, if they were lucky. They allowed no campfires so as not to give their position away to Chambers' scouts.

Walters had had his men bring along a tent, camp chair, small table, and cot so he'd at least have those minimal necessities. But despite his relative comfort, he found himself once again in a foul mood—*Chambers!* Always that damned man escaped his best laid plans. Only his own counterattack back at the tents had been successful, though he had to live with the knowledge it had worked largely because Chambers himself had been busy elsewhere at the time.

And he was sure Chambers had somehow been behind Margaret's escape, along with a handful of slaves. Much too convenient a coincidence—all his dogs suddenly sickening and dying. *Clearly, they were poisoned. Probably by his God-damned Indian! One more reason for a reckoning with Chambers and his soldiers.*

And though he'd had high hopes for the ambush along the road, it had not especially surprised him when Chambers slipped that noose as well. His men were just too good at scouting to fall for something so obvious.

The good news was, his numbers continued to swell, despite the setbacks. More men arrived every hour from the surrounding countryside, most on horseback and armed with hunting rifles, carrying their own ammunition and rations. He'd ordered the

179

word spread that a group of abolitionist sympathizers were trying to incite a slave uprising; they needed all able-bodied young men to help put it down. The fear of another Nat Turner scenario was bringing them out in droves, apparently—even those not inclined to answer the late Colonel Burns' earlier call to arms for the new Confederate Army.

Walters sat and contemplated how to make best use of this new resource. There had to be some way to effectively use it to get the best of Chambers and wipe him out once and for all.

Walters knew he now had greatly superior numbers, though his men's ability to hit a target with a rifle was suspect. He thought about Chambers' devastating use of cavalry armed with multiple revolvers, and of his surprising success at arming and training his slaves. And especially those damned bayonets! Where in hell had he got those? Hard as he thought on it, he simply could not fathom how Chambers had suddenly acquired so many military rifles. He must have secretly brought them with him when he came back from Texas.

Well, Walters had no way to obtain bayonets, but he did now have a large number of mounted men. And though there were but few pistols among them, there were plenty of rifles. Perhaps a large-scale mounted charge, using the rifles at close range. First firing off their rounds, then using rifles as bludgeons in amongst the wagons. That might do the trick. The enemy's bayonets would be of little use against men on horseback. And his greater numbers would nullify Chambers' cavalry. Especially if he instructed his mounted riflemen to target the white men first. Once the white soldiers were down the slaves would put up little resistance; of that he was certain.

The more he contemplated it, the better he liked his plan. He called for his butler, Josiah. "Go fetch Mr. Hawkins and Mr. Brandon. I wish to discuss tomorrow's battle with them."

"Yes, master, I will tell them you wish to speak with them straightaway, sir."

Walters imagined the look of fear and shock on Chambers' smug face when he saw his own death approaching in the form of

Walters' overwhelming cavalry charge. It was such a pleasant image Walters very nearly broke into a smile.

ഇ൧൹ൠ൙൹ഇ൧൹ൠ൙൹ഇ൧൹ൠ൙

It was just past noon on the following day when Zeke came riding back at a gallop from the rearguard to report to Nathan. "Captain … men approach on horseback … a large contingent."

"Large? How large?"

"We estimated … close to a hundred, sir. All have rifles. Some have pistols, too."

"A hundred, mounted?" Nathan looked at Tom who returned a very concerned look.

"Oh, and we spotted a man at their head who looks a lot like Walters, though we couldn't be sure at a distance."

"How far out are they?"

"I was to tell you they were a couple of miles out when we first saw them. That was about three miles out from here, and I came at the gallop to tell you. So … assuming they were coming at a trot, they should catch up to the wagons in about …"

He screwed up his face trying to come up with the calculation.

"About twenty-five minutes from now," Tom answered for him.

Nathan turned and looked back up the road in the direction the wagons were going. It was a long, straight stretch of road heading almost due west, with trees close on both sides.

"Tom … move the wagons to the far end of this current straight section and bring them to a halt. I want them in a square, with the wagons in front going all the way from tree line to tree line. Put all the people and livestock in the middle. Of course, with the women and children in the back row of wagons. And send for Sergeant Jim and the other scouts."

"Yes, sir!" Tom saluted, and turned his horse, trotting off toward the front of the wagon train.

"Zeke, ride back and tell the men we'll be stopping and squaring up the wagons. They can continue to shadow the approaching army from a distance, but I want everyone within the square well before the enemy arrives. Understood?"

"Yes, sir! Shadow the enemy but get back in time to come inside the square," he saluted crisply, and headed back out.

Nathan smiled. It was amazing how quickly the non-military men adopted the military mannerisms in battle. Even the black freemen were now saluting regularly.

Everyone around him was in motion, from Walters bringing a potentially overwhelming force, to Tom riding off to organize the defense, to the cattle, plodding calmly along, oblivious of anything untoward about to happen.

But Nathan sat still on Millie and thought. How best to counter Walters' superior force of men, now mounted and approaching rapidly? And with the Mountain Meadows' infantry force reduced to under fifty men through the continued attrition of the week's fighting. Thankfully, none of his experienced veteran soldiers had yet succumbed. Their superior fighting skills—and a good measure of luck, he had to admit—had kept them safe thus far. He said a quick prayer their good luck would hold.

He decided Walters would try to overrun them in one great charge. Likely his men were inexperienced, unable to hit anything when firing a rifle from the saddle. Walters would know that, so he'd want to close on them fast and have his men fire at point blank range. They were farm boys and such, so likely there were few revolvers among them. So only one shot each, then they'd be in amongst the wagons.

No bayonets ... so they'd use their rifles as clubs, swinging and battering. Not terribly effective if anyone experienced was left standing. Walters would know *that,* too. So he'd target the soldiers. Yes ... of course ... he'd order all hundred rifles to aim at the white men. No matter their courage or experience, that'd be a difficult onslaught to dodge. Hmm ... what to do?

He sat still another minute, then turned Millie and galloped past the wagon train. He wanted to speak with Jim Wiggins as soon as possible.

ಬಂಡಾಣಾಬಂಡಾಣಾಬಂಡಾಣ

"Mr. Wiggins ... how many spare rifles do we have?"

"Oh … a great pile sir, on account o' them fellows we slaughtered back on the field below Mountain Meadows. Enough for at least one spare each, and likely a few extras besides. What do you have in mind, sir?"

Nathan thought for a moment, then answered, "I want every man issued an extra rifle for the coming battle. Form up three companies of riflemen and spread the experienced hands between them. We'll need no cavalry in this battle — they'd be of little use and quickly overwhelmed by the numbers of the enemy. But have the horses saddled and ready … just in case there's a need. And make sure all officers have four pistols each, loaded and ready. Keep all our men and horses safely within the square."

"Yes, sir. Three companies of foot, and no cavalry to start, but have the horses ready for a possible sortie. And issue an extra rifle to each man and pistols to the officers. Then what, sir?"

"Mr. Wiggins … I want volley fire from the three companies. The first six volleys at ten-second intervals, taking advantage of the spare rifles. Each volley thereafter, if any … at twenty second intervals to give the first company time to reload. Tom and I will take any extra rifles and provide covering fire between volleys, taking out any enemy coming in too close. If the enemy closes on us, the officers will resort to pistols and sabers. And if the enemy breaches the wagon wall, remind the men to grab the rifles with bayonets, and attack. Even mounted foes can be taken down with a good bayonet thrust."

Jim beamed like a young child just told he'd get double the presents at Christmas. "Yes, *sir!* Volley fire from three companies, sir. And bayonets when needed! It will be even as you say!"

Stan turned to Tony, who was standing next to him, nudged him in the ribs and said, "Volley fire from companies … much fun! Great noise like cannon battery. Enemy will shit his britches and run crying to Momma," he grinned broadly, and Tony couldn't help but grin back. It *did* sound fun when Stan said it!

"And lastly, Mr. Wiggins … I'll have the first volley at two hundred-fifty yards."

Jim frowned, tipped his hat back on his head and whistled. "Two-fifty? You sure about that, sir? Cutting it pretty close, don't you think?"

Tom also looked concerned. Cavalry at a full gallop would close that distance in less than twenty seconds. They'd only get off their first two or three volleys before the enemy would be on them. Typically volley fire against a hard-charging cavalry might start at four or five-hundred yards. Sometimes further.

"Yes, Mr. Wiggins. I want those first few volleys used to good effect, taking down as many riders as possible. Most of our men aren't capable of hitting anything out any further, and I'd not waste their first two pre-loaded shots. Remember, most of the enemy are green troops, unused to taking fire. They watch a whole row of their comrades go down, I promise you they'll slow. Tell the men to always target the riders farthest out front. It'll tend to discourage anyone from spurring his horse."

"Yes, sir! Two hundred-fifty yards it shall be. And target the leaders."

ಬುಡಿದುಗಳಿಗಳುಬುಡಿಗಳಿಗಳುಬುಡಿಗಳಿಗಳ

Half the Mountain Meadows men lay under the wagons facing east. The other half were above, in the bed of the wagons, kneeling with rifles pointed out over the wood sideboards. Sergeant Jim had ordered them to use the spare rifles first, so the second rifle would be the one with the bayonet. Just in case …

The women and children huddled within and under the wagons on the far west side. They'd secured the horses and cattle tightly within the square, each animal tied to a lead affixed to a wagon. Even if incoming fire hit one or two, there'd be no chance of a stampede.

Nathan put Megs in charge of making sure the women kept their eyes open for any enemy movement out beyond the square to the west or in the woods on either side. They were to come at the run and tell him, or one of the other officers, at the first sign. He also reminded her of the small Colt revolvers he'd given her and Miss Abbey; he was pleased when she showed him they were already loaded and close to hand.

Tony lay on the ground under the wagons, his rifle out in front of him. He'd been assigned to Company A, which was positioned on the left side of the square. Half the company were in the wagon beds above, and the other half underneath.

The hulking form of Stan to his left comforted him. Though he knew a well-aimed bullet could kill even a giant like him, somehow it didn't seem possible; it gave him a confidence he'd not have had otherwise.

He tried to relax and ease up his grip on the rifle, but once again he experienced the twitchy feeling he'd had before the battle at Mountain Meadows; like bugs were crawling all over his skin.

But then he felt something bump him hard on his arm, "Hey, Tony ... relax! Enemy is still ... hmm ... six hundred yards away, maybe. Even enough time to make love to that sweet little filly you're so fond of, yes? And still have time to fight!"

Stan laughed at his own raunchy humor.

Tony smiled and shook his head. Stan was impossible to ignore or to be mad at, no matter what he said.

"Yeah ... I reckon so, Mr. Stan ... I reckon so. Though right now I'd rather be with that 'little filly' than this-here rifle."

"Ha! You say that *now* ... but wait 'til we start volley fire. Most fun man can have with britches still on!" he reached over and slapped Tony on the back before bursting into laughter, which Tony couldn't resist echoing.

They heard the Captain's voice, deep, strong and clear, coming from behind them in the middle of the "square" made by the wagons. He stood so all the people could hear him, not just the men preparing to fight. "In the good book it says, *'Be strong and of a good courage, fear not, nor be afraid of them; for the LORD thy God, He it is that doth go with thee; He will not fail thee, nor forsake thee'!*"

Tony felt a chill go through him hearing those words, as if God himself had spoken them through the Captain's mouth. He suddenly felt more alive than ever before. It occurred to him he was now a *real* man. Free to live or to die as he chose, not by another man's whims. It made him sorely want to survive this battle ... but it also inspired him to fight like a lion against those who would take everything away from him.

"Company A! Present arms!"

Tony, Stan and the men around them, immediately faced forward with their rifles held out front.

"Company A ... Aim!"

Tony looked along the sights of his rifle, pulled back the hammer, and picked out a man riding toward him.

"Company A ... Fire!"

Tony pulled the trigger. There was an immediate explosion of smoke and noise. He looked out and saw several riders tumble to the ground, causing a general disruption of the charge.

He set the rifle aside and picked up the other, already loaded. This time he would only listen and watch, as Sergeant Jim called out, *"Company B ... Present arms!"*

"Company B ... Aim."

"Company B ... Fire!"

Another loud blast of fire and smoke shook the Earth.

More men went down; their riderless horses jostling each other in confusion. He heard single rifle shots from the sides—the Captain and Sergeant Clark firing their shots between volleys, picking off anyone who tried to take the lead.

Company C fired off the third volley and another row of men went down. But now Tony saw the enemy horses were nearly upon the wagons.

"Company A ... Present."

Tony prepared to fire, expecting the order to "Aim."

But there was a loud bang and a crash. The wagon above him shook violently. He heard shouts and cursing coming from above. But he could only see dust, and the legs of horses.

"Companies will fire at will!"

Tony looked for a target, but underneath the wagon all was a swirling dust. A firm tug on his shirt at the shoulder dragged him forward. Big Stan shouted, "Come, men! We must give them bayonet!"

శ్రీఐ🙷🙵శ్రీఐ🙷🙵శ్రీఐ🙷🙵

Nathan watched with satisfaction as the first volley from nearly twenty rifles struck the enemy at a full gallop. Half a dozen riders in the front ranks fell in a tumbled chaos of horses, men and rifles. But the remaining riders hardly had time to react, and continued forward until the second volley hit them, causing another round of chaotic entanglement, human and equine.

At this point there was a definite slowing of the enemy's momentum; avoiding the fallen, and a natural hesitation from the shock of seeing one's comrades felled. This was a particular problem for green troops, and Nathan had counted on that in his strategy.

But despite this, by the time the third volley hit them, the riders were closing fast on the wagons, and their momentum continued to carry them forward. Nathan had fired off two of the three rifles he had beside him, from his position on the far-right side of the line. Tom was on the far left. They stood there to keep an eye out for any enemy attempting to flank them by working their way around through the woods.

But now Nathan knew he'd underestimated the resolve of the enemy; before Jim called out the fourth volley a wave of horses and riders crashed into the side of the wagons, nearly toppling them over. The force of the blow knocked several Mountain Meadows men backward out of the wagon beds. Now enemy soldiers were leaping from their saddles onto the wagon beds; firing off unspent rounds and battering with rifles. Jim called out for independent fire, but his words were mostly lost in the chaos of noise, dust, and gun smoke.

Nathan saw Georgie standing two wagons over to his left; backed to the edge of the wagon, facing three foes approaching him with rifle butts. Nathan grabbed his remaining loaded rifle, pulled his saber and raced across his wagon. Bracing his foot at the top of the tailgate, he leapt across to the next wagon. But even as he did so, Georgie unholstered a pistol and shot all three assailants, *bang, bang, bang!* He turned to his company and shouted, "Give 'em the bayonet, men!"

Nathan landed in the next wagon but crashed into an enemy soldier who'd also jumped in. He lost balance, hitting his head hard against the wagon bed. He'd dropped both rifle and saber in the collision.

For a moment his vision swam, an echo of the terrible blow back in Richmond. But his head cleared, and he rolled over onto his back. A rifle butt rushed toward his face.

The blow never struck, the man crying out in sudden pain. Harry the Dog had buried his teeth in the man's thigh, snarling and shaking his head. Nathan retrieved the saber and thrust upward, impaling the enemy.

He was back on his feet. His men had recovered their initial shock and were now holding their own; it was hand-to-hand combat inside the wagons. But the enemy outnumbered them. More foes were pushing forward, climbing onto the wagons.

Something caught his eye out beyond the milling mass of riders—Walters! He sat his horse well back from the action, a hundred yards away, watching the desperate fighting from a safe distance.

Well back from the hand-to-hand fighting; but easy rifle range—fool! Nathan stooped and snatched up his rifle. He cocked the hammer and checked the percussion cap—still in place. Good! Acquiring his target, he leveled the sites, aiming at Walters' head to account for the bullet's arc at that distance. He slowed his breathing and focused on keeping the rifle steady despite the chaos swirling around him. He took one more breath and held it, preparing to squeeze the trigger.

A woman's scream cut through the din like a sharp knife. He paused, listening again, but heard nothing. He re-focused on Walters, still sitting his horse; an easy target.

The scream again! He turned, looking back across the square. Four enemy fighters, rifles in hand, had jumped down from the wagons and were racing across the open square toward the women and children's wagons.

Nathan pivoted, aimed the rifle at the man in the lead, and squeezed the trigger. Not waiting for the man to fall, he dropped the rifle, reached for his pistols, aimed and fired—once, twice, three times. He paused to make sure all four bodies no longer moved. The last had fallen not ten feet from the women's wagons. *Too close!* he scolded himself. Miss Abbey stood there in the bed of a wagon, gazing toward him, the small Colt revolver gripped in her hand. Their eyes briefly met, before he turned away.

He scooped up the rifle, but realized he carried no rifle ammunition. He grabbed an ammunition bag from a fallen enemy, then stood and gazed back where Walters had been; he was gone.

Damn the ill luck!

The bulk of the enemy on horseback were now pressed up against the wagons. Some still had loaded rifles. Nathan's men in the wagons were hard-pressed. Worse yet, his men underneath the wagons were basically out of the fight, for lack of ability to target the enemy. Nathan feared the situation was about to turn deadly.

He heard a great shout coming from the left side of their wagon wall. Stan was out in front of the wagons leading a bayonet charge against the enemy. Tom was with him as well, saber drawn, as were a dozen of the black soldiers, bayonets to the fore.

Nathan saw the way to victory. He cut down another enemy soldier with his saber then turned and leapt to the ground. Now inside the square, he sprinted toward the center point of their defense line.

He stopped, cupped his hands around his mouth and shouted, *"Companies will prepare to Fix Bayonets!"*

They'd already mounted the bayonets before the battle had started, but the men would understand the meaning; he intended a bayonet charge, so get ready!

"Fix Bayonets! ... Charge!" Nathan ran for the gap between two wagons, leapt up onto the tongue of a wagon and over into the melee on the other side. His men boiled up from under the wagons and leapt down from above. He lashed out at the first rider he encountered. The man knocked the blow aside with his rifle. Nathan raised his left-hand pistol and shot him from the saddle.

A swirling chaos of dust and smoke surrounded him and a deafening roar of battle. Horsemen hemmed him in on all sides as he desperately ducked and dodged their rifle butts. But the riders began backing away from him, clearing a space. Horses pranced and hopped erratically, their riders fighting for control. Harry the Dog was in amongst them, snarling and snapping, biting legs and feet. Horses reared and screamed in fear.

Suddenly the enemy was pulling back, Nathan's own men racing after them. He stopped to catch his breath and survey the scene. The enemy was in full retreat, those unhorsed quickly dispatched with pistol or bayonet.

The Mountain Meadows foot soldiers chased the retreating riders but were soon outpaced. Nathan feared his men would become spread out and vulnerable to counterattack. So he shouted at Tom and Jim, got their attention, and they passed the order to fall back.

The Mountain Meadows fighters were soon back within the wagon square, taking up the same positions they'd held before, busily reloading. The ground in front of them was littered with dozens of bodies, men and horses. They also heard moaning and cries of pain from the wounded.

Nathan quickly located William, who was tending their wounded, as expected. He knew William would have a casualty count, which was fortunately amazingly low, considering the intensity of the fighting. They'd suffered seven wounded, but only two of those were severe. And four killed, including one white man this time, Benny, one of the original farmhands. He'd raised his head to look up from the wagon at the wrong time. Several riders shot him when they pulled up next to his wagon. But the riders paid the price for ignoring the black men and only targeting the one white; the black men in the wagon returned fire, quickly cutting them down.

The enemy, by contrast, had left dozens dead out on the road. Nathan ordered a cease fire on targeting any wounded making their way off the battlefield, or any unarmed enemy coming to carry away or assist the incapacitated.

They reorganized their companies, positioning them to repulse another enemy attack.

But in less than an hour it had become apparent to Nathan the enemy had changed his tactic, presumably deciding another head-on charge was futile. The wagons began taking incoming rifle fire. Sporadic at first, but soon regular and steady, though not volley fire. Walters was learning. If they fired their rifles all at once they'd be vulnerable to a cavalry raid from Nathan's pistol-wielding force.

And the enemy rifles were firing from cover this time, utilizing the roadway ditches, stumps, rocks, and other natural features. But they were back well over four-hundred yards, so Nathan ordered his men to keep their heads down and not return fire. There was little chance of hitting an enemy behind cover from this distance and he wanted to save ammunition. Besides, the incoming fire was wildly inaccurate, only occasionally impacting against the wooden sides of the wagons, but more typically bouncing in the dirt well short, or sailing by overhead.

He told Jim to watch for anyone approaching closer, but otherwise to hold fire. He turned from Jim, figuring he'd walk over to the other side of the square to check on the women. But then he remembered something he'd wanted to ask Jim and turned back.

"Oh, Jim … have you seen Billy? I don't recall seeing him at all during the battle."

"Well, sir, he was inside the square before the enemy's charge. But he told me he was going out into the woods to make sure they didn't try sneaking past us. He left with his bow and quiver of arrows before the enemy charged. I ain't seen him since."

"Oh … well, yes, that's Billy all right. Almost makes me feel sorry for any enemy that *did* try to creep through the woods to get at us."

"Yes, sir … reckon they'd be wearing more feathers than a goose by now."

Nathan smiled at the grim thought, "Yes … likely so. Anyway, let me know if you hear from him."

"Yes, sir."

ৡৢ৵ৣঌ৵ৡৢ৵ৣঌ৵ৡৢ৵ৣঌ৵

They did not see Billy again until nearly nightfall. Nathan had called a quick meeting of the officers, this time including Tony and Big George, to discuss the ordering of the camp for the night.

He wanted his men to get some much-needed rest. But he also wanted to maintain a high level of watchfulness throughout the night in case the enemy had any designs on a nighttime raid. And he wanted everyone back in position before first light, prepared for another major attack.

He'd also ordered there be no campfires. Their light would make his people an easy target in the dark.

He dismissed the men; but before they dispersed, Billy stepped up into the circle. No one had noticed him approach until he stood in their midst.

"Captain ... Sergeant Jim," he said, snapping a salute, which the two returned.

"Have a seat, Billy ... well-earned by now, no doubt. Tell us what you've seen today."

"No, Captain ... I'll not sit. As for what I've seen, that's why I am here. I have found the enemy's camp."

Nathan's eyes widened, "*Oh!* Good work Billy."

But Billy didn't respond to the Captain, instead turning toward Stan, "Come, Stan ... let us make them afraid of the dark."

Stan stood up, grinning brightly. He pulled his large hunting knife from the sheath at his belt and made a point of testing the razor-sharp edge with his thumb.

"I am liking your idea, Billy. I am thinking you will be making good *Russian* one day!"

Billy tilted his head, as if trying to understand what that meant, "All right, Stan ... if you say so. But seems to me I am much too *small* for a Russian."

Stan laughed and removed his gun belt, laying the pistols on the ground.

"Lead way, Billy. But I am warning you, I will try beating your count this time."

Billy had no answer for this, so turned to salute the Captain and Sergeant Jim. He trotted off into the gathering darkness, Stan following closely behind.

ഇൻഇരുഇഇൻഇരുഇഇൻഇരുഇ

"Wake up, Master, sir! I's sorry to bother your repose, but you'll be wanting to know about this, sir."

"What?! What is it, Josiah? What the devil is so important to wake me at such an early hour? And what time is it, anyway?"

"Oh, an hour or more past dawn, I reckon, master. I come because the men are fixin' to leave."

"Leave? Which men?"

"Lots of 'em, sir. Maybe all. Saddling horses and saying they's going back home, sir. Thought you'd be wanting to know."

"Going home? We'll see about that. Hand me my britches and jacket. And where are my boots?"

Walters was soon striding across the camp to find Hawkins and Brandon. There'd been no formal command structure since the untimely demise of the *official* Confederate officer, Colonel Burns back at the battle below Mountain Meadows. So Walters had taken the mantle of de facto commander. John Hawkins and Will Brandon, local farmers who'd each recruited numerous men to the cause, served as his lieutenants.

He found Hawkins, who was busily saddling his own horse.

"Hawkins ... what the devil is going on?"

"We're leaving, that's what."

"Leaving ... why? And what about Chambers and his insurrection?"

"The *why* is the men have had enough. If we try to make them stay another day, there'll be a mutiny. Bad enough all the men killed and wounded in the fight yesterday, but after what happened last night! Even I'm feeling too twitchy to sit still."

"Last night? What happened last night?"

"You haven't heard? Oh ... *I see.*"

Hawkins stopped what he was doing and sat down heavily on a nearby stump with a heavy sigh.

"All was well up to the last changing of the guard in the predawn early morning hours. And nobody realized anything untoward had happened until first light this morning. But then they began discovering ... the sentries ... killed dead; all covered in blood. Their throats slit or stabbed in the heart; and nobody'd heard a peep all night."

"How many of the sentries?"

"All of them. Eighteen in total; and they'd even been paired up this time! But it gets worse ... and this is the part that has unnerved the men and triggered the mass exodus; they got Sam Wilson."

"Sam Wilson ... who's he?"

"It ain't so important *who* he is ... or *was*, but rather *where* he was sleeping. Sam was sleeping under a blanket in the very center of camp, in the middle of a row of six men. They found him in the morning stone cold dead ... with an Indian arrow stuck clean through his heart. And he'd never got out of his bedroll! Whoever done it, hadn't shot it from a bow, but rather rammed it into him with his fist, standing right over him! And no one heard a blessed thing nor woke up!"

"Chambers' damned Indian!"

"Well, damned or not, nobody wants no more of him. A man can walk right into the middle of camp like that and kill a fellow without nobody hearing a thing ... gives you the chills, it does! It means none of us is safe nowhere, never! And as for Chambers, he can go on to the north, or out west if he pleases. And he can take all his feisty damned slaves with him ... and his fucking Indian, I no longer care! Good riddance, I say!"

Walters fumed as he strode back to his tent, "This isn't over yet, Chambers!"

ಬಂಬಂಡಿ ಬಂಡಿ ಬಂಬಂಡಿ

Margaret flinched at a sudden noise behind them on the road. She looked back over her shoulder and saw two riders trotting up the road toward them. Henry also saw them. He grabbed her hand, and they ran to the side of the road and dived under a bush. There they laid still, praying they'd not been seen.

She knew they'd pushed their luck too far this time, staying on the road until after daylight, though it was only a few minutes past dawn.

They'd heard gunshots in the distance the day before—many gunshots off and on for hours as if a great battle were taking place only a few miles away. It had lasted until nearly dark.

They'd walked hard all night and on into the early morning hours, barely pausing to rest. They wanted to get as far away as possible from ... *whatever* it was ... before finding a hiding place for the day.

She held still as the sound of the riders came ever closer until they were right next to them on the road.

The riders continued past, and she let out the breath she hadn't realized she'd been holding. Henry scrambled forward a few feet and looked out. In a moment he slid back down beside her. "Them same two lawmen," he said.

"You sure?"

"Yep, it's them all right. But they was ahead of us on the road. Can't figure how we got ahead of them."

"They must have gotten tired of riding all night and camped somewhere, so we passed them by in the dark."

"Yeah ... I reckon that makes sense."

Margaret slowly removed her hand from her pocket where she'd been nervously grasping the handle of the pistol. Her right hand was soaked in sweat so she wiped it on her skirts, then let out a deep sigh and climbed back up onto the roadway with Henry.

They stood up on the road looking north in the direction the riders had gone. Henry said, "That was as close a thing as I want to risk, Miss Margaret. We best be gettin' under cover."

They started walking again, but this time looking in earnest for a good place to hide for the day. After the fear and tension of the near-disastrous brush with the lawmen had subsided, the full force of exhaustion and hunger hit Margaret. It'd been building for several days, and now she realized she couldn't go much further without a long rest, food, and water.

They finally settled on a grassy hillside next to the road. It was dry, and the grass was soft to lie on. There were also tall bushes growing between the hillside and the ditch next to the road. So they'd be hidden from anyone passing by but could still look out between the branches and watch out for anything unusual. After the battle sounds of the previous day, they were fearful of getting caught in the middle of some momentous event over which they had no control.

They lay down, side by side, though not quite touching, on the grassy hill. Although Henry also felt bone-weary from the travel, he was determined not to fall asleep yet. He gazed up into the blue sky and watched a few sparse, fluffy clouds float by. It was not yet hot, but very pleasant in the sunshine. Later in the day they'd be forced under the shade, but now it felt very comfortable. As he watched the clouds, he thought of his wife once again, for the thousand-thousandth time. But this time it was somehow different from before. Being with Margaret had made him sure the things he'd heard about Northerners were likely true—that they didn't think of black men only as slaves, and that they might willingly help him. Anyway, it no longer felt like such a hopeless dream, as if maybe … if he could only survive these travels without getting caught, there might be a way …

And he now had Miss Margaret to help him. She was an amazing contradiction to him: a high-class Southern woman who was smart and resourceful, but also saw him as a fellow human being and treated him as such. It had never occurred to him there could be such a person, but there she was. And after hearing her story, as they walked for seemingly endless miles, he'd developed a great deal of respect for her. At the same time, his loathing for Walters had increased, if such a thing were possible.

He lay there, lost in thought until he realized Margaret was now fast asleep, making soft breathing noises. He reminisced about lying next to his wife at night, hearing those same soft sounds coming from her. *No time for that now, Henry*, he scolded himself. He carefully rose to his feet, peering out along the road in both ways before quietly moving off into the woods.

His stomach was growling, and he had a mind to find something for them to eat before he had his rest. Probably too early in the year for any berries, but he thought he might try downing a rabbit or a squirrel with a stone. He also had hopes of locating a stream or pond so he could refill their small water bottle. They'd drained the last drop before heading out on last night's walk, and his throat felt cracky-dry. He could imagine

Miss Margaret was suffering it even more, but she'd never once complained. And if there was a stream, there was always the possibility of catching a small fish or two, though he had only his bare hands to do it with.

He walked through the woods for more than an hour. He was careful to keep track of his direction and to note any landmarks, such as odd-looking trees or rock outcroppings, so he could find his way back. And though he'd not found any water, he found a small meadow with fresh rabbit droppings. So after gathering a small pile of egg-sized rocks, he sat behind a bush and waited for any rabbits that might come grazing. It'd be a more difficult throw with the shackles and their broken chain still attached to his wrists, but he reckoned he could still do it, having practiced a few throws with reasonably good accuracy.

He sat still for a half-hour or more with no sign of his intended prey. The sun beating on his back was warming. He started to nod off, his head dipping down to his chest before he'd catch himself, shake his head, and fight to focus and stay awake. But it was becoming more and more difficult as time went by with no movement in front of him, and the day becoming warmer and warmer.

Something woke him with a start. What had it been? He looked out at the meadow, but still no rabbits. He listened for what may have startled him out of his half-asleep state. For a minute he heard nothing ... there it was again! A high-pitched squealing ... or rather ... a squeaking sound. Like ... like a wagon wheel. He stood and looked back toward the road. Now he heard it clear — wagons back on the road. And ... human voices shouting. A large caravan coming along the road.

His eyes widened, *Oh! Miss Margaret! Stay still; I'm coming ...* He dropped the rock he'd been holding and sprinted back in the direction he'd come. He kept enough presence of mind to pay attention to the landmarks he'd memorized so he'd not miss his way. Looking up at the sun he realized his path hadn't led him straight away from the road, but rather more parallel to it, in a southerly direction only a few yards away from the road. That was why he'd been able to hear the wagons. If he ran hard enough, he might get back to where Margaret was before the wagons did. The last thing they needed was for her to be startled awake and sit up right where someone would see her!

He pushed himself to greater speed, his recent lethargy, hunger, and thirst momentarily forgotten. He slowed as he came closer to the place where the woods ended, and the grassy hill began. No good ruining everything by running out into the open as the wagons were passing. He crept to the edge of the clearing and looked out. No wagons on the roadway. He listened but heard nothing. So he decided to chance it and ran as fast as he could down the slope toward where he'd left Margaret. As he ran, he looked back along the road to the south, fearing to see wagons coming toward him. To his relief, he made it back to their hiding place and ducked behind the bushes in the tall grass. Still no sign of movement along the road.

But when he looked down, he suffered a terrible shock! Margaret was gone!

ℰℴℭℬℰℴℭℬℰℴℭℬℰℴℭℬ

Evelyn was in the basement with her head-assistant, Jacob Taylor, one of Jonathan Hughes' men, and Hal Foster, a conductor on the Underground Railroad, both white men. Hal had brought in eleven black 'passengers': six men, three women and two children—a boy and a girl aged eight and ten.

She'd finished welcoming them to the 'station', and had settled them onto mats on the floor, letting them get comfortable and rest a bit after their long walk. She was about to explain what to expect next when they heard a loud noise, like something heavy dropping on the floor somewhere down the hall. The sound was loud enough it nearly made her jump.

She looked at Jacob, but he shrugged, "I'll go see what it was, Miss Eve. Likely the cat knocked a jar off one of the shelves back in the basement."

"Thank you, Jacob."

He opened the door to the hallway, peered out for a moment, and stepped out, quietly closing the door behind him.

Evelyn had turned back toward her guests when the door opened again. Surprised by his sudden return, she turned around, "Jacob, what ..."

But Jacob entered the room with his hands held in the air, head high, and his eyes wide with fear. Two strangers came in after him. Each held a revolver, and the one on the right pointed his in the general direction of Evelyn and Hal.

"Don't nobody move," the one pointing the pistol at her said. He had dark hair and a neatly trimmed beard. The other had long reddish hair and a mustache. Both appeared to be in their mid-thirties or early forties and dressed in very business-like gray suits and hats.

There was a sudden silence in the room. The slaves slid back against the wall. Evelyn and Hal raised their hands and backed away.

"Who are you, and what do you want?" she demanded, trying to sound brave and in charge. "How dare you come bursting into my home and place of business, pointing weapons! You gentlemen don't *look* like common thieves."

"That last part is the only truthful thing you've said," the one on the left said with a scowl. "We know what sort of 'business' you're up to, and we're here to put a stop to it. We're officers of the law, of the Commonwealth of Virginia."

"I ... don't know what you're implying. I run a business to train slaves ... for a fee, of course, that they might learn to be proper household servants, in the traditional, formal style."

But even as she'd said it, she knew it wasn't convincing.

"What a load of horse manure. These ain't no house servants— they're runaways. And this ain't no business, it's a damned house of slave thievery. What y'all euphemistically call 'Underground Railroad'. We followed one of your damned spies to a meeting today. And then we followed you from that meeting to this house. We sat out back and watched this fellow here," he pointed his pistol at Hal, "bring them-there slaves into this house by the back-basement door. What do you have to say to that, little sassy miss?"

Evelyn could think of nothing to say, so she said nothing. But her mind was reeling; how to get out of this predicament? Of all the talks she'd had with Jonathan and Angeline they'd never discussed what to do in this scenario. But … maybe they *should* have, she now decided, a bit too late.

"Well, Phil, reckon we can't go hanging nor even beating no upper-class white woman, nor her white servants—regardless of what kind of black's whore she *really* is."

He sneered at her, but she decided not to give him the satisfaction of a response, though she gave him a glare that could melt wax.

"No … that's true, but nobody said we couldn't make an example of one of these-here runaways. What say *you*, Bertram?"

"I say 'yes' to that."

"What're y'all talking about?" Evelyn asked, a panic rising in her.

"I'll answer no more questions from you, *whore!* Get over against the wall. Nobody moves, or I put a bullet in him, understand?" the one named Phil waved his pistol at the slaves. They nodded their heads in agreement, eyes wide with fear.

Bertram walked over to one man, pointed a revolver at his face, and said, "Stand up."

The man slowly stood, holding his hands up at head level.

"Put your hands together."

The man did as he was told, fear growing on his face. Beads of sweat ran down the sides of his face. Evelyn heard a woman sob softly.

Bertram reached out with his left hand and looped a thick leather strap around both wrists, pulling it tight with a jerk. The bound man flinched in pain. Then Bertram took two steps backward, still eyeing the slave and threatening him with the pistol. He flipped the other end of the strap around a heavy wooden beam in the ceiling and started to pull. The slave's hands were soon over his head. But Bertram continued to pull until the man's feet were barely touching the ground with his toes and finally dangling clear. He groaned from the pain in his wrists, now bearing the weight of his body by the leather strap digging into his skin.

Bertram holstered his pistol, grabbed the strap up high with his right hand, and flipped it up over the beam again with his left. He repeated the maneuver several times until the leather strap had wrapped around the beam a half-dozen or more times—the weight of the man's body, and the roughness of the beam, now holding it firmly in place. He stepped back and smiled at his handiwork.

Bertram looked over at his partner and said, "Phil ... I'll allow you the honors, this time." He made a bow, offering up the bound man to his partner.

Evelyn gasped as the man named Phil pulled a large hunting knife from a sheath at his belt, smiled wickedly and said, "It'd be my pleasure, Bert."

♏♏♏♏♏♏♏♏♏♏

Henry fought to suppress a rising panic. Where could Margaret have gone? He looked back up the grassy hill ... had she awakened, noticed he was gone, and tried to follow? He only saw one track through the grass, the one he'd come and gone using. But if she were trying to follow him, she'd have surely gone the same way, following his trail in the grass.

He looked around on the ground for any other signs. The grass was matted down where they'd laid in the early morning sun. He looked beyond that toward the bushes, and further off to the north toward the line of trees a few dozen yards away. No sign of her.

He sat still, calming himself, trying to think. What to do ... where to look? He had about decided she must have gone after him up the hill when he heard a faint, but familiar sound. The soft sound of steady breathing. He turned back toward the bushes, crawled forward, and pulled back some branches. It took his eyes a moment to adjust to the darkness in the shade, and ... there she was!

Curled up in a ball under the bushes. And still sound asleep. Probably got hot as the day warmed and crawled into the cooler shade. He sat back and breathed a heavy sigh of relief.

He considered his own reaction to the incident. Only a few days ago he didn't even know her, and now ... he was worried sick when he thought she'd wandered off alone. The world was a strange place, he decided. And even as he was thinking those thoughts, he heard noises over on the road.

He slowly sat up and peered through the bushes toward the road. A wagon drawn by a single horse was followed by another, and another. Some carried mostly baggage, but others contained black women and children—a slave caravan. Two white men came trotting by on horseback, moving faster than the wagons, ranging out ahead and to the sides, looking into the bushes and trees at the sides of the road. They had pistols strapped to their sides. One looked right at him and rode in his direction. For a moment he thought he'd been spotted, but he stayed perfectly still without moving. The man pulled up short and turned away, barely giving his bush a second glance.

He watched several more wagons roll by. Then he witnessed a sight he had not expected, a thing he had never seen before nor ever imagined: a whole row of black men marching along ... with rifles slung on their backs! And not only that—there was something odd about these rifles; they appeared to have a pointy metal stick coming out the end, like the needle one used to mend worn clothes, only big enough for a giant. What in the world?

He couldn't fathom why white men would give black men rifles. And further, why black men wouldn't just turn around and use them on their masters and run off. It was puzzling, and troubling at the same time. Was it possible to convince slaves to fight against Mr. Lincoln and the Northerners who only wanted to free them? Would anyone do such a thing? But then he recalled how downtrodden and afraid the slaves had been back at Walters Farm. They'd likely do anything he ordered out of pure fear.

He decided these men must be like that, doing as they were told and just pure afraid to do anything other. And yet ... when he looked at their faces as they marched past ... something didn't fit. Somehow, they didn't *look* afraid ... in fact they actually looked ... *happy*? It was puzzling. He couldn't figure out what it meant, no matter how hard he pondered it.

But finally, he decided it didn't matter. They'd soon be gone on their way, and he and Margaret would get their much-needed rest—unfortunately, with no food nor water. He sat back and groaned, a sudden pang reminding him of his empty stomach.

Henry gazed up at the sky for a moment, then back toward the road. He was surprised to find Miss Margaret sitting up and gazing through the bushes at the wagon train. She looked back at him.

"Slavers ... with a whole lot of slaves," she said in a soft voice, almost a whisper so they'd not hear her over on the road. "Wonder why they're heading north? So odd ... seems like Mr. Lincoln's already sent his troops down south to fight and has got everything stirred up. Wonder where they intend to go?"

Henry looked at her and shrugged. He hadn't been able to puzzle it out either. Margaret turned back toward the road and continued to watch. The wagon train was coming to an end, the last wagon now rolling past. And, to add to the oddness of the whole incident, the last wagon bed was filled with women. One high-class-looking white woman and the rest black women. And they were chatting and laughing genially, like they were all sisters or something. It was a very odd conclusion to a very odd event. Likely a mystery they'd never solve.

Henry continued to watch. The white woman laughed, long and hard, apparently at something funny one of the black women had said. She leaned her head back and seemingly looked straight at him and Margaret. She wore a broad-brimmed straw hat tied on with a sash, her long blond hair flowing out from underneath, braided and neatly tied off with ribbons.

But as he was thinking these trivial thoughts, he heard a gasp of shock from Margaret. "Oh! *Oh! Oh, my God!* It's her ... it's *her!*"

"Her? Her, who?" he asked.

The wagon rolled off down the road, fading out of sight around a sharp bend, just past their grassy hill.

"It's Abigail ... Miss Abbey! Oh my God, Henry ... I must go ... I must go to her," she screamed, and started to scramble to her feet. But Henry grabbed hold of her arm, thinking her exhaustion had finally overcome her senses.

"No! Wait … they'll see you Miss Margaret … the slavers … they'll catch you. Stay low, be quiet now 'til they're all the way gone, don't stand up …"

"You don't understand, Henry … she will *save* us … I must go to her!"

She yanked her arm from his grasp with a sudden strength he never imagined she had. But her sudden release from his grip caused her to slip and fall, hitting her head hard on the ground. For a moment she lay still and didn't move. He feared she'd injured herself.

"You all right, Miss Margaret? Stay still a spell and make sure you ain't hurt or something."

But she gazed at him with a confused, bleary-eyed look on her face and said, "No, Henry, you don't understand. She's my friend. I don't know why she's here, but she will help us. We must go to her!"

She pulled herself once more to her feet, pushed her way through the thick bushes down into the ditch beside the roadway, and scrambled up onto the road.

Henry thought she must be delusional from the heat, hunger, and thirst, and from being sleepy and afraid. But he decided if he tried to stop her it'd only be a fight. And likely the wagons were too far gone by now anyway.

Once Margaret reached the road she began to run. She ran as hard as she could, as fast as her legs would carry her. She thought she had never run so fast before and yet … yet she seemed to be moving ever more slowly, as in a bad dream.

And her legs began to feel leaden … like she could barely move them. She was weak from hunger and thirst and long days of walking, and she could not possibly run any farther. So she stopped, and took a few deep breaths to get her wind. Then she screamed. She screamed more loudly than she'd ever screamed before in her life, "Miss Abbey! Miss Abbey! Please come back! Please come back! Miss Abbey … oh, Miss Abbey … Miss—"

And then she was on the ground, sitting in the road, and she realized she could no longer stand, or move, or scream. She was entirely out of energy and breath. There was nothing more left in her.

Then Henry was there, standing above her, gazing down. He put his hands on his knees, a short length of chain dangling from the shackles still encircling his wrists, sweat dripping from the chains. He too gasped for breath.

"Oh, Lordie, Miss Margaret! I never dreamed a woman could run so fast! It was more'n I could do to catch up to you!"

He stood next to her, breathing hard for a few more moments, "I's afraid they're gone, ma'am. Best we get back under cover and get some rest before someone else comes along the road."

Margaret heard the words, and she knew they made sense, but she couldn't think how to respond or comply. She was utterly drained. Hungry, thirsty, exhausted, and now hopeless. She'd just sink into a deep despair and never get up again.

God had placed Miss Abbey right where they needed her, but they'd missed her. They'd missed her by only a few moments, after all this time! It was so thoroughly, mind-numbingly tragic she could scarcely think or move.

"Come, Miss Margaret … we got's to go."

"No, Henry. I'm tired … can't go any further. I'm … *done.* Go on without me. I'll just lie down here … in the road and … come what may …"

Henry gazed along the road for a long moment. Then he sat next to her and put his arm around her shoulder. "Well, I reckon we're in this together now, Miss Margaret. So if you stays here … well, then I figure I just stays here too."

She hadn't the energy or the clarity of mind to argue. So she sat in the middle of the road, his strong arm around her, her mind a sparkling, swirling mist of smoke and color from pure exhaustion. But as her mind began to sink into a deep darkness, she noticed his arm around her felt warm and comforting.

Chapter 8. Exodus

"I am the LORD thy God,
which have brought thee ...
out of the house of bondage."
– Exodus 20:2

Thursday May 30, 1861 – Richmond, Virginia:

The man named Phil stepped forward, a large knife in his hand. He waved it threateningly at the slaves in the room, intending to terrorize them. But in that instant Evelyn realized he had absent-mindedly holstered his pistol to better handle the knife. Further ... the one named Bert had forgotten to unholster his after securing the poor unfortunate slave to the ceiling beam and giving him over to Phil. And the one with the knife now stood with his back toward Evelyn ...

Evelyn lunged forward and reached around to Phil's right hip, yanking the revolver from its holster. She stepped back and cocked the hammer. She meant to force the men to lay down their weapons.

"Hey! What the ..." Phil spun around, still brandishing the knife, and took a step toward her. "Give me that, *whore*, or I'll—"

Evelyn pulled the trigger. An ear-pounding noise and concussion shook the small room. Gun smoke swirled in the air. Phil's eyes widened with shock and pain, then glazed over. He slumped to the floor. The forgotten knife clattered across the room.

The other man, Bertram, stared at the scene in disbelief. It'd happened so quickly he'd not had time to react. But now he looked over at Evelyn, his face screwed up in anger. He reached for his pistol, "Why ... you *bitch!* You've shot him, you stupid, fucking whore—"

Evelyn turned the gun toward him, re-cocked the hammer, and pulled the trigger, *boom!* The bullet caught him mid-chest even as his pistol cleared its holster. He gasped and clutched at his heart. Blood oozed out from his fingers. He tried to raise the pistol, but his arm no longer obeyed his mind. He pulled the trigger, and it discharged harmlessly into the floorboards. He too collapsed in a heap and lay still.

For a moment nobody moved. Nobody spoke. In the silence, gun smoke wafted up toward the ceiling.

Evelyn stood still where she was, staring down at the slain men, a blank expression on her face.

Jacob stepped up to her and reached out to grasp the revolver from her hand, "I'll take care of that now, Miss Eve ..."

But the sound of his voice seemed to snap her from her reverie. She met eyes with him before snatching the pistol out of his reach. "Nonsense, Jacob! My father wished for a boy; he taught me to shoot when I was barely old enough to walk. I can handle a gun better than most men ..." but then her stern look softened. She teared up, "Only ... I never *killed* anyone before ..."

Jacob gazed at her with sympathy ... and new respect. He stepped back, no longer trying to disarm her. "Yes, ma'am. Not many have. I've certainly never done it, thank the Lord."

Jacob and Hal hurried over to help the slave down from where he still hung, using the dead man's knife to cut the leather strap. He thanked them profusely, while trying to rub the circulation back into his poor hands. A woman came over and embraced him, sobbing. He returned the embrace, murmuring he would be all right.

Jacob looked over at the strangers, lifeless and bloody on the floor, "What now, Miss Eve?"

She considered for a moment. "We must hide all evidence of their being here. From what they were saying it seems they followed me straight here and never had time to report their whereabouts to any of their associates. So likely no one but us knows they came here.

"Jacob ... we must make sure it *stays* that way. Carry their bodies deep into the woods. *Carry* I say ... don't drag them—it'll leave a trail. And have someone walk behind and clean away any telltale blood that may drop. Bury them deep and cover them with rocks that no animal may unearth them and ... separately, well apart—ideally in completely different directions. Disguise the graves with turves, leaves, branches … anything to make the earth appear undisturbed. Be sure to bury everything they brought with them … the knife … this gun … oh, and the leather strap!"

"Yes, ma'am."

"And we must clean this room. Scrub away every trace of blood, but then … dirty it again … with ordinary type clutter, such as people might bring in from outdoors on their shoes—nothing too obvious, though—no mud splatter. Do you understand?"

"Yes … I think I'm getting the picture; make it look as if nothing at all has happened here. Anything else?"

"Yes …" and she stepped over in front of the slaves, now huddled back to the side of the room furthest from where the dead bodies lay. "I'm sorry, but y'all have seen what happened here. So it's no longer safe to stay in this house. Others may come. I must ask you to help bury these … *men* and clean up this mess. And after … I'm very sorry, but you must leave tonight and travel to the next station. Hal, you must lead them again, though you're doubtless already weary."

He nodded, "Yes, ma'am. I understand."

"I know y'all are tired and … oh, *hungry*, no doubt—we *will* get you something to eat before you depart! I'm really sorry, especially for you children, but your travels are not yet over this night."

She and Jacob stepped over to the door, "Jacob, once they're gone we must leave this place. Lock it up and not come back until … well, we'll have to wait and see if it is *ever* safe again. Report back to The Employer. He'll tell you what to do next. I shall do the same."

She turned and looked over the room one last time. Something was nagging her … like she was forgetting something … some last piece of evidence. But she could think of nothing, and shrugged, turning back toward the door.

Then it hit her, "The bullet hole!"

"Bullet hole, ma'am?"

"Yes … after I shot the second man, he fired his revolver into the floor. Jacob, you must find that hole and plug it with an old piece of wood or stick … make it appear as a knot in the wood."

Jacob smiled at her and shook his head, "You are a *wonder*, Miss Eve. It shall be done, even as you say."

She took one last look around the room, noting everyone already in motion, busy carrying out her commands.

Gazing at the dead men on the floor, she thought about how they'd come here to torture and murder an innocent man. She alone had stopped them from doing it. *THIS is who I am!* the tiny voice in the back of her mind said, emphatically. And for once, she agreed.

ℴℴℴℴℴℴℴℴ

"Somebody comes, Miss Margaret," Henry said, again trying to rouse her and get her moving off the roadway. "Two horsemen, from the North."

"It's those wicked lawmen, Henry. You go on, now," she whispered. But there was no energy nor conviction behind the words. So Henry just continued to sit next to her with his arm around her.

Then a small spark of spirit inside her awakened, and she thought, *It's not fair … not for Henry! I'm done, but he's still strong, and they'll put him back in chains, and take him back to Walters and then …*

So she pulled the pistol from her pocket, cocked the hammer, and waved it unsteadily at the riders who'd come to a stop in front of them.

"Don't come any closer. I have a loaded pistol and … *and …*" she knew there was more she was supposed to say, but just now the words wouldn't come to her.

"There'll be no need of that, Miss. We'll not harm you—either of you. Just lay that pistol down on the roadway and all will be well."

No … don't give in, her heart said to her, but her mind argued, saying, *What's the use, anyway? They're bigger and stronger, and they have guns too. And besides … don't I know that voice?*

The last of her strength gave out. The gun slipped from her grasp onto the road beside her, and she leaned heavily into Henry.

She looked up at the man on the horse, but her vision was blurry from crying, so she couldn't see him clearly.

But when the rider saw her face, he gasped, "Oh, my good Lord! *I don't believe it!*"

And then he was kneeling on the ground beside her, steadying her head with his hand and holding a metal canteen to her lips. "Drink, you'll feel better …" he said, and his voice was both forceful and kindly at the same time.

She drank, and it tasted like the sweetest wine she'd ever had, though on any other day she'd have thought the water warm and stale. She drank deeply and gratefully. But then she thought of Henry—surely as thirsty as she. So she pushed the bottle away, intending to give him a drink. But when she looked over, she saw the other horseman had also dismounted, and had handed his canteen to Henry, who was already drinking from it.

She gazed at the man who'd given her water. Concern furrowed his brow, though it was a handsome face—lean but strong, with dark hair and dark eyes and … and … so *familiar* somehow. He smiled, and it hit her, and she gasped, "Why … *Mr. Chambers!* It's *you!*"

He laughed, "Yes, it's me. And thank God I have found you at last! In all this darkness, death and chaos, you are a sparkling ray of sunshine! *Praise God from whom all blessings flow!*" and then he wrapped his arms around her and hugged her, and she hugged him back with all her remaining strength.

And when he pulled away, she saw there were tears in his eyes. He looked over at the other man, who was gazing at the two of them with obvious curiosity.

"Tom Clark, I'd like you to meet … *Miss Margaret!*"

"*Oh!* Oh, my *goodness!* It's such a joy and pleasure to finally meet you, Miss Margaret! And may I say—unless I'm sorely mistaken—you are the world's greatest prison escapist, and the world's *worst* poet … all in one! Well met, indeed, ma'am!" he tipped his hat to her and smiled.

She laughed, for the first time since she could remember. "Thank you, sir ... and the pleasure is all mine, I'm sure. So ... I take it you received my little attempt at poetry, Mr. Clark?"

"Oh, yes ... in fact, I helped de-cipher the message hidden inside your *thoroughly awful* poem!"

She smiled and shook her head in amusement, some life coming back into her.

But Nathan added in a more serious tone, "Your cipher saved countless lives, Miss Margaret. We are eternally grateful."

"Oh, I'm so happy it helped, and y'all are safe."

"Likewise, Miss Margaret, likewise! We've been worried sick about you for the longest time now. When things finally came to a head, we rode to Walters' house for a final reckoning with him, and to get you out of there at last. But he was already gone when we arrived.

"And then I discovered, to my dismay, you had finally made good your escape. And only just the night before we arrived! Tom can tell you I was fairly fit to be tied. We tore the place apart looking for you!

But now you're here, and safe! I can hardly wait to hear the tale of how you accomplished it."

"Well ... in the end I needed help ... from two good men," she looked over at Henry again and smiled. "And somehow God provided them, or I'm sure I should no longer be among the living. I shall happily tell you the whole tale ... but perhaps later ... after I've had a rest."

"Of course! Certainly, my dear! There will be plenty of time for telling tales. We may even have a few of our own," he looked over again at Tom and smiled. Tom rolled his eyes and shook his head in response.

"But, tell me, Mr. Chambers ... I'd thought your wagons had all passed by. I never saw you, but I saw a white woman, riding in the last wagon. I thought it was Miss Abbey, so I ran, and I screamed her name, but she never heard me."

"Not so, my dear ... and it *was* her in that last wagon. She'd given up her carriage to two of the free women with young babes in arms, so they'd have shade from the hot sun. She was riding in the wagon with some other women. And she did in fact hear you, though she didn't know who it was, and doubted her own ears. She sent for me and said she thought she'd heard a woman's voice calling her name. So Tom and I rode back to investigate. And here we are and, here *you* are!

Come, I'll take you to the wagons now and you can see her yourself."

"No."

"No?"

"Not without Henry. We go together, or not at all."

Henry looked over at her and smiled warmly.

Nathan looked over at Tom, who shrugged, an amused look on his face.

"Well, it's one thing to bring *you* along, Miss Margaret. But Henry here … he's a runaway, and we'll be breaking the law taking him, even up North where we're going."

"I no longer care about such laws, Mr. Chambers."

He looked at her another moment, then over at Henry, who shrugged his shoulders.

"Tom … let me ask you a hypothetical question. What with so many freemen in our company, if a runaway slave were to … *secretly* … hide himself among them … well, do you figure anyone could blame us for not noticing? Especially with all the chaos and upheaval that's been going on lately?"

"No, sir. I reckon nobody ought to blame us for that. A man could hardly be expected to notice such a thing … under the circumstances."

They exchanged a smile, and Margaret realized they'd had no intention of leaving Henry behind — she'd been speaking foolishly. Mr. Chambers was not *that* kind of man, which she would have remembered if she'd been herself and thinking more clearly. But Henry smiled at her appreciatively, so perhaps it hadn't been so foolish after all.

She had another sip of Mr. Chambers' canteen, after which he re-stoppered it and returned it to its place hanging on his saddle. Next thing she knew, he'd scooped her up off the ground in his strong arms as if she were a small child. He set her up on the horse in front of the saddle horn.

"Hang on tight there for a moment, Miss Margaret."

She grabbed two fistfuls of the horse's mane, held on tight, and closed her eyes so she'd not have to look down. In an instant he was there with her on the horse and had wrapped an arm around her waist. So she relaxed, and leaned back against him. His sudden, indominable presence, strong and warm against her back, was a glorious feeling. For the first time in months, she felt truly safe and without fear.

She looked over and saw Tom giving Henry a hand up onto the horse behind him, telling him to hold on. Soon they were trotting off down the road, and she thought how wonderful it was to be moving for once without having to walk on her own two feet!

She was startled to see a large animal trotting along next to Nathan's horse. "My *word*, Mr. Chambers ... what kind of hound is that?"

He chuckled, "The very *large* kind."

"Well, that I can clearly see."

"But he is also fiercely loyal to me, for reasons known only to himself. In fact, he has saved my life—two times now, the latest only yesterday."

"Well! I can see there certainly are a lot of tales to catch up on. And if he has indeed saved you, I shall treat him with the proper deference afforded a hero."

Nathan laughed, "I'm sure he'll appreciate that."

᷂᷅᷀ᴥ᷂᷅᷀ᴥᴥ

It was a very happy reunion with Miss Abbey as well, who greeted her with such warmth and enthusiastic affection that Margaret was soon crying like a baby. And Miss Abbey insisted she eat and drink until she was about to burst.

After that, she lay down on a blanket in the wagon, her head in Miss Abbey's lap. She slept for several hours while Abbey sang to her softly, stroking her head and straightening her tangled hair.

It was now late afternoon and Margaret was again awake. They'd been talking for many miles, catching up on all that'd happened in the long months since they'd last met on the veranda at Mountain Meadows. Margaret was wide-eyed with amazement at the adventures Nathan had been through on his trip to Richmond and back, and the battles he had subsequently fought. And Abbey's brow furrowed in righteous anger when Margaret described how Walters had planned to murder her, if Bob hadn't helped her escape.

"That despicable man! I only wish my Nathan *had* killed him! *Oh!* I'm sorry … that was most un-Christian and unladylike of me."

"Oh no, Miss Abbey … I wish he'd done it too!" they exchanged a laugh and a warm smile.

Later the talk came around to Margaret's parents and what her father had told Nathan when they'd met. Miss Abbey wanted to spare her the unpleasant details, but Margaret insisted on the truth, no matter how painful. So Abbey told her everything Nathan had related about the disappointing and nearly violent meeting with her father, after which Margaret was quiet and thoughtful for a long time.

Abbey saw Margaret had a wateriness to her eyes, though she kept the tears from flowing, "I'm … not surprised, I'm sorry to say. I'd hoped and prayed I was wrong, but in my heart of hearts I knew it was so. And Momma is little better — she'll never stand up for me against him."

She was quiet again for a long time. So Abbey sat with her, and held her hand, allowing her to deal with the anguish in her own way.

Finally, Margaret looked over at her, they met eyes, and the tears began flowing in earnest. She sobbed, "Oh … Miss Abbey … I am … so *lost* … so *alone* … I feel … I no longer have a family." She cried with deep sobs, and Miss Abbey held her and rocked her gently, allowing her all the time she needed to let it out.

The black women in the wagon, including Hetty, Cobb's wife, looked on appreciatively. Several exchanged warm smiles and nods with Abbey. And for the first time she sensed there was true affection and comradeship between them, and it warmed her heart.

After a while, Margaret stopped sobbing. She sat up, sniffed back the tears and patted Abbey affectionately on the arm, "Thank you."

"Oh ... never you mind *that*. It is my great joy and pleasure having you here with me at last. Margaret, dear, I have spent endless months thinking about you, worrying about you, and praying for you. And ... frankly, pestering dear Nathan mercilessly to somehow rescue you. So now ... it's ... *indescribably wonderful* to finally have you here safe with me.

"In fact, I was just thinking; I would *never* have abandoned you, even if I'd had to fight that monster myself. And I wish ... well, I wish you were *my* very own daughter."

"Oh ... that is so kind of you to say, Miss Abbey. No one has ever said a nicer thing to me."

"No ... truly, I *mean it*, Margaret."

And then Abbey got a thoughtful look in her eyes. She sat up straighter, "Margaret ... I would like you to join *our* family! You shall be a daughter to me, if you'll have me for your mother!"

Margaret looked up at her in shock, and they met eyes for a long time without speaking. Hetty, who'd been watching and listening to the whole scene, now fairly held her breath to see what might happen next.

"Oh, Miss Abbey ... do you truly mean it? Because I think you are the most wonderful woman I've ever met, but ..."

"Yes ... yes, I *mean* it. I would *love* to have you for my daughter. Will you join our family?"

Margaret appeared stunned, mouth agape. She gazed into Abbey's eyes for another long moment, then broke eye contact and looked down at her hands. When she looked back up a smile lit her face and she shook her head in disbelief. "Yes ... *yes!* Oh, nothing would make me happier! Thank you, thank you, Miss Abbey ... *Momma, I should say!*"

And as they tearfully embraced Miss Abbey kissed her on both cheeks. The other women in the wagon clapped, laughed, and congratulated them with warm enthusiasm. They didn't know the whole story, but they'd heard enough to realize this was a singular event—a special moment such as one rarely sees in life.

Less than an hour later, Nathan came riding up on his horse to check in on Margaret and ask how she was doing. Harry the Dog trailed along behind, as usual.

"Oh, Mr. Chambers ... I am doing ... *wonderfully!*" she said and smiled at him with as bright a smile as he'd ever seen from her.

"Well, you *do* look much better, I must say! Nothing like a little food and rest to restore one's vigor! Not to mention some excellent companionship," he gestured toward the ladies in the wagon and smiled, a smile they readily returned.

But Miss Abbey said, "Nathan ... there's something I'd like to tell you."

"Oh? What is it, Momma?"

"Nathan, dear, I'd like to introduce you to Margaret ... your *new sister!*"

At first, he couldn't comprehend what Abbey had said and appeared confused. In fact, when Miss Abbey had said "sister," he'd immediately thought of Rosa. But then he realized what she meant; Miss Abbey had just adopted Margaret into the Chambers' family.

It was his turn to smile brightly, "That *is* wonderful news, Momma! Absolutely wonderful! Margaret, it's a true privilege to be your brother, and to call you 'sister'!" he removed his hat and bowed from his saddle.

"Oh, thank you, Mr. Chamb—I mean 'Nathan'! And I can't think of a man I'd be prouder to call 'brother'! From now on, with your permission of course, I should like to take the name 'Margaret Chambers.'"

"I would be honored, Margaret ... *dear sister.*"

ಶುಶಾಡ೪ಚಿಶುಶಾಡ೪ಚಿಶುಶಾಡ೪ಚಿ

Tom had dropped Henry off in a wagon further up the caravan, Miss Abbey's wagon being already filled with women. He told him they'd cut the shackles off his wrists as soon as they stopped for the evening to make camp.

They'd stacked the wagon high with various goods, but had left room for a few people to sit in back. At the moment it contained only one occupant, an old slave named Toby.

Freeman, Henry had to remind himself. Mr. Clark had already told him all the black people in the caravan, young and old, men and women, were freemen, having recently been emancipated by Mr. Chambers. It was a thing almost incomprehensible to Henry ... why would a slave owner do such a thing?

Old Toby greeted him warmly, and offered him food, and a water bottle, both of which he accepted gratefully. Toby talked for a long time while Henry ate and drank. He was amazed at everything that'd occurred, especially the great battles in which the black men had actually fought ... and won! With *rifles!*

But after a time, Toby nodded off to sleep. Henry, no longer sleepy himself, jumped down from the wagon to walk. He had a notion to catch up with the younger men and satisfy his curiosity about how it was to fight in a battle! And how it was to be ... *free* ...

ಏ೫ಾೞ೫ಙ೫ಏ೫ಾೞ೫ಙ೫ಏ೫ಾೞ೫ಙ೫

That evening the Captain allowed them to light campfires, but he still ordered the wagons arranged in a defensive square, and a rigorous watch kept up all night. The scouts had ranged far and wide during the day and had seen nothing of the enemy.

A warmth and general hopefulness pervaded the camp. People gathered around several fires, talking, joking, and laughing, though there was no dancing as there'd been back at Mountain Meadows on a Saturday night.

Henry had already paid his respects to Miss Margaret and confirmed she was doing well. And he'd shown her his recently freed wrists; a man named Georgie had cut them off with a hammer and chisel, and another named William had bandaged the bloody, chafed wrists after applying a soothing salve.

He now meant to go join in with a group of men, wanting to hear more tales of the Mountain Meadows' battles and their long trek from the farm.

He strode across the camp passing a campfire filled with women, chatting animatedly, and laughing loudly. A woman approached the fire, coming toward him. When she was within a few feet of the campfire, it lit her features, and he stopped dead in his tracks. *"Lilly!"* he exclaimed.

But the look of surprise and confusion on her face made him realize he had made a mistake; she was *not* his wife.

She tilted her head thoughtfully as she looked at him and said, "Why did you call me by that name ... and ... *who are you?*"

"I'm sorry, it's just ... oh, my name's Henry—I only joined y'all's wagon train today ... with Miss Margaret, from Walters Farm."

"Oh ... the runaway. We'd heard of you but had known nothing 'bout you. Why'd you call me *Lilly* just now? My name's Rosa, by the way ... oh, I should say Rosanna Chambers ... that's my free name."

"My name's Henry. Good to meet you, Rosanna. I'm ... not *yet* a freeman, but I *have* run away from my master."

"Yes, that awful Mr. Walters. We done heard all about him. The Captain's been fighting him tooth and nail for ... oh, more'n a year now."

"Yes ... so I heard. Oh! And I done never answered your question. I'm sorry, but in the dim light of the campfire, for a moment there I thought you were my wife, Lilly. We was together back over on the east side of Virginia before they sold me off to Walters."

"And ... now you see me more clearly ... you still think I look like your wife ... this *Lilly* you speak of?"

"Well ... you're younger, of course ... and maybe a might thinner in the face and whatnot. But ... yes, I still think you could be sisters."

Rosa stared at him for a long moment, an odd, unreadable expression knit her brow. Then she said a thing that sent a chill down Henry's spine.

"Henry ... I ain't seen my Momma since I was a young toddler. I only remember her as a dream of love and sweetness. But ... her name was *Lilly*, and folks from Mountain Meadows say I look *exactly* like she did ..."

Henry's mouth hung open in shock, "You ... you don't suppose ...?"

She gazed at him long and hard. Finally, she said, "Well, if your wife was my mother ... then that would make you ..." she trailed off, and looked at her feet, as if unable to finish the words.

For a moment he didn't understand was she was trying to say. Then it hit him, "Oh! Oh, *no*, Rosa! I only done jumped the broom with Lilly three years back, so I can't possibly be ... well, *you know* ..."

"Oh! I see ..."

Henry couldn't tell if she was relieved, or disappointed.

"But ... as for her being your mother ... could be, Rosa, could be. She told me she had a daughter once, a 'beautiful girl.' But Lilly'd been sold away from the farm when her child was still a babe. She never told me the name of the child, and she wouldn't never say nothing about the father, nor the farm. Seemed like she had no great love for him, or else she was angry with him, or something. Anyway, she never said who he was, and I never asked. But she always missed her baby girl ... and you should know; it weren't by choice she left you. If it *was* you."

Rosa was tearing up, "Oh! This is ... almost too much." She turned away, and hurried off through the dark, leaving Henry standing alone where he was.

He sat down right where he was in the dark, his head in his hands, shaking his head in amazement. *Was it possible?* he wondered. He thought long and hard regarding how Lilly looked when he'd last seen her, and he compared that to Rosa. *Yes ... yes ... they certainly could be sisters.* And then he realized they had the same voice, the same expressions, the same smile. It hit him with a force of certainty, *Oh my dear God ... I've found Lilly's long-lost daughter, all growed up!*

Then he thought, *But ... what should I do about that? What can I do about that?* These were questions for which he had no answer.

ଔଔଔଔଔଔଔଔଔଔଔଔଔଔ

The next day, just before noon, they were within a few miles of the first town they would pass since leaving Lewisburg, a little town called Summersville. Nathan couldn't remember ever being there when he was a child; to him it was only a name on the map.

But given everything that'd happened already, he wasn't taking anything for granted. So he sent a large part of his cavalry ahead to reconnoiter, led by Tom and Jim—Jim to deal with any townspeople who might prove adversarial, and Tom to secure supplies. Nathan wanted to restock their depleted foodstuffs. And to continue acquiring as much ammunition as possible any chance he had, though it wasn't especially needed at the moment.

But in less than an hour the scouts returned, empty handed.

"Gone, Captain … all of them. The place is plumb closed down and boarded up. Ain't never seen the like before, 'cept maybe out in Texas for fear of a Comanche raid," Jim said, shaking his head in disbelief.

"Yes, and when I peered into the general store through the window, the shelves were fairly emptied out, as if to deprive us of supplies," Tom added.

"Hmm … seems like our reputation has preceded us," Nathan said with a frown. "What'd they think we'd do, put them to the sword? Sack and burn the place?"

"Well … that *is* pretty much what I threatened to do back in Lewisburg," Jim offered with a shrug, "could be I overdid it … just a bit." But he grinned, an unlit cigar clenched between his teeth, looking unconcerned.

"Ironic, isn't it gentlemen? Likely those kindly, gentle townspeople would've welcomed that despicable criminal Walters with open arms, while shunning us like we carry the plague."

"Yes, sir … the world is turned all upside down, for certain," Jim agreed.

"Well, fortunately we are still all right on supplies for the moment, though I doubt we can make it out of Virginia on what we've brought with us," Tom added.

So there was nothing to do but continue along the road. But even as the lead wagon was passing through the center of town, the clouds that'd been gathering throughout the morning began to open up—a steady drizzle, accompanied by an unseasonably cool breeze. The murky weather seemed a fitting backdrop to the town's generally depressing demeanor. Not a soul in sight, not even a dog barking at them as they passed houses with shuttered windows and locked doors.

It set the tone for the rest of the day. The hopeful talk and jovial mood that'd started the day ended in a gloomy silence, each person focused on their own wretched discomfort.

And it seemed to affect their outlook concerning the danger from the enemy as well. While they'd started the day positively enough—feeling that the threat was over, or at least greatly diminished—a general sense of dread now pervaded the caravan. A sense of dread that enemy rifles were hiding behind every dripping branch and stone. That an ambush waited around every bend in the sodden, muddy road.

Even Nathan seemed to have become caught up in the gloom of it, ordering no campfires be lit that night, despite the gnawing wetness, and the lack of enemy sightings the entire day.

And the next day was no better. The steady drizzle and breeze of the previous day had turned into a heavy rain—clouds so low it was like walking through a swirling, foggy mist. The trees looming to both sides of the road took on mysterious, threatening shapes as visibility decreased to a few yards in any direction.

Most of the freemen took to carrying their rifles in their hands, rather than strapped to their backs. They gazed suspiciously at the dark woods surrounding them.

And at the end of a long, miserable day, their fears were realized. The forward scouts returned to report another small town a few miles ahead, Suttonsville according to the map.

It straddled the Elk River where the road crossed over on an open wooden bridge. The river was wide and deep, with a swift current—no way to bring the wagons across except using the bridge. But the enemy held the bridge!

"How many?" Nathan asked.

Jamie, who'd been narrating the scouts' report looked over at Jim for an estimate.

For once Jim looked worried. "Hundreds, sir. More than they had out on the road or back at Mountain Meadows. They've got a well-established camp on the other side of the water—rows of tents, and a corral for horses fenced off out in a field beyond. We seen stacks of rifles and have to assume they're well provisioned from the town, and the regions beyond. And ... they know we're here, sir."

"Oh?"

"Yep ... we confronted their scouts out on the road, eyeball to eyeball. Refused to let them get any closer to our wagons. Had to threaten violence if they tried it. No way I was letting them freely scout our numbers, sir. But they know where we are, and it's a good bet they also know *who* we are. The good news, I suppose, is it can't be Walters this time. Unless he's learned to fly."

"Yes ... I suppose that's some consolation. Though frankly I'd like another crack at having him in my rifle sights."

"Amen to that, sir."

Nathan reached in his pocket, pulled out a cigar and lit it. As he puffed distractedly, he looked around at the faces of his men. He saw concern such as he'd rarely seen—certainly not since coming east from Texas. They understood there was no turning back now. And no way past the river except over that bridge.

But they'd all been soldiering long enough to realize attacking a well-prepared, and well dug-in enemy in a narrow pinch-point like a bridge would be difficult, dangerous, and costly in blood. There was simply no way around it. And the bridge was out in the wide open, with fields on both sides and no trees. There'd be little chance for Billy's trickery, or Big Stan's intimidation.

Nathan came to the hard realization, like a cold stone in the pit of his stomach: he was completely out of ideas. For the hundredth time since his return from Richmond, he wished he had a fully manned artillery battery. With plenty of ammunition and powder.

But barring that, he could think of no strategy that might end with them alive *and* on the north side of that bridge. And yet ... that was exactly where they needed to be!

He gazed up at the darkening sky and sighed, "Gentlemen ... it is getting too late in the day for a battle, anyway, I fear. Let's square up the wagons again and get some well-earned rest. Then ... well, then we'll see what the morrow brings."

The next morning the situation had not changed. The enemy was still encamped beyond the bridge, and Nathan still needed to cross. About the only positive thing was the rain had stopped. The clouds were breaking up, and the sun was shining on the wagons, steam rising off the rain-soaked wood.

He'd been hopeful the enemy might let down their guard in the dark pre-dawn hours and they might carry off an assault under cover of darkness the next night. But he'd been up several times during the night to observe the enemy's camp. What he'd seen had depressed him further; they had pickets and sentries at all the vital points, with torches set well away from the bridge to illuminate the approaches. All night, large groups of men were at the ready, marching, rifles in hand. And they'd wisely lit no campfires back among the tents, nor anywhere near the sentries; no light to mark easy targets for him and his men in the darkness.

Nathan called his officers together, and they discussed what to do for more than an hour. But in the end, it came back around to what Nathan already understood; to launch an attack under these circumstances was suicidal.

He stood and paced a few yards away, looking out toward the bridge, though they couldn't see it from their camp. He stood for several minutes, slowly puffing on a cigar. The men sat where they were, mostly staring at their boots. No one spoke, awaiting their Captain's decision on their course.

Finally, he tossed the stub of his cigar into a puddle on the roadway where it briefly sizzled. He strode back over to them.

"Tom ... rig up a white flag. Jim ... you, me, and Tom will ride out and have a parley. Perhaps we can convince them to let us pass—that we are utterly desperate and simply can't turn back. That if they force us to attack ... likely we'll not win but perhaps we'll inflict unacceptably high casualties."

"Yes, sir." Jim said, but he didn't appear convinced. For once he wasn't smiling at the prospect of a conflict.

"I can think of nothing else to do," Nathan concluded weakly, one of the rare times he'd ever felt entirely inadequate.

A half-hour later, Nathan had finished saying his goodbyes to Miss Abbey, Margaret, and Megs. Though nothing was said, they understood the stakes; if his negotiations with the enemy went badly, likely they'd simply seize him, and he'd be unable to return to them.

As he strode back toward where Jim and Tom waited, horses at the ready, a voice called out, "Captain, sir!"

He turned and inwardly groaned—Rosa.

"Hello, Rosa. Are you well?"

"Yes, Captain … but I heard you was riding out alone to deal with the enemy. I … I'm afraid for you."

"I'll be all right, Rosa. Please try not to worry over much. Perhaps you can … say a prayer for me. Pray for God to guide my steps today and show me the way."

"Yes, Captain … that I will do. And I will pray you return safely to us."

Tears welled in her eyes, but he could think of nothing more to say. So he said, "Goodbye … for now … Rosa. Thank you," and turned on his heels, letting out a heavy sigh as he did.

When he got to his horse, the other white men were gathered around to see him off. "Stan … you're in command in our absence. I'd suggest keeping the wagons in the square for the moment.

"But if we don't return by … oh, let's say an hour past noon, you should assume we've been taken captive and will *not* be returning. Then you must use your best judgment as to what comes next. I can give you no good advice other than this: the black freemen who've carried rifles must *never* surrender!"

He looked Stan hard in the eyes, and for once Stan wasn't smiling, "I am hearing you, Captain. The slavers will murder them. Likely in great pain. Better to die fighting."

"Yes … I fear so."

ဆာဆာၷၷဆာဆာၷၷဆာဆာၷၷ

As the three riders, and one large dog, came down the road and onto the flat ground leading to the bridge, no one tried to stop them. An escort of four armed riders formed up behind them, following a few yards behind. When they came up to the south end of the bridge the two sentries posted there parted and stood to the side allowing them to pass unmolested.

But they were only a few paces past the bridge on the north side when other men holding rifles confronted them, blocking the way. The sentries forced them to a stop, though they'd not yet pointed a weapon at them.

"Please dismount, gentlemen. I will lead you to our ... *officers*."

They dismounted, handing the reins to other men who stepped forward to take charge of their mounts. Nathan reached over and patted Millie on the side of her face, "Be a good girl now, Mill. These men will take good care of you," and he gave the man holding her reins a serious, meaningful look, which the man returned with a nod.

Another man stepped forward, "Your hound will have to stay here as well, sir."

Nathan looked at him, then over at Harry, who was sitting looking up at him expectantly, his tongue hanging out one side of his mouth as usual.

Nathan turned back to the guard and made a short, snorting laugh, "*I* can't make him do it, can you?"

The soldier looked over at Harry again, taking in his enormous size and ferocious countenance. He looked up at Nathan and shook his head meekly.

The other sentry said, "Follow me." He turned and strode off toward the tents, his rifle held close across his chest, not bothering to see if they'd comply. But Nathan had no reason to resist, so he fell in behind the man, followed closely by Tom and Jim, with Harry walking beside him.

They marched into the row of tents, toward what appeared to be the very center. There they entered a sort of town square, an area several yards deep and wide, clear of any tents. On the back side of this open space was a tent much taller and wider than the rest, clearly the command tent. At a table in front of the tent sat a bespectacled man in his early forties who appeared to be poring over a stack of papers, examining them, and occasionally dipping a pen into an inkwell and making some notation, or perhaps adding his signature.

Nathan stepped up to the table and stood there, Tom and Jim slightly behind and to the sides. The men with rifles, who'd escorted them, moved around to the far side of the table and stood behind and on either side of the seated man.

The man didn't look up from his papers and was so focused on his task Nathan wasn't entirely sure he was aware of their presence. He resisted the urge to clear his throat or cough—it seemed too trite. So he stood and waited.

The man appeared to finish a particularly lengthy document, set it aside, and looked up. "My name is Pratt. I've been charged with watching this road and preventing any large, armed parties from passing. From what I understand, your group seems to qualify on both counts. Who are you, and what is your business on this road, if you don't mind my asking?"

"My name is Chambers, and as for my business ... that's my own, and frankly, *yes* ... I *do* mind you asking. As far as I'm aware any man is free to travel these roads, which the taxpaying citizens paid for from the government treasury. As such, I see no reason I should answer to *you, sir.*"

The man sat back in his chair and removed his glasses. Nathan had noticed no reaction at the mention of his own name. So either the man already knew it, or he'd never heard of him; it was impossible to tell which.

"A few months ago, that would've been true. But there's a war on now, or haven't you heard? And those in charge have asked me to guard this road until the regular troops can get organized and take over. So guard it I *will*. Besides which, it is *you*, sir, who came here under a flag of parley, which presumes you wish to talk. So *talk* ... if you please."

"Very well, Mr. Pratt. The only thing I came here to say was ... I've been on the road for some days now, and I have my entire household with me. For reasons ... I don't wish to discuss ... I've been forced to *relocate*. And I must cross this bridge to do so—a bridge you seem to have blocked with force of arms. Will you kindly stand aside and allow me to pass in peace?"

Pratt stared at him a moment, then said, "No."

Nathan glared at him but waited to see if he might elaborate.

"Mr. Chambers … we don't seem to be making things plain to one another. So allow me to make my position crystal clear, *sir*. I will not let *anyone* pass this bridge, save perhaps *Our Lord and Savior Jesus Christ* himself, unless he tells me his business and convinces me he has good reason to do so.

"Now, you seem to me a man of some stature, and a certain amount of backbone, I'll grant you. But you are *not* the Christ, as far as I can tell. So if you wish to pass, you *will* tell me your business … *sir!*"

Nathan figured if he told the truth it'd likely go very badly, very quickly—that he was all but an outlaw in Richmond, that he'd been fighting a running battle with militia recruited by same, and that he was trying to escape to the North to join the Union side with a hundred newly freed slaves—men who, by the way, he'd illegally armed and trained to fight.

"Allow *me* to speak plainly as well, Mr. Pratt. I am a soldier by training and vocation, as are many of my men. We are well-armed and experienced in warfare, having recently come from service in the far West.

"I don't wish to fight you, or anyone else. But we *will* cross this bridge, and if anyone tries to stop us, we will resort to violence as necessary.

"Perhaps you will hold your bridge and fulfill your assigned duty, as you see it. But perhaps you will lose so many men in the process your superiors won't look so favorably on your actions."

Pratt turned red in the face and stood up from the table. "You have the unmitigated *gall*, sir … to threaten me?! In my own camp, surrounded by my own men?!" he'd raised his voice and his men gathered around were suddenly on edge, gripping their rifles tighter.

But Nathan had never intended to back down, and the whole purpose for the parley was in fact to threaten these men, exactly as he was doing. Besides, he now had his own dander up. He too was becoming roused and red in the face, "My statement was not intended for a *threat*, but rather a *promise*. I will not be gainsaid from my course without bloodshed, and plenty of it. It's up to you whether or not it will be so ... *sir!*"

But now Pratt was fired up and had taken personal affront. He reached for his pistol holster, unbuckling the safety strap. But before he could draw the pistol, the barrel of Nathan's Colt was staring him straight in the face. And the two riflemen were likewise staring down the barrels of Tom and Jim's guns. Harry the Dog had raised up and planted his front paws on the table. He glared at Pratt, teeth bared and a low menacing growl coming from deep inside him.

But they were in the midst of the enemy's camp; Pratt clearly held the upper hand. In moments, a dozen or more rifles surrounded Nathan and his men. Nathan briefly considered whether it was preferable to be shot now or hanged later.

Behind Pratt, the tent flap of the command tent flew open, and a neatly dressed gentleman in a black suit stepped out. He spoke in the strong, clear voice of command, "*Peace! All of you!* Lower your weapons this instant! I'll have no bloodshed in this camp!"

Pratt appeared to deflate and relax, removing his hand from his pistol holster and sitting back down heavily. Other men lowered their gun barrels toward the ground. Nathan gazed around at them and holstered his Colt. Tom and Jim did likewise. Harry the Dog lowered his front paws back to the ground and stopped growling.

"*Chambers?!* Captain Nathaniel Chambers? Is it really you?" the voice of the gentleman said in amazement and surprise.

Nathan recognized it as a familiar voice ... though he couldn't immediately place it. He looked up and ... "John? *John Carlile!* My good Lord, sir! This is a happy meeting! When last we saw each other we were both fleeing Richmond's secession insanity. Whatever are you doing *here*, sir?"

"Me? Well, these are my men ... or rather I should say, the good loyal Union men of western Virginia ... of which I am one!"

"Union men?!"

"Of course, Union men! Who did you think we were, *Goddamned secess rebels?* Me and others of our persuasion up in Wheeling heard the Southern counties were recruiting pro-secession militias. So we thought we'd do the same for the Union side. We took it upon ourselves to guard the roads going north — prevent those damned secessionists from taking any of *our* territory before the regular Union troops arrive.

"Speaking of, we've had rumors this past hour of an engagement between regular Union troops and rebels at first light this morning, just north of here at Philippi. And, I'm happy to report, the Union troops routed them and sent them running for the hills! They're saying it's the first battle of the war!"

Nathan looked at Tom and Jim, and they exchanged an ironic look — *First battle*, indeed!

"And ... do I understand correctly you've been forced from your home? I am most sorry to hear it. My condolences, Nathan."

"Thank you, John, I appreciate that. It was ... a difficult, painful decision, but in the end the only thing I could do."

"I can only imagine, and am eager to hear all about your escape from Richmond, and your adventures on the road to this point. I'm sure it's much more interesting than my own tale. But before we step in the tent and get caught up on events ... please allow me to straighten out this present matter ..."

He stepped in front of the table to address the men gathered around.

"Men, I want make it clear this has been nothing but a *great* misunderstanding. This is Nathaniel Chambers, late Captain of the United States Army stationed out in Texas. He and I were delegates to the recent Secession Convention in Richmond, and I can tell you for certain, there's not a more loyal Unionist alive."

There was a general relaxation and smiles all around. Even Pratt extended his hand and shook Nathan's, giving him a sheepish grin, and a nod, by way of apology.

Carlile turned to Nathan, bowed, and made a broad gesture toward the North.

"And Mr. Chambers ... esteemed gentlemen ... allow me to be the first to say, on behalf of myself and all our company, welcome home to the North, sirs! And ... welcome back ..." he chuckled, "Welcome back ... *to the United States of America!*"

CHAPTER 9. HOME AWAY FROM HOME

"Where we love is home —
home that our feet may leave,
but not our hearts."
— Oliver Wendell Holmes

Tuesday June 11, 1861 – Wheeling, Virginia:

It had taken another full week of travel after crossing the bridge at Suttonsville before the Mountain Meadows caravan finally reached Wheeling. Several times along the road they passed troops of hard-riding or marching Union soldiers. But though they heard rumors of war everywhere they went, they suffered no further incidents. John Carlile had insisted on providing them a well-armed, mounted escort of twenty men all the way to Wheeling. So Nathan was confident they'd have no further troubles.

Once again, he ordered the black men stow their rifles in the wagons and cover them. For one, he didn't want to unduly alarm anyone they passed. And for another, he wished to avoid an accident or misunderstanding triggering a calamity so close to their destination. Finally, he knew in his heart the Northerners, despite more open minds, were not yet ready to see a large group of armed black men in their midst. He'd rather not press his luck on the matter.

But he was also certain with the war gearing up, it was only a matter of time. Eventually the Union must tap the vast reservoir of able-bodied men they'd acquire by encouraging slaves to escape and come North, then arming them and turning them loose against their former masters. He'd seen for himself, firsthand, how motivated and capable they were in that regard — in no uncertain terms!

Ironically, after their long trek, he and Tom left the group two days before the wagons were due to reach the city. Nathan wanted time to secure a place for a temporary encampment before their arrival.

And John Carlile had requested Nathan arrive in Wheeling before the 11th. They'd begin the second "Wheeling Convention" that day, whose purpose was to discuss the secession of Virginia from the Union. And what, if anything, the western half of the state ought to do in reaction.

Nathan couldn't be seated as a delegate—Greenbrier County was still considered loyal to Richmond. But Carlile wanted him to be there, to hear what was said, and to have his own say, even in an unofficial capacity. Carlile considered Nathan a man of stature, of a certain *gravitas*, whose military expertise might soon be required.

It was mid-afternoon, and the convention had adjourned for the day, having accomplished little more than establishing the rules and procedures, as such things usually went. Nathan and Tom sat their horses on the southern edge of town awaiting the expected arrival of the caravan. Tom had calculated when they ought to arrive, and so they'd ridden out to greet them a few hours before the expected time.

In addition to sitting in on the convention's opening, they'd had a successful mission to find a campsite for their people. So successful, in fact, they wouldn't need a temporary camp after all. While Nathan was hobnobbing with John Carlile and other important citizens attending the convention, Tom had located a good-sized farm, nearly five-hundred acres that'd been foreclosed by the bank a few months prior. And although the farmhouse was a bit run-down, and the outbuildings were in need of fairly extensive repairs, the land itself appeared fruitful. In fact, the crops, mostly corn they'd planted in the spring, prior to the foreclosure, should yield a reasonable harvest in the fall, despite a generally weedy and unkempt appearance.

The property was situated south of town. In fact, only about a half-mile from where they currently waited. It sat on the banks of the Ohio River, surrounded by thick woods on three sides—really quite a pleasant, picturesque setting.

Of course, it was *not* Mountain Meadows, Nathan reminded himself with a heavy sigh. The farmhouse was much smaller and simpler than what they were used to and was showing its age. But they could've done much worse.

Ironically, the only real downside was the farm had never had slaves. That was good in the sense it proved once again a farm could be run without them. But it also meant there were no slave cabins in which to house the freemen, only a small apartment with several rooms in which the former owners had housed the few seasonal farmhands they'd employed.

They'd need to somehow solve the housing shortage. But in the short term it would at least provide them a place to camp. In the morning Tom intended to take several unloaded wagons into town to buy as many tents as possible. He would also purchase as much canvas as he could, so they might manufacture their own. While the tents were being constructed, they could get the freemen in out of the weather by using the barns and other outbuildings.

"I still don't see how we can afford the upkeep of all these people, Captain. It's true we got a bargain on the farm because of the foreclosure. And fortunately, you were prescient enough to transfer most of your cash to New York banks before the secession. Still, most of the family fortune was tied up in Mountain Meadows Farm—in its land and infrastructure. Along with … dare I say it? The slaves themselves."

"Yes, Tom. You're right, of course. We can't continue to support them indefinitely, along with our other men. Fortunately, that's a problem for another day. For now, I'll just have to explain to them the situation. Though they are still freemen, we can't afford to pay them a wage as we'd planned back at Mountain Meadows. I must ask them to work for only food and housing. And, yes, the irony of that being very nearly the same thing as slavery does *not* escape me, Tom. But what else can I do? Other than promise them I will pay them when I may?"

"Yes, sir. I agree. Nothing else you can do right now. But don't forget, though it may *sound* the same, to them it won't be, for one very important reason."

"Oh, what's that?"

"They will be here because they *choose* to be ... and they are free to leave whenever they wish."

"Yes ... of course. And in their position that is no small thing. Thank you for reminding me, Tom."

ഈഞ൝ഒ൝ഈഞ൝ഒ൝ഈഞ൝ഒ൝

Walters brought his men to a halt as they crested the rise and gazed down into the valley beyond. Mountain Meadows Farm spread out below them, the crops still green and the great house still magnificent and stately, despite its recent abandonment.

It was the third time he'd ridden with armed men onto this farm. This time, however, they'd not brought guns but rather torches and fuel oil. And there'd be no Chambers, nor any of his damned soldiers to stop them. This time he would have his revenge, at least in some measure.

It would never be as satisfying as killing the man, or better yet, killing his people and making him watch. Still, it would bring a certain amount of satisfaction. And finally put a positive end to an otherwise unpleasant series of recent events, culminating with the humiliating retreat from the battle on the road north.

He took a deep, satisfying breath, savoring the destruction to come, and he kicked his horse back into motion. He intended to leave not so much as an outhouse standing. And he'd also burn the crops. If Chambers ever returned, he'd know who had destroyed the place he held dear.

But as they passed the slave cabins and approached the main house, it surprised him to see several men up on the veranda, and more walking along the driveway—uniformed men. Soldiers.

They pulled up in front of the hitching post on the circular drive, and he dismounted, telling his men to wait. He strode up to the house and stepped up to the veranda. No one confronted him, nor tried to prevent his passage. He opened the door and stepped inside, gazing about. It was the first time he'd been in Mountain Meadows' great house since his father had brought him on a visit to Jacob Chambers years ago. It didn't appear so impressive now, not compared to his own house. He walked across the foyer and heard voices coming from a room with glassed double doors off to the left. He looked in and saw another uniformed man sitting behind a crude table, on which sat a stack of papers and an inkwell with pen. Another man was standing next to him, and the two of them were examining some document. Walters noted the room had been a library—the walls were lined with shelves. But all the shelves were empty.

He entered the room, and the men looked over at him.

The man who'd been leaning over the table stood up straight, and stepped to the side, as the man seated said, "Good day to you, sir. How may I be of assistance?"

"I ... I am Elijah Walters ... a neighbor. I am surprised to find you here, sir. Why are you here?"

The man gazed at him a moment, as if unsure how to respond.

"Well, Mr. Walters ... I could ask you the same. My name is Colonel Tennison, of the Confederate States Army, and this is my ... *temporary* ... headquarters. So again I must ask, why are you here, sir, and how may I be of service?"

"I came here to burn this place to the ground."

The colonel sat up straight, and exchanged a look with his assistant, another uniformed officer.

"Oh? And why should you admit to me your intention of breaking the law by committing an act of arson?"

"Because this place belongs to a man named Chambers. He's wanted for murder over in Richmond, and he's a traitor to the Confederate cause. Even fled to the North to join up with Lincoln's abolitionist army."

"Oh, *that*. Yes, I see ... well, let me set you straight on a few things, Mr. Walters. Your former neighbor Chambers no longer stands accused of murder in Richmond, in fact, he has been absolved of all crimes."

"*What?!*"

"Yes. You see, General Lee ordered a full investigation, this time conducted by the Army. The investigation concluded Mr. Chambers had in fact been assaulted at gunpoint on the streets of Richmond, and was very nearly murdered himself, even as he had claimed. And, as a result, any subsequent violent actions he or his men may have taken on his behalf were purely in self-defense and thus completely justified. So you see, Mr. Chambers is *not*, in fact, an outlaw."

Walters scowled, but then regained his composure, and resumed his usual, bland expression.

"That may well be, Colonel, but he's still a traitor, and means to fight for Lincoln."

"Yes ... I must agree with you on that point, Mr. Walters. And you'll be happy to hear so does General Lee. That's why he's declared all Mr. Chambers' property forfeit, and has ordered it seized, making it now the property of the Confederate States of America. More specifically, the property of the Confederate Army, until such time as the exigencies of war no longer demand it."

"Well, then, if his property is forfeit, due to his treason, I'll just wait until you're no longer in need of it; *then* I'll burn it down."

The Colonel sat quietly for a moment, gazing at Walters.

"Mr. Walters ... you don't seem to have understood what I said ... this is now the Army's *property* ... by order of General Lee himself. He has declared it will be used as a campaign headquarters, staging area, or field hospital as the situation demands.

"Mr. Walters, the Confederate Army does not take kindly to the wanton destruction of its property. In fact, in time of war that is considered sabotage, a capital offense, sir."

Walters stared at him with no expression and did not respond. The Colonel thought him one of the strangest men he'd ever met.

"Allow me to speak even more plainly to you, Mr. Walters. Since you have come here threatening to burn this place, I am obligated to file a report on the matter. And as such, I am officially serving you notice; if anything at all of a suspicious nature happens to this property, the Army will hold you *personally* responsible. The assumption being, you've either perpetrated the crime yourself or have ordered it done.

"And I must warn you, sir, during time of war the usual rules of *juris prudence* no longer apply. If I order you seized and shot as a saboteur, seized and shot *you shall be!* Do I make myself clear, sir?"

But Walters did not reply or respond, and no expression betrayed his thoughts. He no longer looked at the Colonel but stared straight ahead over the man's head. Without a word he turned and walked from the room and back out the front door, closing it quietly behind him.

The Colonel turned to his adjutant and said, "My *word!* That must be the strangest and most disagreeable fellow I've ever met. Imagine! Coming in here and asking to burn down the place. It utterly baffles me why someone would want to do such a thing to this beautiful home. Even if General Lee hadn't ordered the place preserved, I'd have never allowed it. Captain Chambers was an officer—a proper gentleman by all accounts, and a West Pointer, same as me. If nothing else, professional courtesy demands we treat his home with utmost respect."

ᏴᎣᏓᏉᎾᏟᎽᎾᏓᏉᏟᎽᎾᏓᏉᏟᎽ

Evelyn sat in the library of the Hughes' house where she'd once again been living since the unfortunate events in the basement of her own home. Jonathan had agreed she'd acted bravely and wisely during and after the entire incident. And that leaving the house and staying away until they had time to investigate further was a good decision.

Angeline was sitting with her, and they were chatting amiably, small talk mainly, while waiting for Jonathan to join them. He'd asked Evelyn to meet them in the library for tea in the late morning to discuss what he'd learned. The smile on his face had led Evelyn to believe it was good news. But that was several hours ago, and he'd gone out on some mysterious errand and had not yet returned.

Without warning he stepped into the room, crossed over, and took a seat. He was still smiling, if anything brighter than before. Evelyn was now nearly breathless with anticipation.

"Evelyn, dear … surprisingly I am overflowing with nothing but good news today."

"Well, I am delighted to hear it, sir!"

"And ... were you intending to share, or must we force it out of you?" Angeline asked with a smile.

"Well, the forcing might be fun, my dear, but ... sorry, Evelyn. I'll get right to it.

"First, it appears your house is still secure, and your cover is still in good standing. From everything our people have been able to discover, your assumptions about the event appear to have been correct. The two enemy agents acted alone, and only discovered you by chance, having followed our man to the meeting, and after, following you from there without ever bothering to report back to their headquarters. So thanks to your fortitude and diligence, the two men have simply vanished without a trace. It is a great mystery to all concerned. Even our *observer* has not fallen under suspicion. We can only surmise the enemy agents spotted him by some odd chance and were following him out of pure suspicion without knowing for sure who he was, or what he was up to.

"So all's well that ends well, I must say! You have eliminated two vile and dangerous enemy agents, and no one is the wiser, nor the worse for the wear."

Evelyn frowned at that, "Jonathan, I've been forced to kill two men. That seems a bit of *'wear'* to me."

"Oh, yes, yes, of course, you're right, Evelyn, dear. I speak flippantly of serious matters. I apologize. It's just ... I am so pleased with your actions, and with the outcome I'm almost giddy. Please forgive me."

"Nothing to forgive, dear sir."

"But from what you said earlier, it sounded as if you had other news?" Angeline prompted, knowing her husband well enough to know more was coming.

"I was about to get to that. As you both know, I have certain friends in Wheeling, in attendance at a certain important conference there. And ... you'll never guess who came striding in, larger than life, just as the meeting was getting started."

Evelyn thought about that for a moment then lit up, *"Nathan!"*

"Yes, Nathaniel Chambers, in the flesh! And Tom Clark next to him. And I have since learned he brought his entire household with him to Wheeling, lock, stock, and barrel! Had to fight his way out, from what we understand, wreaking all sorts of havoc along the way. Killed a recently commissioned Confederate colonel and nearly wiped out an entire battalion of newly recruited secessionist militia—a force that was subsequently unavailable to the Confederate side in the lop-sided Union victory at Philippi."

"Oh! Oh, poor Nathan ... leaving Mountain Meadows ... that must have been ... awfully difficult."

Jonathan was puzzled by her reaction, "But ... my dear, don't you see what a *miracle* this is? Mr. Chambers was a virtual prisoner on his own farm—surrounded, vastly outnumbered and outgunned. Cut off from all help. And now, like some kind of conjurer's trick, he's in Wheeling with his whole household! And apparently has freed all his slaves in the process and brought them along with him."

"Oh, Jonathan, of course she understands all *that*, but ... oh, sometimes you're ... such a *man!* Can't you understand how heartbreaking it must've been to abandon his family home to his enemies? And poor, dear Miss Abbey ..."

"Oh ... yes, of course ... sorry. I'm sure you're quite correct. That must have been ... painfully difficult. But still ... you must admit, it is *overall* very great good news!"

Evelyn looked up and smiled, "Yes, yes, certainly Jonathan! Forgive me, you're absolutely right. Nathan is alive and well. And amazingly has escaped his enemies once again. That is a thing beyond wonderful! Miraculous even! Thank you for telling me."

But then a question came to her, "Jonathan ... where in the world is Wheeling, anyway? I've never even heard of it before."

"I'm not surprised. It's a long way from Richmond—a part of the North in fact, despite still being in Virginia. It is in the very northernmost tip of the Commonwealth on the road between Pennsylvania and Ohio."

"Oh. That feels like ... well, like he's now so *very* far away. As if he were now on the far side of the world."

Angeline put a comforting hand on her shoulder, and looked over at Jonathan, and the two exchanged a sympathetic look.

"And, dear, what was the errand you had to run out and do before we sat down to tea? It seemed to me it had some connection with the events we were to discuss, but you've not mentioned it."

"Oh, yes ... I was getting to that ... it seems Mr. Chambers has acquired a farm on the edge of Wheeling, large enough to accommodate his household. Only it has no housing for the former slaves, now freemen. And, I have it on good authority the Army has bought up every tent and every scrap of canvas to be had in Pennsylvania, Ohio, or western Virginia. So Mr. Chambers and Mr. Clark have been entirely frustrated in coming up with a quick solution to their housing shortage with fall weather soon upon them."

"And ..."

"And it occurred to me our shipping firm in Boston has an abundance of the one thing they most desperately need. So I've ordered a goodly supply shipped to them, and delivered as a gift."

He sat and smiled at them, a smug look on his face. But the women looked at each other and shrugged.

"Jonathan ... you look as if you think we should divine your meaning. But really, dear, Evelyn and I have no idea what you're talking about."

He glanced back and forth between the two women, mouth agape; he couldn't believe it wasn't the most obvious thing in the world. "Sailcloth! I have sent them several tons of it."

Evelyn's eyes widened, "Of course! Sailcloth is something a shipping company must always have on hand in great supply, for re-equipping the ships as they come into port. But it can also be used for—"

"Tents," Angeline finished Evelyn's sentence, nodding her head and smiling. "Very nicely done, Jonathan. Sometimes you even outdo yourself, I must admit."

"Thank you, my dear," he sat back in his chair and smiled brightly, a look of great satisfaction on his face.

A few hours later, just after lunch, Evelyn walked alone back to her previously abandoned house. Jonathan had had men spying on it regularly since the incident, and no other policemen or government agents had approached. And, as usual, Angeline had spread the appropriate rumors. This time to account for Evelyn's sudden disappearance—that she'd been called away unexpectedly to tend to a friend who'd suffered a sudden illness.

Jonathan had offered to send her home in a carriage, but she'd declined. It was a pleasant day for a walk, sunny, but not too hot, and she wanted time to think before she arrived and got to work putting the house back in order.

And what she was thinking most about was Nathan. Despite Jonathan's "great good news," she felt sad somehow. Sad for him, and Miss Abbey; truly, having to leave their beloved home must've been heartbreaking. But mostly ... sad for herself. It felt as if something precious and irreplaceable had ... slipped away, never to return. She realized somewhere deep in her heart she'd always assumed ... someday ... she'd be back at Mountain Meadows with Nathan. But now, that dream seemed all but dead. And as she'd told Jonathan ... Nathan now seemed even further away. He was now on the far side of the state. But with the coming conflict that might as well be the far side of the world. As she contemplated returning to her new house, she couldn't help but wish she were returning to a home with *him* in it. She started wondering what he was doing and thinking at this very moment. And if ... if he ever missed her, too. She began to tear up.

Lost in these melancholy thoughts, she did not notice a man had been following her on the street. He was now only a few steps behind her.

"Miss Eve ..."

Startled, she stopped and turned. It was a young man, in the uniform of a policeman. In an instant she recognized he was the young night watchmen Jubal Collins from her old neighborhood, where she was still living with Miss Harriet—and assisting Dr. Johnson in his covert activities.

"Jubal! I'm sorry, I was lost in thought and hadn't even noticed you were there. And ... my, you look *fine!* Isn't that a new uniform? It has been ... some time since we've seen one another."

"Yes, Miss Eve. It has been since you left your mother's house and moved into a house of your own. In a neighborhood outside my assigned patrol."

"Yes, I suppose that's true. And yet, here you are. Have you been reassigned?" but even as she asked this question it occurred to her he knew more about her doings than he should.

"Well, I guess you could say that ... I've been promoted to full police officer."

"Oh! Many congratulations on that, Jubal. That is wonderful news—what you'd been wishing for."

"Thank you, Miss Eve ... but," she thought his usually cheerful face appeared more serious than usual. Or *sad*, maybe. "It seems to me sometimes the things you wish for ... don't turn out as you expect, Miss Eve. Or should I say ... Miss *Evelyn?*"

"Oh ... well, I suppose you *could* call me that. It is, after all, my full given name ..."

"Full name, and *usual* name, I have come to understand."

She gave him a serious look. "Jubal ... it seems to me you have something on your mind, and you wish to talk with me about it. Perhaps you should speak plainly."

He looked down at his feet for a moment, then looked up and said, "You know it was me who discovered what the dentist, Dr. Johnson was up to."

"I'd heard something of the kind. He was ... helping runaway slaves, or some such, wasn't he?"

"Yes. And do you know how I found out about that?"

Evelyn didn't answer but raised a questioning eyebrow.

"I followed *you*, Miss Evelyn."

It was her turn to look away. She had *not* expected this and did not know what to say. So she turned back to gaze at him, waiting to see what else he might say about it.

"I ... never suspected you of anything, I just ... wanted to see you. So ... sometimes I waited where I thought you might be and watched. Sometimes I would catch up to you and speak with you. But other times ... well, other times I only wished to see where you were and what you were doing, but could think of nothing to say. Do you ... understand?"

She nodded, but didn't answer, allowing him to continue.

"Anyway, one night you walked to Dr. Johnson's house. I didn't think much of it … maybe you just had a toothache or something. But then you went there again, and then again, and I started to wonder how many toothaches one person could have. So I started wondering about Dr. Johnson, and I started watching his house. That's when I saw slaves being brought in and out, late at night by the back-basement door. So I reported it. Some officers wanted to go there and quietly murder him and be done. But I … I told them I would not stay quiet if they did, and insisted they arrest him and put him on trial, proper and legal-like. They were furious with me, but in the end, they knew I was right, and they did it my way. I earned my promotion from the incident but not any love from my fellow officers, I'm afraid," he sighed. "And then … then I thought about you …"

"And?"

"And … the thought of you being arrested, or *worse*, by the other policemen … well, I just couldn't imagine it. So I said nothing. And then, you were just … *gone*. I heard rumors, but finally I went to visit your mother, and asked her myself. And she said you'd had an argument, but she wouldn't say about what. And she didn't know where you were either.

"So I kept my ears open, and heard you'd moved into your own house across town and had started a business training household slaves. Of course, I was suspicious, so I came and found your house. And I watched. Well … I don't think I need to tell you what I saw, Miss Eve."

She gazed at him, now deadly serious. "So … what happens now, Jubal?"

She half expected him to announce she was under arrest, and to walk her off to the nearest jail. But to her surprise, tears welled up in his eyes.

"I … I don't rightly know, Miss Eve. I hadn't the heart to turn you in. But if I couldn't do that, then how could I, in good conscience, call myself a police officer? So I've resigned, and have joined the Army instead."

"Oh, Jubal! *No! You* shouldn't have done that. Not because of me! Oh, I'm so sorry ..."

"No, don't be ... it's not your fault. I've come to realize you're a good person, just doing what you believe is *right,* even though ... well, even though in the eyes of the law it's illegal. And I had to decide between my job and ... *other feelings."*

Now she felt herself tearing up. She was starting to understand all actions had consequences, sometimes entirely unexpected. Like using her charm on a naïve young policeman. Because of it she had inadvertently ruined his career and turned his life upside down. Now he'd joined the Army, and if worse came worst, it might even cost him his life. Worse still, he had no idea of her other activities—that she was planning to spy for the Union, a role in which the things she did might threaten the very lives of Southern soldiers like him. He might overlook helping a few slaves run away, but *spying?*

"Jubal ... thank you ... for not arresting me, and for ... making sure they didn't harm Dr. Johnson. He's also a very good man. How ... how can I make it up to you ... make it *right* between you and I?"

"Miss Eve ... you don't owe me anything ... I've made my own choices in this. But since you ask ..."

"Yes?"

"Well, some older fellas I've talked with ... that were in the Army before ... say it's important to have someone at home writing you letters. You know, just about all the little, unimportant things happening back home where things are safe and normal. Helps soldiers forget their troubles for a spell and gives them someone to write back to and ... a reason to keep going."

"And ... you'd like me to write to you ... when you're away in the Army?"

"Well, like I said, you don't owe me a thing, and I've got no right to ask it ..."

"Oh, Jubal! Of course, I'll write to you! As often as you'd like. It's the least I can do after ... well, after all the trouble I've caused you. While you've been such a good friend to me, which I rightly don't deserve."

And then his face brightened up for the first time. "Well, thank you kindly, Miss Eve! Thank you. It'll mean a whole lot to me, I promise you. And ... well, I want you to know I won't ... *you know* ... make *more* out of it than I should. Just ... being *friends* and writing letters ... you understand."

"Oh ... yes, of course, Jubal. Just friends ..." but she knew it was a lie. She could feel his strong attraction for her, like the heat from a flame. In fact, she'd felt it from the first moment they'd met. It'd made taking advantage of him effortless. But now her heart ached for him, knowing she would *never* choose him over Nathan ... *never in life!*

"You write to me, when you get wherever it is you're going, and I promise I'll write back straightaway. And as often as you like!"

"Thank you, Miss Eve. It'll be a real comfort to me when I'm out there fighting."

She felt another twinge of guilt, knowing her spy activities might put him in more peril. But she made herself a promise right there on the spot—whatever else she did, she would *never again* betray a confidence of Jubal's. No matter what he might tell her, she would keep it to herself and not pass it on. She'd do everything she could to keep him safe, or at least not to further endanger him.

But what she said was, "There's no need to thank me, Jubal. It'll be my pleasure. And ... you can just call me Eve ... or *Evelyn*, if you wish, since we're friends," and then she leaned forward, and kissed him on the cheek.

A bright smile lit his face though he was blushing furiously, "All right, if you wish ... *Evelyn*. Oh ... and did I say they's gonna make me an *officer* in the Army ... a *first lieutenant* on account of my police training and all?"

"Oh! How wonderful, Jubal. I'm so happy for you."

"Thank you, Miss ... uh, I mean ... *Evelyn*."

ঙ৪৩ৣ৻৪৩ৣৣঙ৪৩ৣৣঙ৪৩ৣ৻

Nathan sat in the new "library," a small room off the kitchen in the farmhouse, which as yet had no books in it, save one: the Chambers' family Bible. He'd been forced to leave all but a precious few behind at Mountain Meadows—a grievous loss. He had just sat down to relax in the corner on an old, well-worn chair. Megs would never have allowed it in Miss Abbey's elegant home back at Mountain Meadows. But for the moment, they had to make do with whatever furniture the former owners had left behind. It *was* comfortable, he had to admit, and the glass of whiskey he was sipping tasted as good as ever.

He'd only been there a minute or two when Tom walked in and sat next to him.

"Hello, Tom. Timely of you to come in just now; I was just thinking of a question I have for you that I keep forgetting to ask."

"Sir?"

"I've just been wondering if the old owners of this farm had a name for it. You know, like our *'Mountain Meadows'?* "

"Oh, yes they did, sir. Didn't I say before? They called the place *'Belle Meade.'*"

"Ah. French, isn't it?"

"Well … sort of. 'Belle' is 'beautiful' in French, of course. But 'mead' is a poetic shortening of the English word 'meadow,' though they've added an 'e' to the end of it; likely to make it 'look' more French."

"Oh … interesting. So we've moved from *Mountain* Meadows … to *Beautiful* Meadows, one might say."

Tom smiled, "Yes, I reckon so, sir. Seems fitting, somehow."

"And with a French-sounding name your Adilida should feel right at home when she comes to visit. Speaking of …"

"Oh, yes, sir. That's partly why I came in just now," he pulled an envelope from his pocket. "It's a letter I've written to Adilida. I thought I ought to tell her our new location, so she'll know where to write. Not sure if the mail is still going through to the South, though.

"I went to the post office this morning and talked to the Postmaster. He said as of June first, there's a Confederate Postal

Service, and the US Postmaster General has cut off all service to the states in rebellion.

"Oh? Well, we are technically still in Virginia here in Wheeling, so does that mean *we* are also cut off?"

"I asked him that same question myself, and ... well, sir, I'm sure you'll enjoy hearing his answer as much as I did."

"Do tell ..."

"He said his honor, Governor Letcher of the Commonwealth of Virginia, sent a telegram to the mayor of Wheeling ordering him to seize the Customs House and Post Office here in the name of the Confederate States. The mayor sent a return wire saying, 'I *have* seized upon the Customs House and Post Office, in the name of Abraham Lincoln, President of the United States, whose property they are.'"

Nathan laughed, "Good for him!"

"Yes, so needless to say, the United States Post Office in Wheeling is still open for business. And I understand some letters are still going through 'postage due,' when an exchange can be arranged. He said the main route between Washington and Richmond is now completely cut, though. The route has been closed by the Union Army, which now controls Alexandria. He thought some mail may still be getting through out West, down the Mississippi. So it seems there's—ironically—a better chance of getting a letter through to New Orleans than to Richmond."

"Hmm."

"Yes, well ... I had a thought, sir. If you'd like ... I mean, to send a letter to Miss Evelyn ... you *could* include it with mine. I could ask Adilida to send it on to Richmond through the new Confederate mail. Of course, it may never make it through. But then again, it may!"

"Yes ... it's a thought, thank you, Tom. Yes ... I believe I'll do that. I had been pondering how to get her a message, and it seems your idea may just work, as roundabout as it may be."

After Tom left, Nathan continued to sit and sip his whiskey, his thoughts now focused on Evelyn, thinking about what he would say. He wished there were a way to tell her his true feelings, but he'd been warned against it—that it might put her in danger. That, he would never intentionally do. He sighed. Another ridiculous, innocuous letter it must be.

But then he leaned back in his chair, closed his eyes, and envisioned her. Her lovely face and dazzling smile, her sparkling blue eyes and golden hair, her joyous laugh. Her wit and charm. The breathtaking *life* in her! The sweet taste of her lips when he kissed her, and the tender way she held him when they embraced. The subtle curves of her body, soft and warm pressed up next to him. He could almost smell her sweet perfume …

He sat up straight, wiped his eyes, and downed his glass of whiskey. Then he stood and strode out the door, *No good will come of going there, Nathan … no good at all!*

ᘓᘔᕟᘓᘔᕟᘓᘔᕟᘓᘔᕟᘓᘔᕟ

Nathan stood on the front porch of the farmhouse looking out across his new lands.

The house faced south, and he looked straight ahead across the drive to where a small field of grass gave way to the farm barns and outbuildings. There were already signs of repairs being made by his men—freshly patched wood siding on several buildings waiting for a fresh coat of paint, and new shingles patching holes in the roofs.

Over to his left just past the edge of the farmhouse lawn stood two new tents, the first of many to come. Their white canvas fairly glowed in the light of the setting sun. They were large and sturdily built—not a tent intended to be quickly torn down and transported, but rather the type intended to shelter its occupants through a long, hard winter. They featured a raised, wooden floor, and a solid wooden framework over which the canvas had been stretched tightly, with military precision. Each tent even included a port hole for a stove pipe, though the stoves were not yet in place. Jamie and Georgie were still working on manufacturing those.

They were building the tents in a pasture just to the side of the main farmhouse. The future tents' positions had been neatly staked out, row upon row; and several floors and frameworks were already under construction.

The *canvas* for the tents had been somewhat of a miracle in and of itself. Shortly after they'd first arrived in Wheeling, Tom had returned empty handed and downcast from a fruitless expedition to town. He'd discovered there was not a swath of tent canvas available between Ohio, Pennsylvania, and western Virginia. The Union Army had requisitioned every last scrap for their own use.

But then an unexpected gift arrived at the farm: three wagons, heavily laden. When Tom went to greet them, he told the driver, "You must be in the wrong place, mister. We haven't ordered anything." But the man handed him a manifest, and a letter. The manifest instructed the driver to deliver the goods in the wagons to *"Tom Clark, care of Nathaniel Chambers, Wheeling, Virginia."* Tom opened the letter, which read:

> *Dear Tom,*
>
> *Congratulations to you and your Captain on another successful escape from our mutual enemies! I am led to understand it was quite a feat of derring-do and has caused much consternation back in Richmond, which is all to the good.*
>
> *This letter accompanies a little gift from my employer to yours. I trust you will put it to good use.*
>
> *Your friend and obedient servant,*
>
> *"Joseph"*
>
> *P.S. My employer says to tell the Captain "E" is in good health and spirits, and she speaks of him often and with great fondness.*
>
> *P.P.S. Looking forward to further interesting travels together one day, my friend!*

Nathan turned away from the growing field of tents, and looked off to his right, toward the westering sun. The sky was lit with a sunset of fiery orange and red, reflected in sparkling ripples across the wide, green waters of the Ohio River, slipping silently along on its thousand-mile journey down to the Mississippi. It was an idyllic and picturesque scene.

As he stood there, lost in thought, Miss Abbey stepped up behind him and slipped her right arm in his left and gave it a squeeze.

"Oh, hello, Momma. Beautiful, isn't it?"

"Yes …" and then she sighed.

"Yes … *but?*"

"But … well, you know what I'm going to say next, Nathan; it's nice, but it just isn't *home*."

"Then we shall have to *make* it home, Momma."

She was quiet for a long while, and he saw she was crying; no longer looking at the sunset, but gazing off to the south, in the direction of their former home, though of course it was now hundreds of miles away.

"Oh Nathan … they have taken my home! The only place I ever truly loved. Will we ever see our beloved Mountain Meadows again?"

He was quiet and thoughtful for a moment before answering.

"Momma … I haven't led us on this long retreat because I mean to give up or give in to our enemies; rather so we could live to fight another day. And now that you and our extended household—all hundred some—are safe, I mean to take up the fight in earnest and drive it home to these faithless rebels.

"And unlike Billy's hawk, I intend to return one day to the family nest, rout my enemies, and reclaim our home."

"Billy's hawk?" Miss Abbey asked.

Nathan shook his head and smiled, "It's a long story of his people … suffice to say it *didn't* have a happy ending."

"Unlike ours?"

"Unlike ours," Nathan agreed, nodding emphatically. He squeezed her arm and turned once again to gaze out at the sunset.

<END OF BOOK 4>

If you enjoyed *Breakout,*
please post a review.

Insurrection:
Road to the Breaking Book 5

"Gentlemen, let's give these rebels what they've been asking for, shall we?" Nathan ordered.

But it was young Lieutenant Brantley who answered, "I will remind you, Mr. Chambers, I'm in command here. You are simply a civilian advisor."

Nathan turned to his left toward Brantley. The young man, more than ten years Nathan's junior, stood shivering, arms clasped tightly to his chest. The pristine officer's uniform he'd donned at the start of their march, in the dark pre-dawn more than twelve hours ago, was now soaked through and badly soiled from the long scramble up the mountain and through the underbrush. Brantley had said little up until now, leaving Nathan as de-facto commander of the scouting and skirmishing party ever since they'd split off from the main column just after daybreak.

"Certainly, Lieutenant; I stand corrected. What are *your* orders for the men, may I ask … *sir?*" he resisted the urge to infuse the question with heavy sarcasm.

"Our orders were to scout the enemy and report back on their position. We were *not* instructed to engage them, Mr. Chambers. I intend to carry out my orders."

"You mean to only *report* their position, Mr. Brantley? Those orders assumed we still held the element of surprise—clearly that's no longer the case."

"Those are still my orders, sir."

"So you don't mean to fight them?" Nathan growled, "Mr. Brantley, these *secess* bastards stole my home and murdered a number of my men. I mean to pay them back … *with interest!*"

"I hear you sir, but—"

"But what, Lieutenant?"

"They … they ain't fired on us yet, Mr. Chambers. Nobody's been hurt so far. They're Americans too, like us … *ain't they?* Perhaps if they see we got 'em outnumbered they'll just … give it up. Go home peaceful-like, maybe. Don't you think, sir?"

Nathan nodded his head noncommittally but didn't immediately respond. He reached inside his coat and pulled out a cigar, and then a match.

After he lit the cigar, and blew several puffs up through the downpour, he said, "Mr. Brantley … in my experience nobody ever won a war without hard fighting. Me and my men are here to do just that. If I'm your 'advisor,' then I *advise* you to join us. How will it look if us 'civilians' rout the pickets and take the house from the enemy while you and your men are back reporting the enemy's position to the General—a position they will no longer hold, I might add?"

Brantley stared back at him, open-mouthed.

"Lieutenant … nobody ever got a medal pinned on him for following orders. He got it for taking the battle to the enemy. These *secess* rebels have stolen our property, broken our laws, and killed our people. Their officers have broken a solemn vow to defend our country—they'd rather tear it apart. They must be fought where found, and killed when necessary. In war there must be no hesitation, Lieutenant."

Nathan and Brantley locked eyes for a long moment. Finally, Brantley nodded.

"Good. Send a couple of your men back, if you would, to report the enemy's troop disposition and our *present* position to the General. Have them tell him we are preparing to engage the enemy's pickets on this side, after which we'll press the assault across the road and on the farmhouse."

Then Tom Clark added, "And … do just ask him to kindly come along and join the party with the rest of his brigade. At the General's leisure and convenience, of course."

Brantley nodded, then called over two of his privates to carry out the mission.

"Mr. Wiggins … organize our assault."

"Yes, sir!"

"And Jim …"

"Sir?"

"I want it bloody … the bloodier the better. Teach these oath-breakers what happens to traitors and thieves. And show these young recruits what it means to fight a *real* battle."

"With pleasure, sir!" Jim snapped a salute and smiled broadly for the first time that afternoon, despite being soaked to the bone, and shivering with cold. Big Stan, who'd crouched next to Jim so he could listen in on the discussion, broke into a grin, and nodded his head at the Captain, but said nothing.

"And don't worry, Mr. Brantley; I know General Rosecrans … he's a West-Pointer like me. He'll appreciate you taking the initiative."

"If you say so, sir."

Nathan smiled and slapped him on the back, "Good man."

Brantley rolled his eyes and looked up at the sky, which he immediately regretted, receiving a face full of cold rain. He ducked back down again and shook the rainwater from his face, wondering what he'd just gotten himself into.

Acknowledgments

I'd like to thank the following individuals for assisting in the writing and editing of *Breakout*, including reading the beta version and providing invaluable feedback: Bruce Wright, Craig Bennett, Debbie Palmer, Gay Petersen, Leslie Johns, Marilyn Bennett, Mike Bennett, Patricia Bennett, and Rachel Bennett.

And special thanks to my editor, Ericka McIntyre, who keeps me honest and on track, and my proofreader Travis Tynan, who makes sure everything is done correctly!

And, last but not least (at all!), the experts at New Shelves Books; my trusted advisor on all things "bookish," Keri-Rae Barnum, and the guru Amy Collins!

Get Exclusive Free Content

The most enjoyable part of writing books is talking about them with readers like you. In my case that means all things related to *Road to the Breaking*—the story and characters, themes, and concepts. And of course, Civil War history in general, and West Virginia history in particular.

If you sign up for my mailing list, you'll receive some free bonus material I think you'll enjoy:

- A fully illustrated ***Road to the Breaking*** **Fact vs. Fiction Quiz.** Test your knowledge of history with this short quiz on the people, places, and things in the book (did they really exist in 1860, or are they purely fictional?)

- **Cut scenes from *Road to the Breaking*.** One of the hazards of writing a novel is word and page count. At some point you realize you need to trim it back to give the reader a faster-paced, more engaging experience. However, now you've finished reading the book, wouldn't you like to know a little more detail about some of your favorite characters? Here's your chance to take a peek behind the curtain!

- I'll occasionally put out a **newsletter with information about the Road to the Breaking Series**—new book releases, news and information about the author, etc. I promise not to inundate you with spam (it's one of my personal pet peeves, so why would I propagate it?)

To sign up, visit my website:
http://www.ChrisABennett.com

ROAD TO THE BREAKING SERIES: